CW01619230

Clara and Christina

Andrew Cunning

Clara and Christina

JOHN MURRAY

First published in Great Britain in 2026 by John Murray (Publishers)

1

Copyright © Andrew Cunning 2026

The right of Andrew Cunning to be identified as the Author of the Work has been asserted by him in accordance with the Copyright, Designs and Patents Act 1988.

All rights reserved. No part of this publication may be reproduced, stored in a retrieval system, or transmitted, in any form or by any means without the prior written permission of the publisher, nor be otherwise circulated in any form of binding or cover other than that in which it is published and without a similar condition being imposed on the subsequent purchaser.

All characters in this publication are fictitious and any resemblance to real persons, living or dead, is purely coincidental.

A CIP catalogue record for this title is available from the British Library

Hardback ISBN 9781399830218
Trade Paperback ISBN 9781399830225
ebook ISBN 9781399830232

Typeset in Sabon MT by Hewer Text UK Ltd, Edinburgh
Printed and bound in Great Britain by Clays Ltd, Elcograf S.p.A.

John Murray policy is to use papers that are natural, renewable and recyclable products and made from wood grown in sustainable forests. The logging and manufacturing processes are expected to conform to the environmental regulations of the country of origin.

Carmelite House
50 Victoria Embankment
London EC4Y 0DZ

www.johnmurraypress.co.uk

John Murray Press, part of Hodder & Stoughton Limited
An Hachette UK company

The authorised representative in the EEA is Hachette Ireland, 8 Castlecourt Centre, Dublin 15, D15 XTP3, Ireland (email: info@hbgi.ie)

The final belief is to believe in a fiction, which you know to be a fiction, there being nothing else. The exquisite truth is to know that it is a fiction and that you believe in it willingly.

Wallace Stevens, *Opus Posthumous: Poems, Plays, Prose*

Prologue

Clara set the book on her bed, its spine parallel to the speckled ceiling. She pushed it down against the duvet to keep her place. The blue blanket she'd pulled over her knees, one she'd had since she was young, was threadbare, and the cold air streaming through the window hit her bare legs. Her head was busy, her heartbeat elevated. She looked down. The book sat beside her, a lifeless object implausibly unaware of the spell it had just cast. Clara could *see* the girl. The paints. The attic room. She lifted it and looked at the spine.

Christina Darnell.

Never heard of her.

Clara looked again at the back cover, read the praise.

A first novel that comes from some other place entirely.

Compassionate, wise, daring. A book so fully realised, it is impossible to imagine it written line by line.

Her room, a small square her mother had painted green and pink when she left for university three months previously, was still recognisably her own. The bookcase, stuffed with old paperbacks, sat along the wall of the headboard, comfortably within arm's reach. *Dracula*, *The Scarlet Letter* and *The Complete Poems of Robert Frost* remained on top where she had left them in the final weeks of school, sick of the sight of her annotations across their pages. After two years of reading books forced on her by an unchanged and seemingly unchangeable curriculum, Clara felt excitement that on her new reading lists there were books she'd never heard of. Beside her old school texts, a small yellow lamp gave off warm light, enough for Clara to read by even at night. She couldn't have counted the number of novels she'd gone through in that small room over the years. Crime thrillers and horror novels her mother had dutifully taken to the charity shop along with Clara's dungarees and scuffed trainers as she'd outgrown them; literary classics she'd plodded her way through, understanding little but enjoying the rise and fall of their long, winding sentences; apocalyptic and dystopian novels taken from the school library and never returned. The room had been a sanctuary, she thought, even if her new campus quad and tiered lecture theatres made it seem uninhabitably small for the first time.

Clara thought ahead to Christmas, to the usual family visits, tubs of chocolates and small talk, to petty fights over washing up and the distant past. She wondered how anyone lived through it without a decent novel and a quiet room.

She wasn't meant to be reading *Promised Land*. *Orlando* was the first text on the module – 'Gender and Sexuality in Modern British Fiction' – followed by Forster's *Maurice*. They were both in her bag at the foot of the bed. It was only by chance she'd seen it in the bookshop, a single copy sitting amongst the stacks of Woolfs, Austens and Atwoods. Only by chance was it the book her hand brought out of the bag moments before. *Everything* was contingent, she would think, years later, when time made it all seem inevitable. And the thought would bring contentment.

Downstairs, her mother was on the phone making a complaint about a recent increase in their monthly internet bill. Later, she would shout up the stairs that dinner was ready: chips, beans and sausages, and they would speak about Christmas and the unsettlingly warm weather. Her mother might ask what she was reading, though, since Clara had moved to Belfast, Julie had struggled with knowing what to say next after hearing the title of her daughter's latest book. After dinner, they would visit her aunt Ann and talk about her health, the threat of water charges and the upcoming referendum.

Clara looked at her old alarm clock. The one that had woken her up for school every morning for seven years. There was still time.

She wanted to read the opening again.

Clara turned the pages of the book and found her place.

The girl, aware of herself as a girl, set to painting.

She sat upright on a piano stool and faced her blank canvas, one of the many her father had bought for her and stored in the upper room of their summer house, concerned that the solitude of the old building would eventually dement his daughter. This particular room had been unused until the girl required a space in which to paint, and her father dutifully cleared away sodden cardboard boxes of magazines and newspapers and set up an easel by a window that took in the morning's pale light and the eventual gold of the afternoon sun.

If anyone were walking on the beach in the middle of the day, they could look up to the topmost window of the house, which sat watchfully on the rocks just above the shore, and would see the shadow of a girl, statued in contemplation with elbow bent, appraising the development of colour as it unfolded in front of her.

On that afternoon, there was no one below to look at the girl, for it was raining and the clouds had obscured the typical flood of light she had grown accustomed to. In the dim of the attic room, she studied her palette. By then, she had established a layout for the colours available to her and kept to the same system each day. The girl was left-handed and arranged the paint from light to dark, beginning with the left of her board which she held tightly in her right hand. Titanium white, Naples yellow, cadmium red, cobalt blue and carbon black. The tubes sat by her feet with their stoppers pressed shut, and flakes of dull colour sat amongst them on the floor like remnants of weather.

The previous day's canvas sat sideways, discarded, on the other side of the room, leaning on a half-length bookcase, and depicted the girl's third attempt at the beach beyond the window. On finishing it again and disliking it again, she had decided the fault was not her own, for it was the view itself that refused to be painted. Taking it from the easel, the girl resolved never to attempt a landscape again, which in their capricious flurries made static representation impossible and pointless.

When her father took her home for the beginning of the school term the previous year, the girl had taken two of her canvases with her: one for display in their dining room, and one for her own bedroom. The first was an abstract of a horse, the inspiration for which came from a photo in one of the magazines still left in the attic room. The second was a painting from memory of her school classroom.

Emily, a quiet and polite girl from school, did not understand how the girl painted so well. She came to the house to play and glanced at the canvas the girl's father had hung beside the clock behind the large oak table. Emily asked how many colours the girl had, and when she said she had five, Emily said that she didn't believe her.

That afternoon, the girl set to work on painting a self-portrait. It was the first experiment of its kind, and one she would not revisit until she was much older and had a house of her own in which to work. The thought crossed her mind then that she ought to ask her father for a mirror, and suspend it from one of the rafters, or lean it against a pile of thick books on the table as she worked. Accuracy would be simpler to achieve with her own reflection for reference, she thought, but commenced her work without aide, and within minutes found herself considering the use of a mirror repugnant. She painted for one hour, blending the colours to achieve those not available to her, and stopped only when her father called her down for sandwiches and tea. When she returned to the attic later in the afternoon, the girl was afraid of what she had started and hid it from her father.

A Decade Later

I
Queer Writing

'There is nothing more ill-advised than a thirty-year-old with a memoir.' She said it with conviction, sitting tall in her armchair and looking away from Clara to the clock on the back wall.

It was her voice that had pierced Clara when they'd first met, how clear it was, its high ring like struck glass. She had heard Christina Darnell speak many times on the radio over the years, on the few YouTube videos of panel discussions and book events, but in person, she was surprised at how resonant her voice really was, unaided by a microphone and sound engineer.

Christina pulled her cream blazer closed across herself and sat back. It was a conclusive movement, meant to indicate that her point had been made. But by now, Clara knew she could draw her out, that Christina had more to say and would wait to be asked. The time was ten minutes to ten, and they had a little time left.

'Really?' Clara said. 'Surely you don't mean that.'

'I certainly do. And I'm not in the habit of saying things I don't mean.' Clara had laughed at Christina's initial judgment, the performed flippancy, and now leant forward in her chair, serious, one navy-cardiganed arm over her stomach, and waited for her to speak again. 'It's not that they have nothing to say, which is the usual criticism of the premature memoir, isn't it? It's that they almost have too much to say to make up for the little that they do. And all of it nonsense, lies. Often these books aren't really about their author, either. They haven't lived long enough to spread themselves across eighty thousand words. So they tell stories of their poor mothers or the awful bullies in secondary school or they recount the lives of the unfortunate people they've slept with. All second-hand things, really, no genuine sense of a person or, better, of a mind.' She paused as a young couple took seats at the table next to them. 'A memoirist, like nature, abhors a vacuum, Clara, and these young writers fill books with tales that are little better than gossip. I've actually read a couple of them, just to see what the fuss is about. Young poets trying to establish a legacy before they have published a second collection, debut novelists telling the world about their terribly complex inner lives. In reality, they are accounts that ought to have been published in a newspaper column or one of those colourful magazines targeted at women who don't read. These memoirs are called literature, now, which is unfortunate.'

Christina paused to pick up the china cup in front of her.

Clara always ordered them regular-sized drinks now, knowing they would give her the smaller, thinner cups that Christina seemed to prefer. Six weeks ago, when they stood to leave, she saw Christina had left about a third of her cappuccino in the bottom of the large mug, and the image was peculiarly sad for Clara who each week had to readjust to the smaller, frailer woman who met her for coffee; a woman who bore only a passing resemblance to the author photos on the inside of her early novels.

In the silence, Clara looked across at her conversation partner. Her hands looked older than her face, which was perfectly made up with high eyebrows that gave the impression of permanent incredulity. Her hands had a papery quality to them, as though they might permit light to pass through the centre of the palms. The veins on the back were dark purple and clearly defined, rising up from her skin like features on a relief map. She tested the coffee's temperature carefully, raising the cup slowly to her lips, allowing for the small tremors in her fingers. It had been cooling for forty-five minutes, but she was nevertheless cautious, and only parted her lips, painted a soft rose-pink, at the last second. She let out a contented sigh after swallowing and replaced the cup back into the raised ceramic circle in the centre of the saucer. This morning, Christina had her silvery blonde hair pulled into a tight bun that lifted her eyebrows further up her forehead.

If Clara were observing her as a stranger, as someone who knew nothing about her books, she reckoned Christina's appearance and demeanour in the coffee shop would intrigue and repel her in equal measure. There was a unique and intimidating mix of *Vogue* and the principal's office about her, a sort of tight-lipped glamour that Clara now knew was always on the edge of being broken by a proper laugh.

Christina looked up from the cup. Clara nudged the black box sitting between them forwards, sliding it closer to Christina, its unblinking red light facing the older woman. Christina, who was used to the recorder, did not look down.

'I'm wrong, actually. People don't call it "literature", do they, these literary memoirs? They call it "queer literature", or "feminist literature". There's something in that, something worth looking at seriously. The rise of the modifier, this peculiar urge to classify. It's almost as though the writers, or maybe the publishers, know it's not worthy of the undressed term, the naked, pure notion of "literature", so they clothe it in justifications, as though it ought not to have been written except that it has a job to do, that it has a "cause". Maybe that is what irritates me most about these waves of misery tales: that they are written with a sense of utility in mind. *I'll write my story so it can be read at the gay book club or be shared by the online feminists.* It's the reduction of writing to impact, to outcome, to mere demographic. It all feels a bit thin, lowly, perhaps. And even as I've just said all that, I know I haven't quite said what I mean. There's something else to it. Perhaps we will return to this next week, once I've thought it over.'

Clara looked down to her notebook and smiled. She was still getting used to the idea that there would be another meeting, another coffee, another conversation. Memoirs hadn't been the topic for that morning's session. At the top of the lefthand page on her lap Clara had written '*Childhood*'. It was the same heading she'd written for the past four Sundays. But this morning they had discussed penmanship (Christina still wrote letters by hand); the line between pornography and sensuality in contemporary novels (Christina argued that the line was thin, and that the division was about quality, not explicitness: 'Everything is permissible if it's good,' she'd said); and now they were discussing the rise of the young memoirist. Clara would have to listen back to understand precisely how they had moved from 'Did your parents have the chance to read your published work?' to where they were now.

Listening to their conversations was something Clara did after every meeting, usually in a coffee shop on a Monday morning, her headphones connected to her laptop and an open notebook on the table in front of her. She copied out quotations that struck her as useful, made a note of the time Christina said them and then wrote some notes on how it could be weaved into the monograph. It was slow work but Clara loved it. In fact, she found that she often enjoyed it just as much as the actual conversations, because in listening back, she had proof that it had all definitely happened. It really was Christina Darnell speaking with her, sharing her opinions, making jokes.

The recordings, Clara felt, were more real than the conversations themselves.

Clara had arrived early, at about five to nine, as she tended to do so she could queue and order and get a table for Christina to sit at. The first time they'd met, two months prior, it was cold and grey, and the Ormeau Road was covered in a thin haze of rain thrown up by occasional taxis and church-goers in family cars. Clara had turned right at the end of Sunnyside Street and walked the wrong way, passing a closed pizza place and a grocer's before pausing to open maps on her phone outside a Methodist church painted in faded Free-Love orange and pink.

Christina, by contrast, had crossed the road near the park, using the traffic lights at the end of South Parade two minutes from her front gate, and entered the coffee shop to shake hands with a then out-of-breath Clara. Christina handed her a new ten-pound note.

'Cappuccino for me. Cinnamon, if they ask. I'm going to sit down.'

In the emails they had exchanged, Christina chose the coffee shop because she no longer wished to drive, and could leave her townhouse and be there in under five minutes. It makes me sound very miserly, I'm afraid, but these are my terms. Clara, in truth, would have got two buses to Cork each week if it meant having coffee with Christina Darnell. She replied telling her the location was perfect, which it almost was, being only a forty-minute walk from her rented apartment on the Lisburn Road.

Christina was seventy-eight now and age, it seemed, had not granted her patience. 'How long have I got left, realistically?' Christina had said as Clara set the coffees down on that first morning. 'Five, six years if I'm fortunate, one or two if I fall. Forgive me if I don't wish to stand in slow-moving queues with toddlers and dogs on leads wrapping up people's legs. I'd rather like to finish this novel while I'm fit for it.'

Clara had looked up from her filter coffee. A novel. Christina mentioned it so causally, like talk of the weather, and Clara hadn't expected it. She held her face in place. The news that Christina Darnell was writing again after fifteen years would be genuine literary news. Her last book *Wild and Blue* was well reviewed but did not sell particularly well. Clara imagined this wouldn't have bothered Christina, who seemed to have her attention tuned to the afterlives of writers. Sales and early reviews made not a mark in the long run. It was quality she cared about.

Instead of telling Clara stories of her relationships, early life or her parents, Christina spoke of Virginia Woolf and Iris Murdoch, her eyes glistening as she gave glowing judgements on their work. These were her teachers, she said. In particular, she lamented the latter's fall from fashion. 'She should always have been unfashionable,' she said. 'Iris ought never to have been in vogue. She was as strange as she was brilliant. I knew it as soon as I read her. She was always just a little too clever to be popular. Now, she is where she is at her best: at the margins, rebuking the ignorance of her detractors by being infinitely more interesting than their best thought.' Christina paused. She had been still a little out of breath from the short walk. She went to settle back in her seat but instead remained forwards, and raised her finger towards Clara. 'And then they made that awful film of her losing her fucking mind. These things only happen to women writers.'

Christina Darnell had been Clara's way to Iris Murdoch. She read *The Bell* immediately after listening to Christina's appearance on a radio book show in which she had mentioned the novel in passing. Within the month Clara had read *Under the Net* and *The Sovereignty of Good,* then an essay collection on Murdoch's fiction, and got a thousand words for a section in her third chapter on the influence of Murdoch's philosophical prose on Darnell's own ideas-led fiction. Christina's throwaway comments in interview and occasional essay footnotes accounted for large amounts of Clara's reading during her degree, master's and PhD. Without Christina, she would never have read Augustine or Aquinas, or even thought to open a Bible. Christina introduced her to a world of thought Clara would have considered exhausted, or unfashionable. She read large volumes on the history of Western philosophy to learn about Plato and Hume and Heidegger. She learned the names of the female mystics and committed entire passages to memory. *All manner of things shall be well*, she found herself repeating after a phone call from her mother. Thanks to Christina's fiction, Clara knew what Occam's razor was, she could hold a conversation about table tapping in Victorian England and recognised that good thinking was rarely reducible to binary options.

In the end it wasn't so much the sentences of Christina's work that Clara sought after, but the mind that produced them. By borrowing just one more book, reading just another article, she would be permitted access to the holy of holies: another reference Clara only understood because of Christina.

The novel before Christina's last had won awards, something she hadn't accomplished for a decade or more before that book. The collection of non-fiction that followed it, *The Shape of Clouds: Essays on Art, Truth and Fiction* was widely read on university campuses at the turn of the millennium and appeared for a few years on reading lists in English departments across the UK, but following that, it was only her first novel, *Promised Land,* that stuck around on undergraduate modules and in university bookshops. By publishing only four works of fiction, critical attention had been dense and concentrated, and had fallen away as quickly as it had risen. The publication of another novel after all this time would be an event, Clara thought.

'It's all a bit hush-hush,' Christina had said with a wave of her hand. 'My agent has told me not to mention it until the manuscript is in her hands. She's concerned it'll be unpublishable, I think. Or that I'll die before it's done.'

'I am sure it will be incredible,' Clara had said.

'It won't be.' Christina said. 'It will be perfectly credible.'

'Oh, sorry, I just meant that it is brilliant news.'

'I know. I'm being funny. People never can tell.'

Clara smiled. Her heart rate had risen, and she looked down to her phone on the table and fought the urge to message her old PhD supervisor, her editor.

Christina crossed her hands on her lap, pleased with the effect her news had had. 'I have about forty thousand words or so. It's usually at this point that I can tell if it's worth anything.'

Clara nodded. She knew the word counts of Christina's novels. *Séances* was eighty thousand, *Promised Land*, eighty-five. At forty thousand Christina was already about halfway.

'And how are you feeling about this one?' Clara asked.

Christina pursed her lips and tilted her head. 'Not bad.'

After that first meeting, Clara had spent the afternoon back in her cold apartment researching other famous breaks in novel writing. It could be a nice appendix to the book, she thought. She clicked on the top article from her search and jotted down a few findings. Donna Tartt typically took a decade between books. Marilynne Robinson had a twenty-four-year hiatus between *Housekeeping* and *Gilead*, and Henry Roth published *Call it Sleep* in 1934 and then, sixty years later, released the first of the 'Mercy of a Rude Stream' series. Fifteen years was significant and Clara knew that if a new novel were to be published, she'd have to give an account of the prolonged silence between books. Between Malachi and Matthew there was about four hundred years, the article stated, though their authorship, divine or otherwise, depended on the religious convictions of the reader. Clara wrote it down anyway.

Much would be written about Christina's fifteen years of silence, her move from London to Belfast, her largely hidden life, her return to the novel form. Most scholars thought she'd given up, or retired, that she was a relic from a previous age with nothing to say. The *Guardian* ran a piece in the last year entitled 'Forgotten Geniuses: Why Your New Favourite Might Be an Old Favourite', and Christina Darnell was third on the list, sandwiched between two writers from the mid-century that Clara had never heard of. It felt like an affront after three or so years of a doctoral dissertation. One of the comments below the article said *Some real gems here, but Darnell is a man-hater. RIP*. It amused Clara that someone could be so wrong about Christina and her work, even assuming her to be dead. She wondered what Christina would make of these sorts of comments and pictured her laughing, eyes closed and head back.

From the moment Clara had turned the recorder on that first Sunday morning, she'd recognised that Christina was not finished; in fact, she was startled to discover the real Christina Darnell was furiously alive, passionate in conversation and about her interests, which spanned world religions, coffee cake, Susan Sontag, the films of Richard Linklater, cosmology, Freud, feminist theory and theologies of the Incarnation. She emailed her editor that same afternoon and told him that her idea was going to work, that Christina Darnell was writing again, and that she seemed to be open to conversation, open to having herself recorded, transcribed, written about.

Good news! Well done. Keep me posted! Get some juicy gossip. All best, Chris.

Clara broke the short silence that had settled between them. 'I have some questions about the memoir stuff.'

'I thought you might.'

'Well, I'd hate for you to be misread, or misinterpreted. You know the environment now.'

'You're worried I'll be the subject of an online mob,' Christina said, with a small smirk. 'Perhaps what I mean is that these young writers publish too early. I think that once they finish their manuscript they realise there's nothing really in it save for discussion of an "issue", so their publishers set to work on marketing it to the right audience. It is thin, thin work, Clara. I don't think Baldwin or Morrison would like the identitarian nature of publishing these days, the diluting of writing into narrow labels.'

Clara tilted her head at this. She was comfortable enough in Christina's company now that the compulsion to nod after everything she said had subsided a little.

'But Morrison was explicit in her work about race. It was her theme, her whole life's work.'

'To only teach Morrison on "Race and Literature 101" would be to lose so much of what makes Morrison a genius. Her books are about history, truth, forgiveness, America, faith, redemption, sex and trauma. They aren't narrow treatises on a political point. She was an artist, not a polemicist. Same for Baldwin. He can't be confined by one category, the way people might like.'

'I take your point, but you could definitely get in trouble with that line of thinking these days.' Christina nodded once.

'I understand that. And that's why I said we'll need to revisit these topics. I haven't quite worked out my thoughts on them.'

Clara wrote something down into the notebook on her knee. 'Yes. I'm pre-empting some raised eyebrows when people read you being disparaging about queer literature. You know people don't need much of an excuse to start posting about a writer's views.'

Christina sat back into the leather armchair and crossed her hands on her knee. 'How on earth could they ever think I am disparaging queer writing, Clara? I just about invented it.'

Clara stopped writing and looked up to the serious expression on Christina's face. They looked at one another for three unbroken seconds, Clara's pen hovering over a blank line.

The fine-lined sides of Christina's mouth twitched as she looked down to the younger woman's notebook, and finally gave way to a smile, and then a short laugh. 'And there's the quote for the back of your book,' Christina said.

Clara laughed, closed the notebook and reached to turn off the recorder.

'Radical Queer Feminisms or Conservative Canon-Keeping?' Critical Perspectives on Christina Darnell's Fiction

It is not in the nature of scholarly opinion to present a homogenous view of a writer's work, intent or interventions, and it would surely be a facile point to open a discussion of critical opinion of any body of work. However, every rule has exceptions, and such is the stark divide in scholarly approaches to Darnell's work — both fiction and essay — that we cannot hope to understand the interpretations at play without first attending to the peculiar binaries that seem to dominate critical writing about her output. [does this need the thesis stuff on lack of biographical readings in Darnell criticism?] To exemplify this divide we can turn to Miranda Moore, one of the first academics to take up serious study of Darnell's work. She argues, in the first published essay on her fiction, that 'Darnell represents that most precious thing in the arts: the hint that new ground may well have been broken.' She argues in that article that Darnell's early work, Promised Land and *Séances*, *'articulate the perpetually unfinished nature of feminism, that the only way for any justice movement to maintain momentum, both politically and morally, is to remain open to the stranger, to the new, to that which might once have seemed like an enemy.' Here we have Darnell the visionary: the artist who can see beyond the smaller wins and losses of the feminist movement to a sort of utopian future, where the initial seed of equal rights has flowered into something utterly, radically new, where unlikely allies could sit in the shade of a garden planted by women who might never have imagined such a community possible. [Is tone too formal here given the interviews to come? Maybe mention how Christina would scoff at these high praises?] There are other scholars who subscribe to this version of Darnell: Buckley, Wright and Browning, who all, in their way, see the radical edge of her work as the horse that pulls the cart. We shall turn to each of them in what follows. But this is just one side of the scholarly appraisal. On the other, there is Darnell the conservative, the older artist intent on the maintenance of her influences' reputations and canonisation. Gibson, for example, leads the charge here. He writes, 'In both interview and essay, Darnell seems preternaturally keen on defending a sort of feminist, queer canon of her own making. Woolf, Murdoch and Lorde come up most often, to the loss, it must be said, of newer, more radical voices. It raises the question whether Darnell gave up reading work published after the 1990s.' Gibson here outlines a familiar criticism of Darnell's later work and thinking, namely, that it has a tendency to look backwards and seems slow to credit contemporary voices. Gibson's article has been influential for Darnell studies and Stevenson picks up where he left off, arguing, 'In self-consciously naming her influences, Darnell seeks to choose how she is read. With Woolf, a literary experimentalist; with Murdoch, a philosophical thinker to be taken seriously; with Lorde, a visionary. Of course, the danger in associating oneself with such towering figures is the inevitability of falling short in the course of the comparison.'*

In this book, I wish not to dwell on this divide in scholarly opinion, for to do so would surely risk losing the value of Darnell's work in itself. But at the outset, it is worth noting, if only to immediately move beyond it. Scholarly opinion exists, often by necessity, at a massive remove from the flesh-and-blood writer it takes as its subject. In this study, I intend to move scholarship closer to the person who exists, without reference to journal articles and academic conference papers. In the overview that follows we will take a brief and, I hope, informative journey through the terrain of Darnell studies as it stands which will, in turn, pave the way for the subsequent chapters, which take up the work of Christina Darnell in parallel with notes from conversations I have had with Darnell herself. It is the aim of this book to unearth some of the biographical riches scholars have been so far unable to lay claim to, and to use the life and thinking of Christina Darnell to enliven and enrich how we read her important, vital and, at times, prophetic work. [Put in something here about the debate around biographical readings of other writers. The limits, the potential. Examples: Sylvia Plath? Emily Dickinson? If CD doesn't open up about life and past, is there any point in putting this bit in?]

Clara closed the laptop and went to switch on the kettle. She had a solid, weighty satisfaction in her stomach as she moved slowly into the kitchen. It was a bright afternoon beyond the apartment, and she allowed herself a look out the window towards the communal garden she had yet to visit. There was a father playing catch with his young daughter and Clara watched her practise one-handed catches for a moment, feeling slightly outside time as she observed them from above. She felt like she was under water, her mind and movements slow, as though she was watching people on the surface who were moving freely and quickly. Her head felt calm and still, a feeling she had only previously experienced as a student after sharing a joint with her old flatmate, Sophie.

That she was getting the same kind of high from writing an academic monograph made Clara content with the choices she had made. The lack of money, the absence of job security, the shame of answering the question 'What do you do?' at parties. The last time this had happened – the question coming from a relatively handsome accountant who worked in his dad's firm – Clara had the confidence of two gins and laid out in uncharacteristic detail the job of an academic, the studying, cross-referencing, the teaching and discussions, the conference attendance and endless emailing. His response – 'You get paid to read books? What a gig' – made her make excuses the next time she was invited to a party. For the few months Clara had taught in a secondary school, though, she felt she had something more concrete to offer strangers. Everyone had been to school, had had a favourite teacher, could tell a decent story about a prank that had got out of hand. Being a teacher was comprehensible to people, an obviously useful job. When people asked about her work she would get well-meaning sympathy. 'I could think of nothing worse,' people would say before realising how rude it sounded, inevitably adding, 'You must be a saint.'

Looking back on that time, Clara reckoned a lot of her colleagues, tired and full of compassion, probably were.

She let the tea bag stew in the 'Dr Clara Wilson' mug Daniel had ordered for her in the first weeks of their relationship. Clara had complained that her friends had all, unanimously and in isolation from one another, said the same thing when she told them about him and his job: 'He's a *real* doctor then?' After the third exposition of the history of the doctorate from the Middle Ages to contemporary universities, Clara recognised that any argument she could put up for herself and her degree seemed only to confirm her friends' gently held prejudices. Daniel kindly referred to himself as a 'physician' for a few days in the lead up to the mug arriving and, when it did, Clara felt a liking for Daniel concurrent with the predictable shame. She only used the mug when the apartment was empty, like it was now. Clara removed the tea bag with the reverse end of a fork, squeezing it against the inside of the mug, and put it into the bin she'd opened with her foot. She took milk from the fridge, added a small amount and replaced it. Clara took the mug with her to the sofa.

The stillness in her produced by the writing session was already waning. Clara knew if she switched on the TV and began to flick through the usual American sitcoms and European thrillers it would be gone within seconds. She felt resistance rise up and then fall within her. In these moments Clara was aware enough to realise there was more than one self, that there were at least two, and they tended to work against one another. Each one with its own allegiance, its own precise alienation, its own demands on her. That Clara had to house these selves and smooth over their inconsistencies and contradictions felt like a unique struggle, though she knew it was more likely a basic and universal human problem, and that she was mistaking the specifics for the problem itself.

Put another way, Clara didn't feel at home anywhere, not in a seminar room, not in her family home. And the problem, as all the theorists said, was something that started within the self: it was an outward manifestation of something fractured and broken inside her. Put yet another way, the thought of calling her mother would occasionally enter Clara's mind, unbidden and with such force that she would not be able to relax, or read, until she had. They would talk for three or four minutes about work and Clara would listen to her complain about a minor injustice. Then, once the call was over, relief would flood her veins like saline and, for a short time, all would be well.

Years ago, Clara came across a verse in the Bible as the epigraph to an academic article on free will and determinism: *I do not understand what I do. For what I want to do I do not do, but what I hate I do*. This was the fundamental problem of being alive, she thought. Clearly had been for thousands of years. She felt a little less special realising that what felt like a particular neurosis might in fact be a general one. The verse planted itself in Clara's mind then and re-emerged in her thoughts every few days when she found herself doing something she didn't want to do, or avoiding the things (good food, friends, conversation, exercise) she really wanted.

The verse returned to her again as watched her hand move for the remote.

2
The Death of the Author

The next Sunday morning was the warmest of their days together. Clara had no need for her bedroom or bathroom light as she pottered between the two rooms, hanging her black towel on the back of the door, remembering moisturiser and heading back to collect it from the dresser opposite her bed. She had also taken the portable radio into the bathroom and set it on the shelf beside the toothpaste and the two toothbrushes and waited for the water in the shower to run hot. A honey-voiced Radio 4 presenter accompanied her shower with barely audible interviews on same-sex blessings in the Church of England and a short piece on Hindus in frontline British politics. Afterwards, on opening the shower door, the mirror was obscured with condensation and Clara lifted the white sash window a little to circulate cool, breathable air and saw that the ground below was dry. Like Christina, Clara didn't have a car, so had become used to the typical Belfast mizzle, and still felt a small burst of contentment on the days when there was no rain.

Her outfit was hanging on the back of the bathroom door. A pair of black pleated trousers, white blouse and tan leather jacket, and she noted with pleasure that she would not need a coat. For the first meeting she'd had with Christina she had chosen a navy blazer and smart white trousers, the same outfit she wore when she lectured. Somehow a blazer felt appropriate when talking to undergraduates about Zadie Smith. But when that first hour was up and Christina had left for home, Clara had felt overdressed in the coffee shop and walked home to change before meeting Daniel for lunch in a noodle bar by the old cinema.

Clara was glad her meetings with Christina took place at a remove from the university: it meant there was something of a separation between their conversations, the writing of the monograph and Clara's teaching. Years later, when she was consciously aware of being happy, Clara would realise just how important it was that Christina had suggested they meet off campus. But at the time, Clara was only faintly aware that there was a significance in where they weren't. Universities were strange places, after all, and Clara had yet to feel totally at ease on a college quad. Her interviews with Christina Darnell would not have been out of place in one of their seminar rooms, though, in front of hunched academics making hasty notes and little noises of approval as they listened to Darnell's musings on morality and the invention of character. That they actually happened in the presence of single mums wrestling prams into tight spaces and pensioners discussing radio dramas and local politics made Clara feel strangely content, that maybe her life wasn't planted on an illusion, that there was something tangible, something weight-bearing about her life choices. It was the sort of coffee shop her mum could have sat for an hour and made comments on passers-by.

Clara often wondered what her mother would make of her conversations with Christina. The thought of her hearing them filled Clara with a feeling of embarrassment that made her involuntarily raise her shoulders. She imagined her mother sitting beside them, interrupting their conversation every now and then to point out a ridiculous outfit worn by someone outside the shop before settling back into her typical fidgety silence. Clara wondered what might happen if she went to the bathroom and left them alone for a few minutes. It seemed unthinkable, the two of them talking, though she had a persistent suspicion that they would get on better without her there.

She's nice, isn't she? her mum would say later. *A lot more down to earth than I'd assumed.*

Clara could hardly bear the thought of it. She found her keys on the dining table and, as she walked down the hall to her front door, she forced her mind back to her meeting.

Christina's insistence on not wanting to travel more than a few minutes beyond her house was genuine, Clara thought, though it also had the benefit of keeping the murky business of literary criticism at arm's length. The only suggestion of Clara's primary intentions for the conversations were the red light of the recorder and the open notebook that sat on her knee. After a while, Clara noticed Christina barely registered the electronic recorder and when she did look to Clara's lap, it was with an expression caught somewhere between amusement and curiosity.

The air on the Lisburn Road had lost its chill when she opened her front door and stepped into the quiet street. Clara unbuttoned her jacket. She connected her headphones to her phone and played the remainder of a podcast she'd started late the night before, pulling the time stamp back six or seven minutes to something she recognised. The host – a young, early-career researcher in cultural studies – had a professor of American literature on this week. She remembered his clipped southern English accent from just before sleep now that she heard him speak again. The host was called Hassie, and despite Clara's initial eye-roll at her obvious attempts to get noticed in an impossible job-market, she realised that at some point over the last three months she was listening no longer out of spite, but because Hassie was genuinely good at interviewing academics.

She had a pleasant Yorkshire accent which had been tempered by time spent at Kings College London for her doctoral research, and the result was a northern voice that had few class markers. She could well have been the child of working-class parents, a mining family or shopkeepers, or she could have been an upper middle-class daughter of dentists or pharmacists, and her accent would give her listeners few clues. Clara found herself, in spite of herself, liking Hassie. Initially her voice, its oscillations and seeming refusal to commit to a definite place was off-putting, and Clara felt ashamed as the thought passed through her mind that someone with a Yorkshire accent — no matter how diluted — wouldn't ever sound like a proper academic. Clara's eventual change of heart came with the realisation that any prejudice that would keep Hassie out of a university job would apply all the more to Clara herself. In any case, she found herself rooting for Hassie, and her aim was now to get on *Rescuing Rapunzel* (she still shuddered at the name) in the next year and publicise her book on Darnell, once it was finished.

It was the sort of thing that could help in a job interview. *Impact. Outreach.* The sorts of words that made Clara feel disassociated from herself, like she was floating above her life, watching herself as a stranger listen to lectures and write conference papers, as though she were somehow both the observed and the observer, or, worse, that she was really the empty space between. Every way of life exacted payment of some sort, Clara reasoned to herself, again and again. Civil servants had to put up with tedium; teachers and police officers, abuse; doctors and nurses, long hours and bodily fluids. Perhaps the cost of being an academic was perpetually feeling like a person who only half participated in the world.

As Clara rounded Stranmillis University College, Hassie was asking her guest about the connection between transcendentalism and contemporary American poetry. 'It seems that American writing just can't seem to get beyond Emerson, Whitman, Dickinson etcetera. I was thinking this week of what Whitehead said about European philosophy, something like, it almost entirely consists of a series of footnotes to Plato. Is contemporary American writing guilty of something similar? Is it all just footnotes to the American Renaissance?'

'Now that would be a massive overstatement, Hassie, which is why I think you've phrased it like that. You're provoking me.'

'Of course!'

'Well, I'll take you on. It really is a key question and there are a number of ways we can think about offering a response. First, if the entire impulse of a literary and philosophical movement – the Transcendentalists in this case – is to essentially begin over, to start again and conceive of some foundational principles of American writing and thinking, then it is difficult to see how any writer in America could ever do anything that does not at least touch on the issues those formative writers discuss. They took as their project the rethinking of consciousness, freedom, religion and so on. In some ways they ensured they will always be part of the discussion by inserting themselves so obviously into how Americans think and write. Even by diverging from Emerson or Thoreau, the contemporary writer has not escaped them: the story becomes how they broke from American tradition.'

Clara listened as the discussion went from contemporary poetry back to Walt Whitman and Herman Melville. Professor Wright – that was the guest's name – talked about how the first generation of 'American writers' set in motion an ambitious task of rethinking fundamental human questions without assuming that the Europeans, the much older civilisations, had the answers. 'They were eager to invent,' he said, 'invent a nation, a country, a new way of thinking.' Clara had taken one module of American literature in her second year, but hadn't enjoyed it, and now, as a supposed 'expert' on contemporary fiction, she felt her ignorance of whole areas of literature sharply. As a result, her body reacted viscerally to any information – written or spoken – that she felt might plug a gap in her burgeoning expertise, and on these occasions her peripheral vision would disappear as an animal focus came over her. For the remainder of the walk, the two podcast voices faded to background chatter as Clara found her mind buzzing with connections – tangential and tenuous though they were – between what she had just heard and Christina Darnell's work, how the questions the canonical American writers asked were similarly threaded through Christina's novels. Clara had a familiar spark of excitement at the possibilities of the half-ideas and allowed them to accompany her on the final stretch of the Lisburn Road.

This was the architecture of Clara's mental world and had been for years, she realised. Christina's novels were the usual terminus of her thinking, where her thoughts always led her to, as though the work of Christina Darnell was a scratch in vinyl Clara's mind couldn't help but follow.

Arriving at the usual place ahead of schedule, Clara was pleased to see there wasn't a queue beyond the glass double doors. She took a quick look around for Christina before approaching the tall man behind the counter. Clara ordered a cappuccino and black filter coffee, tapped her phone on the card machine and waited for the soft beep. He smiled at her as she lifted the two cups and then he wished her a great day. His smile had something in it that made her wonder if she'd been teaching him on 'Introduction to Contemporary Fiction' this semester. There was almost a hundred of them enrolled on the module, so he could easily have been amongst the other eighteen- and nineteen-year-olds with their copies of *White Teeth* and *Shuggie Bain* sitting in front of them, spines shamelessly uncreased. She'd keep an eye out for him. Next Wednesday's lecture was on Sarah Waters and for the journey from counter to table, Clara ran over the slides she'd already made, picturing the quotes from *The Little Stranger* she'd typed onto a black background, testing her recall for what she wanted to say about each of them: Influence of Henry James and *The Turn of the Screw*; effect of blurring of the psychological and the supernatural; the house in feminist writing.

Clara had to fight to keep *The Little Stranger* on the course. It was fifteen years old now, and the argument for it as 'contemporary fiction' was weakening with each passing month. But Clara adored the book when she first read it in the summer between first and second year of her undergraduate degree. When she was offered the module last year, Professor Robertson had suggested she take if off and replace it with something just out: Megan Nolan or Naoise Dolan. Clara replied to the email to say she would take it off next year, if she was still around – she just wanted one chance to teach it before it disappeared into the abyss between contemporary fiction and rediscovered classic.

Clara wondered how much money someone like Sarah Waters had in her bank account. It must be millions, with the TV adaptations. Clara thought about what she would do with that sort of money and once again ruled out taking a break from her work. Online appraisals varied from two to five million, but there was little doubt Christina Darnell too had made a significant amount of money over the forty-five years she'd been writing. Prize money alone was in the tens of thousands, and the film deal for *Séances* was surely worth a large amount. Her current three-storey house would have been one of the more expensive in South Belfast, and Clara couldn't imagine Christina Darnell with a mortgage. She'd have bought it outright, with the money from the sale of her apartment in Belgravia a few years ago. Pocket change by comparison, she reckoned; regardless, though, Clara bought the coffees, getting there early to prevent Christina handing her another note.

She brought them to the table at the very back of the shop, a circular, marble-effect surface wedged between two brown leather armchairs. She brought out an old tattered copy of Eagleton's *Literary Theory* she'd packed in her rucksack that morning. Clara hadn't read it since she was an undergraduate, but remembered enjoying his style. The book was sitting at the end of a shelf in her bedroom, its glossy black spine and white, capitalised font appealing to her as she packed the laptop and recorder in her bag that morning. It was the kind of book Daniel scoffed at when he cast his eyes across her bookshelves in the bedroom after they'd finished and before he fell asleep.

'Literary theory? People seriously make money out of that stuff?'

'It's interesting. And the author is a lot cleverer than the consultants you worship.'

'My boss is an avid reader.'

There was a wounded tone to Daniel's voice Clara only recognised after he'd left and she'd replayed the conversation back in her head.

'*Tuesdays with Morrie* isn't literature, Dan.'

'You're a snob.'

'Maybe so.'

The arguments over her books were an ongoing conflict, but they were typically light-hearted skirmishes, with Daniel making fun of Clara's bookish obsessions, and Clara taking them as opportunities to mock doctors' tendencies to overestimate the transferability of their own intelligence.

When Daniel returned to his own place in the east of the city and she was left alone, Clara occasionally considered that the jibes and jokes were not just playful banter, but evidence of a total mismatch in values. His clumsy attempts to understand this part of her life frustrated Clara in the moment and then endeared him to her when he was at a distance. Years later, she would look back on him with uncomplicated affection. Now, she distracted herself with wine, with new and expensive books of literary criticism, with the writing of lectures and emails to students, and texted Daniel when she'd exhausted her mind enough to want sex and company again.

She leafed through the book now, stopping when she saw a line drawn in black under some text: graffiti from a younger Clara. She remembered underlining some of the sections. In truth, she was startled by how a line below a line could so precisely evoke the feeling of exhilaration at finding just the right quote to make her point; how it could bring an entire blur of weeks and months back, as powerful as the smell of her childhood room or an old friend's detergent. The uneven, twice drawn line under the last quote, one about emotion and religion, returned her to her student house in her second year, a grotty three-bedroom apartment on Lower Windsor Avenue with flaking brown leather sofas and electrical fittings in danger of falling off the walls entirely. It was all contained in black biro: the mould in the top right corner of the kitchen, the smell of boiling instant noodles and yellow-sticker wine, the loud laughing of Felicity and Sophie as they came up the stairs after the pub and called in to see how Clara's studying had gone. She flipped back in her copy and saw another marked section, this time highlighted in yellow.

She had used the quote in her first ever essay on Christina's work. It had been a first-year module, and Darnell's first novel, *Promised Land*, was on the reading list. It was the first one she'd bought, fate arranging it that she saw the paperback sitting on the table at the front of the university bookshop as she walked in after lunch with a new friend. Clara was only nineteen then, and, looking back, she wondered how much of the novel had actually made sense to her, for it was a strange book, full of biblical allusion and philosophical argument and even now, at thirty, there were sections she still couldn't grasp. But there was something magic about the prose even then, the reticence of Darnell's style, how she would refuse to get in the way of her reader, how she would hold back the emotional centre of the novel, cloaking it in abstract language or image. It had Clara hooked from the first dozen pages and she read the whole thing on her childhood bed, back against the wall with her knees drawn up to her chest.

A few weeks later, back in Belfast and in the midst of lectures and seminars, Clara emailed her tutor with a proposed essay title: 'Rewriting Eve: Visions of post-patriarchal religion in Christina Darnell's *Promised Land.*' She didn't share the title idea with her mother. Julie raised an eyebrow the first time she came into her living room to see Clara with her confirmation Bible on her knee, leafing in Leviticus for the punishment for witches. It was something her mother would never fully understand. Her Bible had sat unopened in the display cabinet for more than thirty years until then.

Religion was more of a matter of culture for Clara's family. Catholicism was in the air, as clear and undetectable as carbon monoxide. Any tangible commitment to it, any public discussion of original sin or atonement, was tacitly seen as taking the whole thing too seriously. Christina, however, seemed to have the opposite approach to religion. The ideas of theologians held her attention, she treated the language of scripture with the utmost reverence, while any sort of commitment to institutions or overarching moral system was rejected out of hand as obviously missing the point. The counter-intuition of Christina's thinking was one of the major reasons Clara fell so hard for her writing. If she could lead her by the hand into theology, what other worlds would she open?

Clara's title had been approved the following week and she had set to work on the first piece of her academic career that she would take some pride in.

'And I thought *I* was early this morning.'

Clara looked up from her book at the sound of the smooth, familiar voice of Christina Darnell. Her accent, while undoubtedly English, was hard to place precisely. At times, Christina's way of speaking seemed like a throwback to radio broadcasts used in documentaries, the sort of Received Pronunciation that could have announced the death of a monarch. It was the kind of voice reviled in Derry City. But Clara had little intention of bringing Christina Darnell – award-winning British author – to her hometown, despite Christina's views on the border being totally at odds with the associations her childhood friends would have made with the accent. This morning she was wearing a long white coat over dark trousers and a white blouse, and the subtle stoop in her back was harder to spot.

'You *are* early,' Clara said, with a look at her phone. 'Three full minutes. How are you?'

'I'm fine. It's a little warmer today, isn't it? I didn't need this at all.' Christina took a rose-coloured scarf off her shoulders and draped it over the armchair. She liked to sit with her back to the window. It helped her concentrate on the conversation, she said. She sat down and nodded in the direction of her cinnamon-dusted cup. 'Lovely. Thank you. Now tell me, how are you?'

Clara put the book back in her rucksack and opened her notebook to today's page. Christina caught the title of the Eagleton book Clara had been reading and her lips twitched into a near-smile.

'Good, thank you. I had a lovely walk here. It's pleasant.'

Christina nodded. 'I had the doors in the kitchen open to the garden this morning as I had breakfast. We've almost wintered it out, haven't we? Now' – she gestured broadly to Clara – 'to business.'

Clara imagined Christina sitting side-on to a large, long, heavy wooden table, eating toast and jam, her body swivelled towards an old tree and patches of wildflowers, the pale sky in the distance framed by trestles of pink climbing roses either side of the sliding doors. Often, it was difficult for Clara to believe Christina was alive now, and not, essentially, a Victorian. She often looked at her as though she were a time traveller, someone not quite at home in the age in which she found herself. In Clara's imagined scene, Christina was doing a crossword, her elbow on the table, drinking tea from a fine, hand-painted china cup. And while Clara had never seen Christina do any of these things, there was something true about the picture.

She turned the recorder on and sat it in the centre of the table between the two cups. 'I was thinking about *Promised Land* this week.'

'Oh, you were? I like that one.'

'Me, too. It was the first of yours I ever read.'

'Yes, it seems that it is still taught in some places. That's a nice thing.'

Clara was keen to stay with her line of questioning this morning, and had considered that perhaps the best way to get to Christina's life was through her fiction and not, as she'd first thought, around it.

'*Promised Land* opens with a child painting her own portrait.' Clara spoke quickly to avoid interruption. 'And she only has the primary colours available to her, and white and black. I know you've talked about that many times over the years, but I wonder how much of that scene is autobiographical? Were you a painter when you were a girl?'

Christina looked at Clara as she formed her question, and continued to look at her for a few seconds after, in silence, as though waiting for more. She looked away.

'I suppose I'm not all that interested in those sorts of questions.' Clara put down her pen and went to speak, but Christina continued: 'You're right that I've been asked many times about that novel, and about that scene in particular. *It's a powerful image of girlhood, of having to form an acceptable version of yourself out of the colours available to you*. They tell me that all the time, as though I didn't know it when I wrote it. But questions about whether I am the little girl? What possible interest could they be to anyone? Who has ever read a novel and found their reading experience enriched by knowing the author was drawing on her own life? This is a very modern thing. And I mean in the last ten, twenty years. The obsession over autobiography, this sort of passionate pursuit of the author behind the fiction, like Dorothy in *The Wizard of Oz*. What could ever be gained by looking behind the curtain? A brief sighting of an ageing, fallible artist whose work is more interesting than they are.'

Clara made a few notes as Christina spoke and looked up at her as she finished. It was the first time Christina had given any real justification for her reluctance to talk about her own life. There was a hint of shame in what she said, almost as though she was fearful of her biography because the mystique around her work would cast the *real* Christina Darnell as mundane, ordinary, unworthy of attention. Clara wrote the thought down before speaking.

'But what about someone like Emily Dickinson?'

'What about her?'

'Her biography enriches the reading of her work.'

Christina pushed back into her chair. 'In what way?'

'Well, knowing about the wilful confinement of her own life in that house and then, later, in her room, gives me a fuller sense of where her poems come from, why they are so slight, so walled in.' Clara felt a little exposed by putting forward an argument, and found her right arm had moved across her stomach.

'But, Clara, they are walled in whether you know anything about the woman or not. The work is still the work, and in this case the connection between form and life is easy to draw. But what if we suddenly discovered she was a socialite who went to every New England party? You would be sitting here saying how she deliberately contrasted her public life and private life in her poems. It's arbitrary, in other words. You see,' Christina leant forward in her chair towards Clara, her hands pressed together, 'your generation seems to think literature is like a puzzle, and that by getting some sort of secret answer, the whole novel or poem or body of work will be unlocked, all because you uncovered where the writer bought her groceries or something. I'm afraid it's rather less scientific than all that. Literature, or at least good literature, has very little to do with the person who wrote it. As soon as a work is finished, it sits in a place between writer and reader, and both can lay some claim to its meaning, but there is no monopoly. The writer is only one reader among many, in the end.'

'This is all starting to sound a little "Death of the Author"-y,' Clara said. Christina smiled at the younger woman.

'Well, I'm nearly eighty, Clara, as strange as that may seem to look at me. But I am finding new meanings to Barthes as I approach my ninth decade.'

'But seriously, though, do you not . . .'

'I am being serious. As I get closer to my own death, I realise that Barthes was closer to the truth than a lot of the critics and professors now would allow. When I die and the literary vultures start picking away at the facts of my life, they'll see how impoverished their position on literature has been all this time. They'll want to forget everything about me if they wish to read my work and enjoy it. Maybe only by dying can a writer's work be read properly. If, that is, she is left to rest in some sort of peace.'

Clara was writing again, for she could immediately see a use for what Christina was saying. The introduction of her monograph could house a discussion on Darnell's death, and her musings on her literary afterlife. That Christina was already considering how her biography would be read and assimilated into the appreciation of her novels after her death was an interesting brute fact for a critic. It suggested there was something to read, something to find out about Christina's past, something she was trying to discourage the discovery of. Writers could often be private, but Christina Darnell was squeamish about biography to a near-ludicrous degree.

The thought crossed Clara's mind, as it had a few times in the past few weeks, that Christina knew that her famed reluctance to talk about herself would inspire a biographical reading all the more. Clara wondered if Christina wished to encourage it through fierce reticence.

As she was finishing scribbling her notes, Clara realised Christina had stopped speaking. She felt a jolt as she wondered how long there had been a silence.

Christina was looking at Clara's notebook the way a mother cat might regard a kitten, her head tilted to the side.

'You think that books are better read without regard for their authors?'

'I wouldn't put it as baldly as that but, yes, I do. To read a book because you find the author interesting, or to avoid a book because you find the author objectionable, is just about as neat an example of prejudice as I can summon. It is prejudice in its most literal sense.'

'But books *are* written by people, though.'

'Clara.'

'No, I mean, your position seems to deny the personhood of the writer, but I'm just saying that Hitler wrote *Mein Kampf*. It didn't invent itself.'

'You're right. And are you saying that if I didn't know anything about Hitler's biography I would fall in love with the ideas in that book? This is precisely the point: the utter loss of respect for the reader to actually read. What you've suggested there, Clara, is that we only know the book is bad because of the gas chambers. What I am saying is that the book was bad before it was retrospectively bad.'

Clara smiled. She had plenty to say in response, but an argument over the relationship between author and text would be a waste of her time with Christina. Very little of it would go into the book, which was meant to focus on the life behind the work, not the elaborate defences Christina put up, as interesting as they were.

'Is all fiction not just autobiography, though?' Clara went on. 'Does it all not come from some lived experience that finds expression in an invented narrative?'

'Huh.' Christina made the noise involuntarily, it seemed, as she looked up towards the air conditioning vents in the roof and leant back into her chair. 'Now we're getting somewhere,' she said. 'I thought we'd get here sooner, this idea of all fiction as biography. There might be something in it, but I think I'm allergic to it, because I've seen where that line of thinking leads.'

'Where?'

'To autofiction. Whatever the fuck that is.'

Clara was caught off guard by the swearing, as she was every time Christina swore, and laughed.

Christina narrowed her eyes and smiled.

'What's wrong with autofiction?' Clara asked, and Christina said nothing for a few seconds, picking a piece of lint from her trouser leg.

'There's nothing *wrong* with it, per se. That makes it seem like it's all a matter of taste, which it isn't. It runs deeper. It's that autofiction isn't actually a thing at all. It is a contradiction in terms, like a married bachelor or a square circle. Fiction, by necessity, is invention. Auto, by contrast, is rooted in some sort of established reality belonging to the author. To combine these things is to reduce fiction to autobiography, and ruin the only good thing about a memoir, which is its implicit claim to historical truth. There can be nothing good about combining invention and personal history in the one genre, like some sort of Frankenstein's monster. People may well pretend they find it beautiful, but we all know it's ghastly and will pass away soon enough.'

'Why do you think it's so popular now?'

'Because every twenty-three-year-old in the West is doing a PhD in creative writing, that's why. And what's more, they all seem to discover by their second year that they have nothing to say, that they have no actual imagination. And, strangely, they haven't experienced enough in their short lives to successfully make something up, so they turn inwards, and when they find nothing of much worth there either, they decide to invent a new version of themselves and call it autofiction. Why else is every second book nowadays set on a university campus? I'll tell you: because genuine fiction is very difficult. All of those sorts of novels read like writing exercises. *Take the architecture of your life and change it a bit*. That's all fine, but don't mistake an exercise for something worth publishing.'

Christina spoke without moving her head, as though she had written the response, memorised it and then recited it for Clara.

In her notebook, Clara wrote down: *CD aware of new trends in publishing – she does read new stuff?* Clara always had a suspicion that Christina was more invested in staying abreast of the contemporary literary world than critics assumed. While her novels could be austere and had a kind of old-fashioned fussiness about them, Christina the woman was much more image-conscious than her books made out. It was little surprise to Clara to find that Christina had well-shaped, considered views on present-day debates; but it was uncanny, nonetheless, to realise she had been watching and appraising, a kind of Deist God who elected not to intervene in human affairs.

As Christina continued to talk, Clara trusted the recorder to preserve what she was saying, as she found her thoughts had turned to the bookshelves in Christina's townhouse. This happened often, when she was watching Netflix, or trying to write. Somewhere, in those rooms, were the stacks of books, vertical, horizontal, leaning, that Christina had read, had cast aside, had loved, had made her weep. In that house was a collection of books that would tell a story that Christina resisted telling.

When Christina stopped speaking and reached for her cup, Clara flicked back in her notebook to the previous page where she had written some bullet points. She looked up at Christina.

'Aren't you writing a version of yourself in some of your novels? I'm thinking of the sexuality of your protagonists, which seems to align with your own.'

Christina set the cup down and did not look at Clara. When she spoke, she spoke to the floor.

'No, Clara.'

'Sorry, I am just wondering about the connection between you and the women in your writing.'

Christina sat back, upright, and looked at Clara. 'And why just the women? I have written male characters, too. A priest, a teacher. Would it be too outlandish to ask me if they are versions of me, too?'

'I guess it seems more realistic that your female protagonists are closer to you.'

'The key word there, Clara, is *guess*. That's all literary criticism is, nowadays. Guessing. You know, I once was invited to read at an academic conference on philosophy and literature – years ago now – and in the panel before my reading, a professor of twentieth-century poetry stood up and gave a twenty-minute paper on Anne Sexton's dentist. No, I'm not joking. Apparently, one of her poems mentions teeth, so that set him on a wild goose chase to discover who her dentist was and that, of course, led to a thrilling ten-minute concluding discussion of Freud's theory on teeth, and how this exploded critical judgements of the work of esteemed American poet, Anne Sexton.'

Christina threw her head back and laughed, the sound filling the room.

3
The Society of the Spectacle

Clara was in her apartment again. There was a scented candle burning on a table beside her that smelled of clean linen, and the radio from the bathroom had been set behind the sofa and played the sound of a muted trumpet. She retrieved her laptop from her bag, opened it to the file named 'Darnell Monograph' and cast her eyes down the screen. The bottom left corner read: 51,263 words. The radio played a tune that Clara recognised and she turned it up before taking her shopping bag to the kitchen, wanting in a strangely insistent way to hear the presenter say Miles Davis or John Coltrane.

Although it ought not to have been, the light outside was already waning. The kitchen was cloaked in sullen grey and the apartment was cold again, despite the warmer morning. The rental paint scheme of cream walls and white doors often had the opposite effect of what was presumably the intention of brightening the property. With the sad sort of light on offer on days like these, the walls seemed to give up their colour and turn to shadow. Clara went to fill the kettle for later and as she waited for the water to run cold, she noticed soapy watermarks splashed across the lower half of the window. It was usually only when she had someone coming over that she became aware of her apartment's preventable imperfections. She told herself it was because she lived so much of her life inside her own head that her windows were often neglected for weeks at a time, and laundry was often only finally done when she caught herself considering shorts in the middle of winter. On her way back to the dining table, Clara turned on the portable radiator by her chair to its first setting.

The walk from the coffee shop had felt short, as Clara had been turning Christina's words over in her mind and was keen to get back to writing. As a result, she found herself inside the supermarket without remembering crossing the road or lifting the basket she was then carrying through the fresh food aisle. She picked up a courgette, and the more expensive fresh pasta from one of the refrigerated sections, and then halloumi and a glass jar of green pesto. Clara was in the queue for the self-checkout before remembering garlic bread for Daniel, and would have turned back had the lady not asked her, 'Cash or card?' and directed her to the tills on her left with a nod of her head. She walked home without listening to music or a podcast, and her mind was quiet and alive, capable, for once, of thinking of just one thing at a time. She took the keys from her jacket pocket and felt a satisfying, bodily craving for what she had: an empty afternoon in which to write. Clara climbed the stairs at speed for fear that the feeling would leave before her laptop was open.

She blamed climate disaster, political corruption and both the threat of war and actual war for her relatively recent attention deficit. As an undergraduate, she remembered being able to work on essays for three hours at a time without needing a break. Back then, she played albums on a CD player her mum had bought her for her first Christmas as a university student; a sleek black square with two speakers connected with red and black wires. She had set the player and the speakers on a dark chest of drawers that smelled of the floral air freshener refills that had leaked in the top drawer, left there by the previous tenant – an anthropology student called Lisa, based on the textbook she'd also abandoned below the squeaky single bed. Clara stored her small collection of CDs in that top drawer, considering it better to put it to some use since it couldn't house clothes, smelling as it did. Ben Howard and Laura Marling accompanied her 3,000-word essays on Joyce, Freud and Brontë which were typed on an old mahogany desk she found in a charity shop and set at the far end of her thin student bedroom. Now, nine, ten years on, Clara lamented the loss of her attention span and occasionally considered its cause. There had been social media back in those days, too, which ruled that out as an explanation and she decided after speaking with friends that it was not a problem specific to her. Sophie said she couldn't watch a film without her phone in her hand and often checked the time on her screen, put it back in her pocket, only to realise she had forgotten to look at the numbers. It was a relief for Clara. She wasn't alone. She said that it couldn't be a sign of some deficiency on their part; that it was more likely a symptom of living just before the apocalypse.

'Imagine what it must be doing to our nervous systems,' Clara had remarked to Sophie one evening, as they sat drinking wine in Sophie's living room. 'We're on constant high alert. Our bodies respond the same way to a missed call as they would to a bomb scare.'

'I think I'm just addicted to my phone,' Sophie had replied, shrugging.

Sitting down on one of the hard, cheap pine dining chairs that came with the flat, Clara read through the first draft of her introduction. There was some editing to do, she thought, but it was solid. The first few paragraphs were lifted directly from her dissertation and, save for a few word changes, they had remained largely intact. Introductions had a very specific job to do, her external examiner had told her, and hers was ticking along fine.

Nothing she and Christina discussed on their Sundays would change the fact that she had to begin with a survey of Darnell studies, exploring the articles and arguments scholars had put together over the last forty or so years. The time she'd spent writing her doctorate had given her a bird's eye view of the field, and as she flicked her eyes down the paragraphs, she felt a sliver of pride that she could write this sort of material without much trouble. Her proposed monograph was fairly unique in that it would blend critical, scholarly writing with narrative and more personal prose based on the conversations she had with the author herself. Clara's PhD supervisor told her that by not committing to the usual academic monograph she was damaging her employment opportunities, but the literary studies editor at a reputable academic press had replied within ten days of the proposal being sent.

We're always on the lookout for new forms of scholarship, and ways to reach beyond the academy, he'd said in the email, before signing it off: Yours in books, Chris, which Clara cringed at. She saved the email in a folder named 'YES!' along with the email she'd got four years previously telling her that her PhD funding had come through. She looked at these emails every few weeks to keep her going. On those occasions the very typeface of the offer letter returned her to the loud staff room of the all-boys school she was in during teaching practice. The notification sound had ruptured a conversation about a playground fight. Clara opened it, her stomach lurching as she read the subject line: CONDITIONAL OFFER.

I've escaped.

The thought came unbidden, so Clara told herself there was no point in feeling bad about it; but she did, as often as the memory came to her. The geography teacher, a kind, middle-aged woman who seemed always on the verge of a smile, saw the look on her face as she read the email and touched Clara on the shoulder. It took her a few seconds to look up from her phone to the woman's warm eyes.

Still, the exhilaration the email brought her that afternoon returned to her, albeit in smaller and more complicated ways, each time she reopened it. Now, she still felt happy for the woman who received it, who took her mother out for dinner that night to celebrate; who answered her mother's questions about funding, the price of rent in Belfast for a single woman and the now wasted year doing a teaching qualification; who picked at her chicken stack with little interest, and who insisted her mother have the sticky toffee pudding she knew she would have wanted though wouldn't have considered ordering. But Clara's happiness was not without grief. The email attachment represented a block of time, a solid square three years of purposeful life. Now it was over, and the letter represented new, sad and melancholy things. The fact that time kept moving, for one; the realisation that the future never found her much different, for another.

There was a subtle change in the air as clouds parted outside Clara's apartment, and a stream of yellow light warmed her table. She closed the document, having saved the minor adjustments she had made, opened a new one and started to type.

Behind the Curtain: The Writer Beyond the Writing.

She highlighted the text and enlarged it, then changed the font to match the one she was using for her monograph. Clara screwed up her face at the screen and leant back in her chair.

There were two contradictory spatial metaphors in the title she'd written. Was she trying to say Christina was *behind* her own writing or that she was *beyond* it? She would come back to it once she had a draft of the chapter. The 'Behind the Curtain' part could remain, though. Christina had said it herself just an hour ago, and it struck Clara as an appropriate way to read

Christina's reluctance to open up about her past: the image of the older, smaller woman crouching behind a veil hoping to retain her reputation by never being uncovered.

Not for the first time, Clara wondered about the ethics of the book she was writing. Tabloid journalist she was not, but for the briefest moment, Clara had the image of Christina speaking intently to a woman who had her head down, thoughtfully and thoughtlessly writing the connections and implications that had just popped into her head. She felt something approaching embarrassment and readjusted herself in her seat. Increasingly, Clara found her conversations with Christina clashed with the version of herself that spent the rest of the week writing them up, interrogating them for clues and key words.

Clara looked down at her notes from earlier and started to type.

One of the most enduring scenes in Darnell's fiction, the self-portrait opening of Promised Land, *sits at the centre of the philosophic and political vision of her work more broadly. As an undergraduate, those opening paragraphs were my first encounter with the mind of Christina Darnell, with the patient, teasing quality of her prose, and I still find something new in those lines each time I go back to them. For example, that we never see what the girl has started to paint in that novel strikes me as important, for it is just one example of many in Darnell's fiction of her resistance to climax, or 'drama' as it is typically conceived. It is, in other words, a distinctly feminist approach to narrative structure.*

As I have got to know the woman who wrote the work, the image of the little girl painting her self-portrait has returned to me, freshly layered with significance. The little girl – perhaps Christina Darnell herself (we shall return to this later) – never shows the reader her rendering of herself, and the novel moves on from that initial scene with no further reference to the unfinished portrait. This metaphorical, almost fable-like opening is, I would argue, an instructive passage for understanding Christina Darnell herself. Recall that the girl in that scene refuses the help of a mirror, instead preferring her own imagination over the reality of her reflection. This is a very interesting turn to the imagination and to memory over the verifiable and – for want of a better word – 'reality' of sight, and it will be worth pausing over its significance. It is with this in mind that I wish to turn our attention to Darnell's opposition to biographical readings of her own work; to her own, as it were, refusal of the mirror.

Clara stopped typing and looked beyond the glow of the screen to the open kitchen door. The radio was playing an Ella Fitzgerald song and the lyrics had made it difficult to type. Clara lifted her phone from the table where it had been sitting, silent and face down. The time was 14.41 and she had a message from Daniel.

I'll be round at 4. Sleepover?

The aubergine emoji he ended the message with made Clara laugh.

OK. I have courgettes.

Daniel came online and read the message and then went offline. Then he came back and put a heart on Clara's message.

Clara closed her laptop, went into the kitchen and turned on the overhead light. She hadn't put the courgettes or the pasta in the fridge and they were sitting on the counter in their packaging, the plastic wrapper spotted with condensation that looked like frost. The chopping board was on the drying rack and she gave it a perfunctory wipe with the drying towel her mother had bought for her last year. It said 'PhDone' on one side in blue slanted writing, and on the other side there was a graduation cap which her mother insisted on calling a mortarboard. Julie had accompanied a friend to her son's graduation years before and had heard the other mothers talking about gowns and mortarboards, and the new term was seemingly all she took away from the experience. On the phone the night before her undergraduate gradation she asked Clara if she had remembered to rent a mortarboard.

'People don't really call it that, you know.'

'I don't care. I want a photo of you throwing it into the air,' she had said.

Clara pulled the plastic off the courgettes and began to slice one into satisfying circles. After the first was complete, she remembered to turn the air fryer on to preheat, and then she cut the other. After coating them in oil, she tipped the courgettes from their bowl into the basket and set them to cook for twenty minutes. Clara brought the radio into the kitchen and changed the station. She opened the fridge and removed a red pepper, listening to a man ask academics about the Salem witch trials. Clara chopped as he talked. She dropped them into the basket with the courgettes and took her phone from her pocket. There were no notifications. No further messages from Daniel. Clara opened their conversation thread and clicked on 'Media, images, docs' and scrolled through the photos they'd sent one another over the last four months. She tapped on the photo she was currently using as a cover photo for social media. It was of both of them, slightly obscured behind wine glasses, smiling, Daniel's arm across her shoulders. They looked happy. Daniel had taken her to an upmarket restaurant on the more expensive side of her road, and they shared a bottle of red wine over dinner and then another after their plates had been taken away. They had nothing to celebrate that night, which comforted Clara. She was occasionally concerned she had fallen into a relationship that relied on nights out to celebrate birthdays and promotions, glued together in the more mundane moments with weekend takeouts and good sex.

When she voiced this concern to Sophie, she had laughed. 'You're *complaining* about having good sex?'

Clara scrolled back further and clicked on another image. It was Daniel's penis, hard, taken from above, with his left hand holding a Coke can, its base held tight against his pubic bone. She clicked on the image again to bring up the texts and scrolled up.

All men say that.

Maybe.

Go on then.

What?

Prove it.

Clara looked at the time stamp on the messages. There were three minutes before Daniel's next reply, which was a photo.

I'd forgotten how big these cans were.

I respect the commitment to the cause.

Straight from the fridge. It's freezing. No judgement.

They'd been on three dates by then, and Clara hadn't yet seen Daniel naked. When they had sex after their second date, it was in the early hours of the morning, it was dark in Daniel's bedroom and they were both drunk from the wine they'd had with dinner. The next morning, she woke to him dressed in sweatpants and a Sum 41 T-shirt, holding a steaming coffee pot and an empty mug for her.

'I thought you might be dead,' he'd said.

The photo had intrigued her initially. It was strange to see him naked only after they'd slept together, and the Coke can made her laugh, despite the obscenity of the image. Clara was opposed to those sorts of photos in the abstract, perhaps even on principle, and she was quietly surprised at herself for not deleting it, and grew gradually more comfortable with the number of evenings in which she went back to it. Looking at it again, now, leaning with her lower back against the kitchen counter, she realised that it wasn't his penis that she was drawn to, but the flat of his stomach, the shape of muscle below the skin, and the subtle trail of hair that split it all in two. Daniel wasn't a gym-goer like his university friends and colleagues on the ward, but he ran twice a week and played rugby for an amateur team in East Belfast. It gave him a realistic look: a body that, if it was lit properly and from the right angles, could be popular on social media. When he left her bedroom after sex and Clara observed him from the bed, he looked just right to her; that is, not so sculpted as to make her self-conscious, and with just the right amount of visible muscle in his back to make her feel sad he had already come and was heading to get the wipes from the bathroom.

Clara typed a message to him.

Food will be ready anytime. Do you want an early or late dinner?

A reply came a minute later.

Brill. I can come anytime.

Well, I know that.

Clara put her phone back in her pocket and climbed the stairs to her bedroom. *Séances* was sitting where she'd left it on her bedside table, with a black bookmark keeping her place about a third of the way in. The cover of the novel was creased, and the corners were folded up and had recently started to split. It made the book look faintly ancient. The novel was her favourite to take down off her shelves and riffle through, smelling its now powdery pages. She was confident she could recognise a significant majority of her books by smell, by how their scent would bring her back to the chair she was in when she finished it, or to the person she was with when she bought it. Clara had been rereading Christina's novels since they started their Sunday conversations and, last week, she had finished *Promised Land* and had immediately moved on to the next novel. It was the sixth time she'd read *Séances* in five years and when she told Daniel that at the weekend, he'd screwed up his face.

'Are you not so bored of it by now?'

'No,' she said. 'When I was writing the dissertation I was reading like a PhD student, dissecting them and reading for arguments and everything. Now I can read them as they are meant to be read. But, anyway, they're so good it doesn't really matter how you read them. They never get boring.'

Daniel had tilted his head. 'To be fair, I've watched *Mad Men* three times.'

Clara had watched it with him. He'd espoused its virtues so powerfully in the first weeks of the relationship that she'd felt obliged to give it a go.

Daniel had lost patience with her after the fourth episode. 'Why are you on your phone?'

Clara looked at him and back to the phone. 'I'm making a note of something! It means the show is good,' she'd said. Clara had found the series' lack of obvious moral outrage at the period's misogyny and racism interesting. She'd jotted down some initial thoughts about how art can engage with controversial issues without needing to loudly proclaim the obvious point being made. Clara thought it could make for an interesting discussion with undergraduates who often only wanted to talk about art that totally agreed with their recently formed worldview, or – and this was even more common – a piece of writing universally praised for its quality that they could lambast for its out-of-date attitudes. At a conference in Durham during the final year of her PhD, Clara had fallen into conversation with a man called Sam, a teaching fellow in Philosophy of Religion in Sussex. After comparing research interests, Sam had told her that he was ready to leave academia following two terrible years of teaching. Clara hadn't heard anyone at this stage of their career openly admit a desire to move beyond the academy and felt instinctually repulsed by the idea. She found her opinions on Sam change instantly as she looked for evidence of some deficiency on his part, though, she had to admit, he seemed well-adjusted, humble, intelligent. She'd asked him about his experiences and his animated response had made her laugh.

'So I've been teaching Reformation and Enlightenment to final years. *Final* years. Got that?' Clara nodded, smiling in anticipation. 'We do the usual stuff, beginning with Luther, Calvin, Zwingli. The second half goes into Schleiermacher, Hume, Kant, blah, blah, blah: you know the usual stuff. But here's the thing – I checked out after the first four or so weeks.'

'What happened?' Clara asked.

'The students had no interest in any of the module's content. We read Luther's *On the Freedom of a Christian* for the first session, and I gave what I considered to be a pretty good introduction to the module, talking about how we were at the beginning of a theological, political and social explosion, how Luther was about to light a powder keg that we are still reeling from to this day. Exciting stuff, no?' Clara smiled again as Sam stood up straight from the doorframe he had been leaning on. 'Well, when we got to the discussion I asked them all about their response to the first text. We deliberately choose an easier reading for the first weeks, even though they are final year students. *Final year*: don't forget that. Anyway, the first person says she hates Luther already as she read that he was rude to his wife. Another person in the second row pipes up and says he'd read that too. So, the stage is set for the remainder of the module.'

Sam crossed his arms and looked at Clara.

'What do you mean?'

'I mean for the rest of the course, the discussion about the key texts of the Reformation was based almost entirely on if the writers would be acceptable on a twenty-first century university campus. Calvin was criticised for using male pronouns for God, for example. Now, as a theologian, I recognise their frustration with patriarchal language. In fact, I teach a master's course on queer theology. But my God, the fact that *final year* students couldn't see past their own concerns to get the genius of Luther and Calvin made me depressed. I found myself opening my fourth lecture with something like, "OK, folks, so today we look at the Counter-Reformation. Like the previous three weeks, you'll no doubt have come across material that might not align with your contemporary language or contemporary political opinions. I would encourage you to approach the theology on its own terms, just for the sake of a good discussion. And so you have something to write about at the end of this module." Stony silence. The discussion after my lecture was terrible. So I gave up. For the rest of the weeks, I deliberately set them stupid, inappropriate questions for group work and I sat at the front and looked for jobs in politics or policy research. The final nail in the coffin was seeing how much they loved the questions. Which, remember, were written as a piss-take.'

'Give me some examples, please.' Clara was enjoying the conversation and found herself happy to listen to this man, who was a few years ahead of her and willing to be honest. It was refreshing, and she found her view of him changing again.

'Oh, it was things like "If the Reformation had been led by the wives of the theologians, how would it have been different?" And "If the Reformation was to happen now, what would the Ninety-Five Theses be?" Stuff that might be fun to chat about in the pub, but not really questions for a module meant to be about learning the ins and outs of the Reformation and Enlightenment.'

Clara had laughed again at Sam's exaggerated frustration. He was exactly the sort of teacher she'd have loved. They continued to talk for a few minutes, and Sam asked about Clara's plans for after her PhD. It was difficult to talk for an extended period of time about her desire for a monograph and academic job to someone who had done all she was aiming for and yet was preparing to give it up. But Sam was not competing with her, so he really listened, and this meant that Clara didn't need to sound quite so certain of herself as she talked about the idea for her book. He nodded in all the right places and sincerely wished her luck. Clara looked him up a year later and saw his name listed as a policy advisor for a political party.

Clara sat down on the maroon-coloured duvet and rearranged the pillows on her bed. Leaning back, she again felt a pleasant stillness come over her. She picked up *Séances*, careful not to cause any more damage, and opened it at the bookmark.

'Ghosts didn't wear black until the nineteenth century,' the priest said, looking at her through the steam rising from his mug. Father Forbes seemed taller and wider in her kitchen than he did in the church, and his voice sounded cavernous and wide, too, as though it came from an open place down deep inside him. It had the echo of implicit authority, whether he was saying a prayer or, as he had done moments before, asking for a biscuit.

Marie leant in at this point, intrigued by what the man was saying at her table. 'What do you mean?' she asked, putting both hands around her cup.

'Up until the Victorian period, ghosts tended to be seen in white,' he said.

'They still are,' said Marie. 'The white ghost is still the way a child would draw one, Father. A bed sheet with eyes. You know the sort.'

'I suppose you're right,' he said, and bit his bottom lip.

'Sorry, I cut you off.' Marie dipped an oatmeal biscuit into her tea and looked to the priest.

'Well, as we near the end of the century, sightings of ghosts in black, particularly female, begin to be reported. Isn't that interesting? I've read various theories on the subject, and no one is quite sure why. Before this period there was a belief that a ghost would have progressed through Purgatory, and would have come out the other side purified, hence the symbolic white dress.'

'And what happened that made ghosts change their clothes?'

Marie smiled as she spoke and didn't take her eyes off the priest, until she suddenly felt the biscuit fall apart between her fingers. She looked down to the cup and back to Father Forbes.

'Well, I suppose the answer to that hinges on your theology. I, for one, am more inclined to think that what a ghost looks like tells us more about the person who did the seeing than it does about the nature of the afterlife.'

Marie put her thumb and index finger in her mouth and used her tongue to clear them of crumbs.

'And you're meant to be a man of God?' she said, a smile spreading on her lips. 'You're a doubting Thomas, Father!'

The man smiled back and took a sip of his tea. 'I have my doubts about ghosts, having never seen one myself. And I suppose I do sound a bit like Thomas, don't I?'

'Verbatim.'

Marie swirled her cup on the table, hoping to dissolve the biscuit she knew had gathered at its base.

Father Forbes straightened himself in her chair.

'Well, regardless. I do think you should stay away from the occult. The implications of dabbling in those practices are unclear to me, but scripture is unambiguous. Bad things await, witches are to be stoned and so on.'

Marie sat back and appraised the man.

'You call round, I make you tea, give you biscuits, and you threaten me with stoning. Is it any wonder priests aren't allowed to marry. The prohibition seems rather unnecessary if this is how you talk to women.'

The priest laughed and covered his face. 'Oh God,' he said.

The woman smiled and let a silence fall between them.

Father Forbes spoke again, a more gentle tone entering his voice. 'Well, Marie, I've done my job. I've told you the Church's position. It's up to you now.'

Marie looked at the man, the white of the collar and drained her cup.

Clara had put square brackets around the 'Doubting Thomas' dialogue years ago, when she was working on the second chapter of her thesis. Beside it, she had written 'Irreverent?' but nothing else. In her dissertation, Clara had quoted from the passage, using it to make a point about Darnell's writing of religious figures. They were exclusively male, and were often paired in conversation with a woman who used humour to undercut their otherwise typically assumed authority. In *Séances*, Christina's protagonist was a thirty-eight-year old, unmarried woman who, by the novel's close seduces the priest into bed. The surprise for Clara on her first read was not the priest breaking his vow (hypocritical clergymen were hardly a literary bombshell, even in the early nineties), but rather that Marie, the woman who claimed to have contacted the dead, was a lesbian.

Much had been made by early reviewers of the unexpected 'heterosexual turn' in the novel. Up to that point, Christina's work had not dwelt on love or sex between men and women, instead offering up what one reviewer called, 'sensitive explorations of transgressive love, that gladly sacrifice narrative breadth for moral depth.' *Séances* confused the critics. On a BBC radio show, one academic expressed his disappointment with the novel. Clara transcribed his comments and quoted them at length in her thesis. He said, 'Darnell had been gaining momentum as Britain's premier radical voice. The characters in her sublime first novel refused social and moral convention, and the text quietly challenged the settled conclusions of our culture through serious, compassionate characterisation. This latest novel undoes all of that work, as it seems Darnell has ceded to the reactionaries. Her book ends in the most conventional of scandals and seems, rather concerningly, to invalidate the sexual orientation of her own character.'

Clara, along with a majority of scholars now, disagreed with the initial reception of the book. It had been grossly misunderstood and, Clara suspected, part of the misunderstanding had been wilful and carefully calculated. If anything, *Séances* was Christina's most radical work, which, Clara suspected, was written in the full knowledge of its own likely misreading. For a modern reader, the book was properly termed 'queer', a word that was more spacious than 'gay', that had room for the movement and fluidity of the novel's principal character. Crucially, this was also a descriptor that Christina had claimed for herself in conversation, allaying any fears Clara had that her hero might have disappointed her with a late-in-the-day turn to conservatism. It happened often enough to justify the worry, Clara thought. Clara wrote in her thesis that had British literary critics had awareness of the potentials of the term back then, the novel would have been read properly from its publication. Clara also noted that by the time Christina's third book had come out, reviewers and academics seemed intent on offering only a rebuttal, a semi-'takedown' of the newest successful woman writer. It was a pattern that repeated itself every few years in the literary world, Clara noted. A woman could write an excellent novel, a prize-winner perhaps. But she would have to be prepared for her second or, if she was lucky, third book to be criticised and maligned. It was a natural fact of the earth's workings, like the water cycle or the summer solstice.

Clara looked up towards the open door at the sound of the doorbell. It was a harsh, grating sound, like the noise on a gameshow meant to indicate a wrong answer. Clara retuned the bookmark and set the novel down on the bedside table. She smiled into the mirror on the door of the wardrobe and then ran her tongue along her front teeth. There was another loud buzz. Clara lifted the novel and put it in the drawer. She went to the phone on the wall and lifted the receiver. A car flew past that Clara could hear through the static and from below the living-room window.

'Hello?' Daniel said, into the fuzzy silence.

'Come on up,' Clara said, pressing the red button.

4
Das Unheimliche

Fragrant pinks stars had begun to bloom on the magnolia tree in the university quad. A tall student with his hair in curtains blew cigarette smoke over the Sartre he was reading, his back against the tree's base. A group of women walked to their next class, takeaway coffee cups in hand, talking loudly about a holiday to Marbella. A mature student with a phone to his ear organised childcare on a bench. Inside the lecture building, it was quieter than it had been. It was the last week of lectures before reading week, and Clara had lost at least two dozen students, returning, she presumed, to their family homes and parents' washing machines in Strabane or Omagh or Coleraine. She had released the essay questions for the module assessment earlier in the week, and now realised it had been a terrible mistake. With the precise rubric now circulated, the students knew exactly what they had to do and, by extension, had worked out exactly what they *didn't*. Attend lectures, for one. Read any more books, for another.

> Choose one title from the list below. You must write on two novels from the module and make use of secondary criticism (at least five articles).
>
> 1. Contemporary fiction is more interested in political and social debate than 'art'.

2. 'The contemporary novel is a vehicle for genuinely free expression.' To what extent do you agree?
3. The biography of a writer is an essential component in interpreting a piece of contemporary fiction.

The one hundred or so students enrolled on the module now knew what questions were available, and many of them had clearly made up their minds. By now they had read five novels, and could reasonably justify not attending any further classes, instead writing their essays on two of the novels already covered. Looking out at the newly empty seats dotted around the lecture theatre, Clara chastised herself for not including a stipulation on the choice of texts. You must write on one novel from the first half of the module, and one from the second. Without it, Clara feared the last five weeks would see fewer and fewer students attending her lectures and, given the unethically small amount of money she was paid to deliver the module, the attendance of students was, in part, her encouragement to persist.

The module was in one of the larger lecture theatres, with tiered seating, multicoloured fold-out chairs and long rows of white tables that ran unbroken between the lines of chairs. There were no windows, and the cleaning products used in the room made it smell more like a science classroom than a literary one. Every other week, Clara would have to wait at the door for a nursing lecture to finish. She would stand at the entrance, half in the room, half in the hall, and watch the students, nearly all women, take notes right up until their teacher stopped talking. The woman who taught on the module was friendly, and always spoke to Clara on the way out. 'Sorry, I went over there. It's all yours now.' The nursing students took three or four minutes to file out after her, full of chat and clutching textbooks to their chests.

By the time Clara was setting up her presentation, a few of her students had already decided to leave the building and get an early lunch.

Clara reached her arms high above her head, joined her hands and stretched out the muscles in her back. She had sat in this lecture theatre eight years previously and watched a lecturer perform this same set of movements. She was a tall, blonde-haired woman, an expert on aesthetics. The lecture theatre had been full and loud that morning and Clara watched the woman fetch a USB drive from her bag and then open a presentation on feminist literary theory. Her name was Dr Kate Breton, according to the title slide. Clara had googled her as she waited for the lecture to begin.

> Research interests: critical and aesthetic theory; Adorno; post-Kantian idealism; theory of emotion; philosophy of literature. Open to PhD students in any of the areas listed above.

Dr Breton had slowly raised her arms and linked her fingers above her head. Clara had watched, breathless, as she pushed upwards, her eyes closed, stretching further and further, as though pushing a heavy box towards the ceiling. Kate was swan-like and deliberate in her movement and a few of the students had stopped their conversations to turn towards her. When she opened her eyes she let her arms fall, slowly, down by her sides and began to speak in a quiet, English accent.

'Good morning. We start this morning with Woolf's *A Room of One's Own* and we aim to finish, in an hour, with a Lacanian interpretation of a story that appeared last year in the *Sun* newspaper. Are we ready to begin?'

Clara looked out at her students. Only some of them had bothered to bring their copies of *The Little Stranger* with them, and a handful had laptops sitting open in front of them already. During the lectures she could never tell if the noise of typing was from the students making notes based on what she was saying, or if they were shopping for shoes. It would be draconian to email them all and ask them to bring notebooks rather than laptops, she thought, but it did cross her mind every week as she stood in front of them and felt a familiar powerlessness come over her.

Behind Clara, the screen displayed the cover of the book along with her title 'The Little Stranger: *Freud, Frights and Feminism*'. She had her name – Dr Clara Wilson – on the bottom right of the slide, opposite her contact email and office hours on the left.

She exhaled, tapped the microphone and started to speak. 'Who here believes in ghosts?'

There was still chatter in the room and only the front row heard what she had said. 'Good morning, everyone.' She clicked on the keyboard and a picture of the film *Poltergeist* came up. 'Who here believes in ghosts?' she asked.

Four hands went up.

Clara instructed the students to huddle into groups of three or four to discuss a question amongst themselves, which they did with little movement and loud talking. The first ten minutes had been frustrating, more frustrating, in fact, than usual. Their faces – those who actually looked towards her as she spoke – displayed an almost keen uninterest, or so it seemed to her. The clicking of laptop keys and the sounds of a muffled laugh from the back row finally caused her to change course. Perhaps they needed something to engage them, to lift the energy in the room. Instead of moving into the section on *The Turn of the Screw*, Clara decided to get them talking with one another about the book.

'You have five minutes to discuss the following question, after which, I'll want to hear some of your ideas,' she said. Some of the students began to whisper to those beside them. 'Quiet, please. Otherwise I'll have to repeat myself.' There was silence. 'Thank you. I want you to discuss the character of the narrator. Some reviewers have found him to be a surprisingly, perhaps even a conspicuously, dull figure. What role does he play in the narrative? Why has Waters written him in the way she has? What is she up to here?'

After Clara stopped speaking there was little talk. The students turned towards one another, some with guilty expressions; others shrugged and shook their heads.

Clara left it another few seconds and then interrupted. 'Okay, stop. It seems like this is the wrong question. Perhaps not all of you had time to finish the book. Can we try this, instead: discuss the metaphoric potential of a poltergeist. What could it signify in a narrative? Does it have to be proven to be real, or is there literary value in its ambiguous existence or non-existence?'

This time, to Clara's relief, there was talking. She took a sip of her water and breathed out. This year's cohort were hard work, certainly tougher than the previous year's group. She'd heard her PhD supervisor complain about them to the Head of School in October. The faculty had met for a wine reception to celebrate the publication of a book written by one of the senior professors. The book was a thick, tome-like study of metre and form in Irish poetry and was described by the professor as his 'life's work'. Clara only went to the reception to be seen to be there and as she listened to the man give an account of his last seven years of research, she felt an urge to cry, or to give him a tight hug. He was sixty-eight then, and looked older. He smoked cigarettes before and after every lecture, which he typically gave with no notes and without even a single reference to the assessment questions attached to the module. His students were frequently flummoxed by the essay titles when they were released, and then angered by the lack of reading lists or guidance. 'Go and read widely,' he would say when asked for some recommendations. 'Follow your interest.' It didn't seem to cross his mind that they might not have any. Clara had taken his course on Irish modernism years ago and regretted it. He pronounced the word 'theatre' as 'thee-ate-her' and told long, non-sequiturial anecdotes about his evenings and chance encounters with Heaney, Longley and Muldoon. Once Clara had got over his impressive performances in the lecture theatre – the uncanny recall of entire Yeats poems – the erudition and obvious expertise, she felt a hollowness come over her. The man was once-removed from his own life, living on scraps produced by the real talent. In lieu of writing his own poems or plays, or giving talks about his own fiction, he was doomed to become a master of other people's genius, to learn every detail of their lives and present them to a captive audience of nineteen-year-olds. His whole sense of himself was founded on a facade, she thought, a false belief that any of this mattered. That she was on track to do the same bothered her. But she would do it differently, she thought.

As she had watched him talk about his book, practically iridescent with pleasure, the thought crossed her mind that if this man retired, he would drop dead within the month. Clara had pushed all of those thoughts down and away. After the reception, she had stayed for the free wine and listened as her supervisor lamented the inattention of the new students to the old professor and Head of School.

'They all want to be English teachers,' he said.

'And what's wrong with that, Paul?'

'Nothing. In theory. I went around the room in a tutorial last week and asked them their favourite piece of art ever. Could be an album, a play, a film, a book, whatever.'

'That's a nice idea.'

'It helps me remember their names. Anyway, by the fourth student I already had three *Gatsbys*.'

'And what? It's a terrific novel. Pretty near perfect, in fact. Do you contemporary-lit people reject it out of hand because it was published before 9/11?'

'No, Linda. Schools teach it at A-Level. It's the only fucking book they've read. And, listen, when I asked why they liked the book so much, they all talked about how they fell in love with the Jazz Age.'

'Yes?'

'My arse they did! They all had nice teachers who made them cups of coffee and let them discuss what they thought the big eyes in the novel meant. It made them all want to be that very same teacher. Not a shred of evidence of any interest in literature, as far as I can see.'

Clara was comforted by the conversation. It meant she had a justification for when she found herself underwhelmed by the quality of discussion or by the blank expressions on her students' faces as she spoke from the front.

During her teaching course, she'd spent three months in an all-boys secondary school back in Derry City. There was no discussion of literary allusions or authorial intention in the English classes she observed in the first week, and she was told on her second day that to have kept all the boys in the room by the end of the lesson was a day's work well done. She began teaching the next week and had never felt nerves like it. But after her first class in which one boy, Sean, had done a headstand on his desk rather than tell her his name, Clara settled into the chaos with a feeling of unexpected satisfaction. She got used to pretending not to hear all the *fucks* and *cunts* as the boys bickered with one other on the way into her classroom. She became practised at not showing fear, and eventually, fell in love with each class she had been given. The boys largely came from the same estate she had grown up in, and, though they didn't know this, they seemed to sense something authentic in her approach to them. She found some other teachers patronised and condescended to the boys, saying things like, 'Would you do this sort of thing in your own home?' to which Clara knew instinctively the truthful answer was, 'Yes, miss.'

By the middle of the placement, Clara was surprised to realise she found teenagers genuinely interesting: the apocalyptic dramas, the tragedies, the sheer conviction they all seemed to have about everything when they were asked the right question. After a master's degree spent discussing psychoanalytic theory and the crucial role of the literary critic, Clara found herself relaxing into the gentle and tired conversation in the staff room, and the genuine laughter of the boys once she had gained their respect.

The routines of a classroom were peaceful: the handing out of books, reading pages from a novel, teaching the boys how to write short stories. She might have stayed in the profession for the rest of her working life save for a stray comment. Near the end of the teaching practice, Clara met a woman from the master's in Belfast for a drink. Helen had ambitions of being a literary critic and talked at length over a cocktail about her connections in journalism and the near disappearance of serious reviewers. She would revive the old art, she said, in a questionable attempt at irony. During the master's Helen had been vocal, as mature students often were. She would raise her hand during seminars, ask for precise definitions of words. She somehow acquired the lecturers' mobile numbers and texted them between sessions, telling her classmates stories of her latest exchange with the Fulbright scholar in the pub after a seminar. Clara knew she was brighter than Helen, and the unspoken realisation allowed her to permit Helen her excesses. Near the end of their drink, Helen mentioned a book her sister was reading. It sounded interesting and when Clara asked if her sister was involved in literary circles, Helen laughed a little and said no, she was just a teacher.

An observer would not have realised the extent to which the comment collided with Clara, her unblinking eyes, the slight tightening of the lips. But, internally, Clara's mind was whirring. She thought of all the things she could say, the boys she taught every day who would hate this pretentious woman.

Helen kept talking, but Clara had switched off.

They said their goodbyes by the station and Clara spent the train journey home trying to focus on a novel. Eventually, she took out her phone and searched up doctoral programmes.

Moving from the classroom to the lecture theatre had been a real challenge, and she found the polite lack of honesty in university students hard to take at first. Sometimes, when she stood in front of the unimpressed, largely grammar-school educated adults in the lecture hall, she found herself summoning the faces of children she'd met in the classroom. Boys she would never forget: James, the first to come out in his year group; Alex, the good footballer who never had money for school trips; Toby, who had lunch with the librarian as she was the only one who could get him to eat. They felt more real to Clara than the students who came to her lectures.

Clara looked around the lecture theatre and found herself able to pick up phrases from the discussions.

'Reminds me of the novel The Exorcist *– not the film. Anyone else read it?'*

'It's a way of anxiety or mental health expressing itself.'

'Why does it have to mean something? Why isn't it just a ghost?'

'Freud has this whole thing about doubles. We did it last semester.'

Clara let the students talk for another few minutes, passing the time with a look at her notes for the rest of the lecture. She still had Freud's 'The Uncanny' to cover (most of the students would have read the essay in their first term in 'A Journey in the History of Ideas': a cumbersome, uselessly broad module all students were automatically enrolled in for their first semester) and, if she had time, she would lead them on to five minutes on alterity in feminist theory, giving them a reading of the novel with gender in mind, an alternative to the class-based readings the students would encounter in their wider studies.

Clara spoke clearly from behind the microphone: 'Okay, well done. That'll do.' She gave the students a few seconds to finish their sentences and turn themselves back to face her, which they did. 'Excellent. I was listening and overheard some very interesting chat.' Clara motioned to the second row. 'Can this group here talk to me about ghosts. Give me a couple of ideas to get us started.'

At this, a small woman from the group raised her hand. Clara recognised her from the previous term and remembered her being quite good. Lucy? she wondered. Hannah? 'Yes, go ahead,' Clara said.

'We actually started with the question you asked, Dr Wilson. We were wondering why a ghost or a poltergeist has to automatically be read as a symbol. It seems like the question relies on an assumption that needs to be discussed first. What if it it's just itself?'

Clara beamed at the young woman. 'It's Hannah, isn't it?' She nodded. 'Hannah, this is excellent thinking. Did we all hear what she said? Hannah's group have raised a brilliantly clever issue with the question I asked. Why does a ghost have to be a metaphor? Why can't it just be a ghost?' She paused and looked around the room. 'Well? I'm not here to answer questions.' Clara was pleased to hear a few laughs. A young man in a quarter-zip fleece raised his hand. 'Yes, go on.'

'Isn't the whole point that a novel is written by a person, so, if it's a good book, we should assume everything is there for a reason, especially something like a ghost? It has to mean something, especially since normal novels don't have ghosts all that often.'

Clara smiled. 'You've taken us back another step. I like it. Now we have to consider why anything at all would end up in a novel. Surely it's all pure intention, the writer's will, their desire to "say something" to us? What do we think?'

Another hand went up in the back of the lecture theatre. Clara gripped the edge of the table in front of her and swayed. It was the first time she'd ever felt anything approaching joy in this particular lecture theatre. She pointed to the woman at the far end of the room.

'I don't think everything is in a novel by intention,' she said, in a loud, clear voice. 'That assumes that every writer is like an all-knowing machine. I don't think that's right. It leaves no room for chance or accident, or . . . I've forgotten the word.'

'Mystery?' Clara guessed.

She nodded.

Clara smiled. 'Thank you. We're getting somewhere.' She paused and glanced around the room. There was a new energy in it, enough, possibly, to venture another question. 'Indulge me,' Clara said. 'Raise your hand if you think everything in a work of fiction is there intentionally.' Seven hands went up immediately, then another four or five, and then one or two others who were sitting close to other people who'd raised their hands. Clara nodded appreciatively. 'Can any of you tell me why?' She looked at each of them, watched their eyes cast towards their laps. To Clara's relief, a young woman in the third row gave a little wave of her hand and Clara nodded to her.

'How else would anything get there? If a writer has to choose the name for a character, she may as well make it mean something. And, even if she doesn't care, that is still an intention, isn't it? Whether a detail is important or not, even that is up to the writer.'

A man behind the woman made a face of approval, nodding his head as she spoke.

Clara was impressed with the woman's clarity. 'Good,' she said. 'Really well put. You're saying that even though not every detail of a novel – the specific colour of bed sheets for example – are appropriate raw materials for an interpretation of a novel, that doesn't mean that the author has given up their claim on the text's overall meaning.' The woman nodded her head slightly. 'In the way you've conceived of it,' Clara went on, 'even the writer's decision not to care about certain details is still a product of intention. That's really clever.' As Clara spoke she saw a few people shaking their heads. 'Go on,' she said, nodding to a tall woman to her right.

She had crossed her legs into the aisle and put down her pen as Clara spoke to her. 'I think that that way of thinking is a bit dead, or scientific or something. It reminds me of being in school when my teacher would tell us that the colour of a carpet said something about the emotional lives of the characters. I hated it then and I think it ruins reading. It leaves no room for the reader, for the uncertainty of what a good book means. The novel we read this week is all about ambiguity, and the reason I loved it so much is because the writer left everything, even the story's closing scenes, totally up to us. Two readers could have read the novel at very different levels: one, as a simple ghost story; another as a psycho-domestic story of the upper classes' anxiety about class in post-War England. It works as both, and the writer leaves it totally up to us. Even in an interview I watched, she said that one of the things she liked about writing the novel is that the meaning of the poltergeist is up for grabs, even for her.' The woman paused, as though suddenly aware of where she was. 'Sorry, I've gone on for too long.'

Clara balled her fists in the air and shook them. 'Oh, you've all made me so happy,' she said, through comically gritted teeth. The students laughed.

*

Clara stopped for a coffee on the way from the lecture theatre. For the past two years an independent coffee business had rented a space on the ground floor of the building and established a pop-up shop, selling hot drinks and tins of Coke, or pre-made filled croissants to students who had skipped breakfast. The filter coffee was cheap and strong, and Clara could typically only stomach half a cup before throwing the rest in one of the big bins by the automatic doors. On one occasion, the staff had let the coffee churn all morning and the resulting cup Clara was offered made her right eye twitch after just a few mouthfuls. That afternoon, the sofas and tables were all taken and the space was loud with chat and laughter. Clara asked for a small filter and nodded at the barista who had nodded at her.

If Clara was honest with herself – which at times, she was – the real reason she queued for coffee was because she enjoyed the feeling of being looked at by the students she had just taught, or by those she'd taught the previous year whom she could just about remember. No matter how the lecture or tutorial had gone, Clara would feel the glances of admiring eyes on her as she scrolled through her phone. It made her feel important.

Unlike the boys she'd taught in the school, Clara's new students didn't need anything from her. Not really. And in the absence of being needed, feeling admired was a decent substitute. She told herself it was genuinely good practice to make herself visible in the foyer, for how many times had a student approached her in the queue and asked a basic question that Clara could answer in seconds? She reckoned she headed off possibly time-consuming email exchanges simply by being present. Clara was so accommodating and friendly to these students she likely inspired them to write the emails she often received a day or two later, with further questions, such was their satisfaction in finally communicating with an approachable lecturer who seemed to care.

Standing in the foyer, Clara let herself enjoy the adrenaline and dopamine rush. The lecture had been the best of the semester.

One of her students – the tall woman who had spoken at length about the novel (she was called Aithne, Clara learned) – had made her way tentatively to the front of the lecture theatre as Clara was packing up. She had thanked her for the lecture and said it had given her many ideas for her essay. Clara said she was glad it was useful, and remarked on how valuable Aithne's contribution had been. She batted away the compliment and asked Clara if she would be better pairing *The Little Stranger* with *The Gathering* by Anne Enright, or if she should wait until they'd covered *Milkman* in week nine. Clara recommended waiting and making an informed choice, telling Aithne that she was intelligent enough to write a brilliant piece in a short period of time if necessary. Aithne had left the lecture theatre with a smile on her face.

Clara knew it had gone well, for she recognised the energy she was feeling had come directly from the students. She put her phone in her pocket and looked around at the occupied tables. It was at these precise moments – the twenty or so minutes following a lecture – that Clara was most acutely aware of the doubleness of her life. Coming from a council house in Derry, Clara recognised she did not really belong amongst the sons and daughters of doctors and barristers she had studied alongside during her undergraduate years. Her lecturers said she had raw talent when it came to writing essays and discussing texts, but when the seminars ended, Clara found she didn't quite have the language to comfortably join the groups going for lunch or to the poetry events. Early on in her first semester, Julianne, a second-year literature student, suggested lunch to Clara after a lecture on post-structuralism. (Julianne downloaded the timetables of lecturers she liked and sat at the back of lectures she thought would be interesting. 'They don't take attendance,' she'd said to Clara who was bemused not by her eagerness but with her seemingly shame-free commitment.) Clara sat opposite her as they shared a bottle of wine Julianne had insisted on buying. She wrote 'spoken-word poetry' – Clara wondered if this was a contradiction in terms but pushed the thought away, assuming she had misunderstood something – and had been up all night rehearsing for a slam event she said Clara should come along to that evening.

'I would usually have had the evening to myself, but my dad had the Chief Justice over for dinner, so we were all called to be around the table for seven.' She took a long drink of wine and tucked her long dark hair behind both ears. 'I hate it when he does things like that.'

Instances like this, to greater or lesser extents, highlighted to Clara that she was, to use the term her professors had insisted on using in every lecture, an outsider. And when she turned her attention away from campus, back to where she grew up, Clara found she no longer belonged there either. Her mother and her aunt had never fully understood the little girl who gobbled books up by the day and now, as an adult, looking back, Clara found she had never really understood them either: how they would gossip and complain about the neighbour's loud music; become obsessed over something one of their friends had said; spend hours watching soaps on TV. Only on moving out of her mother's house did Clara recognise that they had been largely strangers to one another; that if her mother had had no caregiving responsibility for Clara, she would have had lots to say about the odd little girl who obviously thought she was something.

Now, Clara was playing a new part. Standing in the foyer of the lecture building, Clara once again felt the subtle shame of standing in the foyer of the lecture building. She was surrounded by students who, she knew, had come from a diverse set of backgrounds, from beyond Ireland, from estates like hers, from a whole range of possible beginnings. But, when she looked around, part of her felt like it was still her first day on campus and she was once again intimidated by the big words the other students seemed to know (*post-colonialism* and *new historicism*), by the extroverts who ran the societies and already seemed to know everyone, by the girls who would have rolled their eyes at her in school when she answered the teacher's questions. It was ridiculous, she thought, and the feeling retreated slightly. She was meant to be where she was, meant to be writing a book, meant to be teaching at a university. And, she thought, looking around at the students, she would be meeting Christina Darnell on Sunday.

As Clara turned away, she found herself smiling, a child protecting her secret. Despite everything – the undergraduate essays, the master's thesis, PhD dissertation all dedicated to Christina's work – Clara found she still felt the same way about the novels. They felt like the familiar walls of her own private world. No amount of studying and writing would change that.

There was a reason, Clara thought often, why Christina's novels fell on such fertile soil within her. The precise moment of her first reading *Promised Land* coincided powerfully with the recognition that she was in exile, caught between two versions of herself she had yet to successfully assimilate. Christina's fiction sat at the 'between-ness' of things too, or, as Clara had put it in her PhD: 'Darnell's work occupies the liminal spaces between the privileged and the ostracised, the insiders and the expelled.' Clara liked the sentence and would have copied it into the monograph word for word had she not watched a Zoom panel on literary criticism that featured her editor, Chris, a few months before: 'The word "liminal" is the one term I would happily throw into the garbage heap of academic lingo,' she remembered him saying. 'Its unending use, particularly within literary studies, suggests it fills a hole until an academic has something actually interesting to say.' He said it with a smile and the small audience laughed at his exaggeration. On hearing it, however, Clara immediately opened her laptop and used CTRL F to find all her uses of the word and synonymised them as best she could. Still, Christina's novels *did* occupy those spaces, they *did* examine the psychology of being ill-at-ease in the world, of being homesick for an imaginary past, impatient for a romanticised future, the feeling of being caught or stuck or impossibly stretched between too many things. Clara wondered if she fell for Christina's writing not due to its aesthetics or its intelligence or its subtlety, but rather by instinct, at some deep level of human experience. For while she had little in common with the novels' characters, their professions and traits, she felt that the mind who produced each of them would surely recognise her as kindred.

Clara pushed the button by the door and stood back as its glass lumbered open into the foyer. She felt a chill in the wind as she stepped out into the courtyard and pulled on her headphones. She had an old BBC recording lined up and had been looking forward to listening to it again on her walk home. It was recorded at the turn of the millennium as *The Shape of Clouds* was published in the UK and was one of the few interviews Christina had done for the book. Even then, essays didn't get much attention. Clara pulled the time stamp forward to 2.13, which she knew from memory was when the interview started. She braced herself for the slightly higher pitched, quick delivery of Christina's younger self.

Christina, you've said in the past that woman have, traditionally, been the superior writers.

I have, haven't I? Now, I don't want to be taken as encouraging some sort of battle of the sexes. I'm just looking around and looking into the past and telling people what I see. It's not a prescriptive judgement, I don't think.

Is it an essentialist one?

In what sense?

You're not saying that there is something more natural about a woman writer, or that a woman has some essential qualities that predispose her to writing well that a man does not share, are you?

Oh, God, no. How could we ever prove such a thing, anyway, even if it were true? No. My point is simple. Muriel Spark, Penelope Fitzgerald, Iris Murdoch, Doris Lessing. These were the great writers of my childhood and young adulthood. Yes, there were the men, too, but I have to say, I find those women superior. It isn't a biological thing, no, but there must have been something in the cultural waters. You're going to ask me what that was and I'll tell you before you ask, I have no idea.

Well, how does feminism feature here? Does feminism help explain the rise of the woman novelist?

I think it does. But, I once heard A.S. Byatt say that it also helps explain the recent near-disappearance of serious women writers. I think she might have overstated the case, somewhat, but her point was that as women writers began to be taken up as subjects of academic theory, there was a subsequent dip in the quality of the novels being written by women. It all became self-conscious, writing became 'women's writing'. And that is a significant shift.

You don't like the term 'women's writing'?

I can't see much use for it except within the cloisters of academia. There is a growing binarisation happening in the arts. What I mean is that critics seem to be increasingly interested in the identity markers of the artist and less and less keen to approach the art itself. That seems to me to be a great loss.

I imagine those sorts of people would say that by focusing on artists' identities, a lot of otherwise under-represented groups of people are now signing book deals, making films, having their plays produced.

Which is wonderful. It really is. I benefited from the removal of gendered barriers back when I started writing in the 1980s. But if people really cared about opening access to the arts to everyone, they would get on with that and wouldn't beat the artists over the head with an increasingly more specialised set of adjectives once their work is published. The work is the work. Remove barriers, let artists produce work and stay out of their way.

Clara took her phone from her pocket and paused the interview. Hearing Christina talk yet again about the obsession around the lives and identities of writers had sent her mind spinning. She had long suspected that the aversion Christina had to this particular line of inquiry was not just a matter of taste, but a thing in itself – a substantial factor in her thinking that needed to be accounted for. There *must* be something she was missing about Christina's life. Not for the first time, Clara's imagination invented a secret daughter or a son, an illicit affair with another writer, or a politician, even a series of money-making pseudonymous novels Christina would rather not be associated with. The interviewer had only had about twenty minutes with Christina, but Clara had months. She had no excuse not to get something; although, as their meetings had gone on, she found the impulse to pursue Christina's secrets was sated simply by the sound of the woman's voice.

Clara resumed the interview.

Margaret Atwood won the Booker last year, Jhumpa Lahiri won the Pulitzer. It's a good time for women in writing, isn't it?

It is.

On a slightly different note, who excites you these days? Who stands out to you?

Lahiri's book was a deserved winner. It was exceptional. Atwood's, too. *The Shipping News* took my breath away, but that was a handful of years ago now. I'm currently reading Spark's new one, *Aiding and Abetting*. I can't be objective about it yet, or maybe ever. On the male side, I think McEwan writes well. He's probably the most interesting of that group. Kingsley's son wrote one good book, as far as I can see. The rest is style. Women can't get away with that, by the way. It seems we have to prove ourselves afresh with each new publication.

You see real differences in how women and men are received as writers?

Of course. Men's literature – which is a term that is never used, by the way – is universal, with implications for every person, for the cosmos itself, in some cases. A man can write a novel about one day and it is seen as the Word made flesh. Women's literature, by contrast, is read as entirely bound by the biography of its author. Women authors cannot make universal declarations. We are too busy writing about marriage. Perhaps this is where I, like many others, make my departure from conventional thinking.

And this new publication of yours is a departure of sorts. A collection of essays. Where did the idea for the collection come from?

In truth, from two full spiral books of handwritten

notes. The essays are taken from scraps and writings I've been making for years, the earliest notes from the writing of my first book. My agent read the notebooks and sent me a letter suggesting I organise them into something, and that's what I did.

And despite the time period over which you have written the source material for these essays, the collection is striking in how cohesive it is. Did that surprise you?

Writing is fundamentally mysterious, Marcella. It really is. When I read through the manuscript of the collection, I have to say I was surprised it all hung together quite as well as it does. Writing gives the passing of time a sort of coherence it might not otherwise have had, or, perhaps, it reveals a coherence that might have gone unappreciated, I can't be sure which it is. But when I read these essays, it feels like they were written all together when I know, in fact, that they were written in all sorts of different times and places. I usually only have that sort of feeling with a novel, once it's finished. The kind of arc it gives to the time given over to working on it. But all writing is writing fiction, isn't it, so I shouldn't be too surprised at the experience with this book.

You've subtitled it *Essays on Art, Truth and Fiction.* Are these the main concerns of your thinking all the time?

There isn't much left out by a subheading like that, is there? But it did give me freedom to include pieces on music, for example. To answer your question directly, I suppose the answer is yes. When I'm not caught up with groceries and washing countertops, my mind tends to turn to the relationship between art and truth.

Actually, perhaps it is especially when I am cleaning countertops that my mind turns to that. Chores have a remarkable way of encouraging the mind to slow and think carefully. It probably comes from the same place as all those repetitive religious practices, like the rosary.

And religion has come into these essays, hasn't it? That might surprise some readers.

I can't imagine why it would surprise them, though you're right that it might. Religion and literature are allied phenomena. I know I should be railing against the conservative confines of organised religion, but I confess to having few hang-ups about the whole thing. A blessing of a non-religious upbringing, perhaps – that I can approach old texts with optimism rather than trepidation. For me, religion is like an old chest full of artefacts. We don't want to lose touch with what it has for us. Truth matters to me, as a writer of fiction. As strange as it may seem to your listeners, I do think the ancients cared about that too.

You seem to find striking consistency across human thought. Where a lot of thinkers want to emphasise the particularities or the divergence between cultures, time periods, one thing this collection does is focus on the surprising coherency of human thinking. Is that a fair reading?

It's an interesting one. I think I would agree with you if I can emphasise the importance of subtlety and nuance. I am not blind to the very real diversity in the way groups of people assert their identity, worship their gods and so on. But you are right, I am absolutely fascinated with how the fundamental problems of how to live in this world remain fundamentally unchanged given the millennia that have passed. At one level, most human thinking – the very best of it, anyway – is trying to articulate its answer to the question 'How can we be at peace?' Major themes in our thinking can be seen through this lens. Love thy neighbour, the rise of democracy, the strange emergence of grace in the midst of very hard times, the exploration of space, the rise of the arts, of the novel. All of these things seem to be an articulation of an authentically human desire: the desire to be at peace, to make our lives with one another a little easier, to understand why our behaviour falls short of our highest thought. You see, Marcella, I consider people good, not evil. I think most of our problems today come from a lack of peace and misguided attempts at gaining it.

It's as simple as that? A search for peace?

Well, I'd be surprised if you considered that simple. Very few people find it.

You do write in the essay 'On Time and Memory' that an authentic life, a life 'at peace', as it were, comes from realising that living is an artful pursuit, not a logical one.

That seems to me to be fairly obvious. We create our lives out of the most spare raw materials, don't we? The anxiety that pervades our culture today comes at least in part from thinking there is some 'right' way to live. There is no finally correct way to write a novel or paint a landscape. I take this as an instruction.

And what about you, Christina? Does this writing come from experience? Have you found peace?

Like I said, I don't tend to write about myself.

5
On Relativism

The following Sunday, Christina spoke quickly, in one long, unbroken monologue. That morning, she had been irritated by a poet speaking on the radio as she ate her breakfast. When she arrived in the coffee shop, Clara asked her how she was and did not speak another full sentence in the three minutes that followed.

'I know it's a small and pedantic thing to home in on, Clara, but the man's voice was so off-putting. He had this slow, clever, American accent. I'm not good with placing those sorts of things, but he sounded like he'd be from a big city and probably writes his work in a university. Certainly not in the south. There was no warmth to his voice. But the way he answered the questions got underneath my skin. He spoke as though he were better than the questions. And he started his answers with superior little phrases like, "I suppose I didn't really consider those sorts of things when working on the book." Although when I say that now, it doesn't sound all that bad. But the *way* he said it irritated me. Almost as though he was really saying "This question is stupid. Of course I didn't think about this when I wrote my work of genius." That was just one thing. But the main thing was the way he actually spoke about poetry. My God. You could be forgiven for thinking he was talking about continental philosophy. Phenomenological, ontological, the impossibility of the contemporary poem escaping irony. Oh, Clara, it made me glad not to be a poet. Do they really consider all of that before they sit down to write? It was all so manly, so without feeling. I don't go to many poetry readings now, and I never really read much poetry, but I heard Seamus Heaney read in London somewhere, in the nineties. I know that it's unfair to compare a younger poet to someone like Heaney, but listening to that man today, I couldn't help but think of him again. To say he doesn't quite measure up would be to miss the point entirely. I thought to myself, he isn't even working in the same field. What has happened to poetry that men like this one are now the ones being interviewed on the BBC? When he got round to reading the actual work, I was speechless, Clara. It wasn't a poem. It was some sort of riddle, as far as I could tell. He introduced it by saying it was about becoming a father. Then he read it. He may as well have said, "My first is in boat but not in canoe." There was nothing of any substance in it, no heart. And I'm not saying that all good books are full of emotion or something like that, but when you introduce your book as about fatherhood and it's all abstract philosophising, it does give you a sense of the writer. Maybe even the father. But I digress. When did literature become an intellectual game? I really do think that's a fair question.'

Clara sat relaxed as Christina spoke, and nodded and smiled occasionally to show she was listening. She did not write anything down.

When Christina finished, she took up her cup, still shaking her head.

Clara spoke up: 'I suppose postmodernism is where it all starts, isn't it?'

Christina narrowed her eyes. 'I hate these sorts of words.'

'Well, it's relevant here, I suppose.'

'Go on, give me the academic jargon.'

Clara laughed as Christina put her cup down and looked over at her. 'Well, I guess that postmodernism celebrates the fragmentary nature of consciousness, the randomness of thinking, the lack of a coherent whole to life, and the art that follows it is looking to represent those things in some way. The poet you heard this morning might be a postmodernist, or a post-postmodernist.'

'He was a snake-oil salesman, Clara.'

'Well, some critics think that might be a distinction without a difference.'

Christina nodded. 'Nicely put. I think that's right. This denial of selfhood, the obscuring of a person's perspective, just feels empty to me.'

'I agree. But what if it's true?'

'Go on.'

'What if the postmodern representation of reality is accurate? What if the world really is, at base, chaos without meaning?'

Christina considered what Clara was saying. She moved her tongue across her bottom lip a number of times. Her eyes were thoughtful, moving. 'Ah,' she said softly. 'But this is exactly what they are arguing against, isn't it?'

'What?'

'That an accurate portrayal of reality is possible. If we say that the postmodernist vision is true, aren't we also saying that postmodernism must therefore be false? We can't let them say that objective truth is an illusion while also claiming that their claim is, by some fortunate coincidence, the only true thing. That way fascism lies, Clara.'

Clara's mouth tightened into a line and she looked down towards the table and then back to Christina.

'Isn't postmodernism meant to be an attempt to get rid of totalitarian thinking?' Clara said. She was trying to think back to a critical theory class she'd sat in on a few years prior, but all she could remember were the words 'sign' and 'signified', and the tutor pointing to the clock on the wall to illustrate the difference. It hadn't made much sense then, either.

'It may well have been. But look at the world you've inherited. No objective truth, fear of meta-narratives. And I agree that those things can be bad, and that evil things can be done in the name of truth and a grand story, like nationalism or colonialism. But the denial that truth exists is not only incoherent, it is dangerous. Sometimes some people are just wrong, Clara. And sometimes some people are right. We can't live comfortably in a world where facts are reduced to mere interpretations. And the irony of it all is that a lot of people your age rush to call things fascistic when they don't agree with you, but very few step back and see where it all comes from: the basic denial of truth.'

Clara lifted her cup and blew on her coffee.

'Do you disagree?'

Clara set her cup down. 'No, I don't. I was just thinking of how this relates to literature. Surely as a writer you believe that interpretation is key, that a book's meaning exists only by interpretation.'

Christina nodded. 'Of course. A book's meaning is not a stable fact. But it would appear that, nowadays, the physical existence of one of my books on a table might be up for debate. *That* used to be taken as a fact.'

Clara squinted. 'I don't think anyone would deny the existence of a book if it was sitting in front of them.'

'Nor do I, in most circumstances. But if it is politically expedient to deny the existence of a book, I believe there is a growing number of people who would do just that. In the past, the number of people who attended an inauguration or a political protest was taken as more or less a fact. Now, politicians and media consultants will lie about the number of people in a photo while it is being displayed right there in front of them. It seems to me to be moment of great danger here. I do still have the stomach for debate on how we interpret facts, but I confess I am losing hope in our species if our public conversation has digressed to the extent we are now debating not the *interpretation* of established facts, but the actual *existence* of them.'

'I agree with you,' Clara said. 'But then there are people arguing that nuance doesn't exist, that there are simple facts and that any attempt to discuss interpretation or a different way of looking at something is just blind ideology.'

'That's right. I am talking here about cold, hard facts. Numbers, percentages, that sort of thing. Those things are provably true or false. But you're right, Clara. There are whole swathes of people who seem intent on reducing complex, nuanced things to simple binaries. That has never led to good thinking. Your generation seems a little better at dealing with nuance than my own, I'll give you that.'

'You think so?'

'Well look at the worst offenders, the people who deny truth in the most blatantly absurd ways. They tend to be of my generation, don't they? Maybe we had life a little easier, or something. I think it's impacted our ability to handle ambiguity.'

Clara went to speak but Christina continued.

'I say "our", but I hope I've managed to avoid it. Writing helps, I'm sure.'

Clara looked down at her notebook. Weeks before, Christina's passion in conversation would have unnerved her, made her retreat a little and soften her next question. Now, Christina's unfiltered honesty made her feel something like gratitude. She could navigate a conversation with her without fear. Clara had three questions for their interview that morning and they had not touched on any of them. During the week, she had planned to ask Christina about the role religion played in her fiction, and aimed to get her to speak about her own personal relationship to Christianity, or lack of it.

Getting to Christina's life might be easier by beginning with ideas, she thought. At the very least it might remove abstraction as a means of escape.

'I'm sorry, Clara,' Christina said then, looking at the younger woman's open notebook. 'You haven't got to your questions.'

'Oh, please don't apologise. Everything we talk about is interesting.'

'I blame that pretentious little shit on the radio.'

Clara smiled at Christina and looked down at the first question on the page. 'I've been thinking a lot about how religion sits at the edges of a lot of what you write. *Promised Land* has a full chapter set in an Anglican church; *The Hiding* has Professor Stewart losing his faith entirely; Marie in *Séances* has a dalliance with a priest – and obviously there are all the occult practices throughout that book.'

Christina laughed. 'When you do those sorts of lists it makes it seem like I'm obsessed with God.'

Clara shook her head. 'I know, but everything I said *is* in there, and it's a thought that surprised me: that religion always makes its way into your fiction. Why do you think that is?'

Christina looked impressed by the question, sitting back in her chair and looking at Clara. She made a shape with her mouth. 'Well, I suppose another way of asking that question of a different novelist would be, "How do you manage to *avoid* religion in your work?" Wouldn't that be truly remarkable?'

Clara tilted her head to the side as she wrote in her notebook. She didn't look up as she spoke. 'Are you saying religion is pervasive, that it ends up in your books just because it's part of everyday life?'

Christina shook her head. 'No, I don't think I am. That would be a horrifically boring answer, wouldn't it? And inadequate, I think. Perhaps another way of looking at it is this: religion has been the container for our most interesting questions for a long time. Until fairly recently, I'd say. Questions like: "Is a person free or determined?"; "Is forgiveness distinct from forgetting?"; "What is the nature of time?"; "How does a person retain a sense of themselves given the shocking contingency of the physical world?" Those questions interest me, Clara. They still do. And for centuries it was religion that posed them for us, and, at its best, it was religion that gave us space to think about them properly. The problem, of course, is that religion, as Feuerbach said, is simply mystified anthropology, and, sooner or later, it runs into the problem of every human system of thought, in that it thinks itself to be the theory of everything.'

Clara looked up from her book as Christina spoke. Despite the lack of personal information, this was Christina at her most engaged, talking about abstract ideas, intellectual history. When Clara knew she would be meeting Christina Darnell, it was these sorts of conversations she found herself hoping for before she drifted off to sleep each night. Clara wanted to be frustrated that her question hadn't delivered the sort of response she was looking for, but found she couldn't feel it. This was a treat.

'The religious figures in your work are so obviously fallible,' Clara said now, reading from the page. 'They fall short of their ideals continually. I'm thinking of Father Forbes allowing himself to be seduced by Marie, a sort of reverse of the serpent and Eve scene in Genesis. Are you interested in exploring the humanness of religion, rather than the theology?'

'You spoke earlier about a distinction without a difference. Well, there's another one. The theology of a religion and the humans who seek to live by it are one and the same, in my view. The doctrines of Christianity are no more divine than the plays of Shakespeare or the poetry of that man on the radio this morning. The advantage religion has over modern writing is that the sifting of history has improved the quality of religious thinking and separated the wheat from the chaff, as it were. That's why good contemporary novels are often forgotten about and then rediscovered: there needs to be some appraisal that can only happen given time. Novels that are hyped with publicity teams and barrels of cash are never the books that live past their natural first life. I can't think of one, anyway. But I've gone off topic. What I mean is that religion, like politics or literature, is human from top to bottom, and I suppose my work is interested in exploring the implications of the humanness of it all. In some ways, the temptation scene between Forbes and Marie is a celebration of the human capacity to overthrow narrow ideology.'

Clara was writing the thoughts running through her mind, reduced to single words and short phrases, and nodded her head again to show she was taking in what Christina was saying.

Two men sat at the table beside them then, as Clara was writing. They were having a loud conversation about property. Clara tried to focus on writing down what Christina had just said.

One man asked the other about his tenants.

In response, he rolled his eyes and crossed his legs. 'Vermin,' he said.

Clara took a breath in and looked up to Christina.

Christina looked to her left, away from the men, and then turned herself to look at them. 'I'm so sorry, gentlemen,' she said. 'We are waiting for two of our friends to join us. I forgot to put my coat on the seat.'

The man who had just spoken looked at his friend, and then at Christina. 'I don't think you can reserve seats in here.'

'No, I don't suppose you can. I wasn't telling you I had. I was just asking if you would mind sitting over there.' She glanced over her shoulder to the long table by the window.

The other man sighed and got up.

When they had moved to their new seats, Christina sipped from her cup and set it down carefully. 'Postmodernists will say that it is not a fact that those men are bastards, Clara. I say that this is where postmodernism is wrong.'

Clara let out a laugh, involuntarily loud, and the two men looked back at the women. One of them shook his head.

Christina's cheeks had a little colour in them. 'I've never owned more than one house at any one time,' she said, looking directly at Clara. 'I could have, of course. But no. Only the one. I don't boast about much, but I do like that fact.' Christina paused and laced her fingers in her lap. 'Now, go on. I only have fifteen minutes left and I want to be useful to you. Then I need to ask you something.'

Clara thought for a second, looked down at her notebook and then back to Christina. 'You've said that people were too interested in the artist and increasingly uninterested in the art itself.' Clara looked up to Christina, who had her eyes fixed on her. 'Is that still the case?'

Christina laughed. 'Of course it is. Much more so than whenever I said that. The recent industry of autobiographical fiction is a result of critics focusing entirely on the writer's life, the books they've written about "the real Shakespeare" or Beckett's love affairs. Who cares who Beckett slept with, by the way? I don't care about that any more than I care about how often my neighbours have sex. Which is very little, by the way.'

'Your neighbours have sex very little?' Clara asked.

'No, I meant that—' Christina glanced over the table to Clara. 'Oh, you're joking. Very good.'

Clara smiled at another rise of colour in Christina's cheeks. A swell of pride in her chest for having wrong-footed Christina for the first time. The image of her younger self came to her then. Clara in a coffee shop near campus, Christina's novels sitting in a neat pile at the far end of the table, some book of literary theory to her left, an open notebook with scribbled thoughts in front of her. That she was happy then made Clara feel a swell of compassion for the younger woman, who had no idea what was to come. She wished she could whisper it in her ear*: You'll meet her! You'll make her laugh!*

Across from her, Christina continued. 'What I mean is that why should any reader care about what a writer gets up to? This obsession gives young writers the impression that all of their experience is interesting to write about. It isn't. Go and read some debut novels if you want to test the truth of my hypothesis.'

Clara sat forward. 'I think in some senses it's a compliment to the writer. The readers are saying "I loved this book so much, I need to know more about the person who wrote it." '

'That way leads to disappointment for the reader. What are they expecting? Some extra-terrestrial with superhuman powers? In reality, the writer will be some quiet little person who has spent years of their life in solitude thinking about human experience. There is no revelation, Clara. There is nothing to see except what the writer has allowed us to see. What all this does is produce writers who think themselves celebrities. Which leads to some terrible books written by people whose principal desire is not to write but to be seen to write.'

'You think that applies to writers nowadays?'

'Certainly not all. By no means. There are still writers concerned with authenticity, with the importance of fiction.'

Clara nodded her head and glanced down at her notes. 'Can we stay with the truth thing for a minute longer? I'm wondering about an interview you gave years ago, just after *Promised Land* came out.'

Christina's lips pulled into a small smirk. 'I forget you've read everything.'

Clara looked away as she laughed. 'You said something like "fiction is not separate from life. It is every bit as real as what we usually take for reality." I haven't got the exact quote, but I think it was something like that.'

'Yes, that sounds like something I'd say,' Christina replied, sitting back.

'Well, is that not in tension with your views of relativism? If you think fiction is all there is, in a sense, are you not as post-modern as anyone?'

Christina smiled again, more fully. 'That's a wonderful question. Let me think.' Clara felt a fluttering in her stomach – a feeling she got every time Christina said something affirming to her. 'OK. The reason it appears to be a contradiction is, I suppose, because of the way postmodernists talk about truth and fiction. Or maybe the way critics of postmodernists talk about the way they think. I can't be sure. But typically, when people talk about postmodernism, they tend to talk in terms that reduce fiction. For example, if it is the case that there is no objective truth, then everything is diluted into fictions, little versions of the ungraspable "real thing".' Christina used her fingers to form the quotation marks around the phrase. 'Implicit in all they say is that fiction is synonymous with lies, or failed efforts at something more grand. This just isn't the case, and this is my problem with it all. Perhaps it's not a philosophical issue I have, but a linguistic one.'

'What do you mean?'

'I mean there is a world of difference in saying that "Truth" – with a capital T – is really only fiction in the end and, on the other hand, saying that it is actually fiction that shows us what truth really is. These statements are exactly the same but with the emphasis reversed. It is the emphasis that is key here. I do not see fiction as a reduction of the world it happens to be about. Fiction is the only kind of truth we can put our hands on.'

Clara was quiet for a moment. 'It's a beautiful thought. Complicated, though.' Clara smiled and Christina returned it.

'It's not complicated so much as complex. In a nutshell, I guess what I'm saying is that through fiction, through art in a more general sense, we get to a very interesting paradox: that the artifice of good art reveals in its made-up-ness, the artificiality of everything else which is, perhaps, the one thing we can rely on. This must lead us to the conclusion that fiction is not a distraction from reality, but a way *into it*. Because reality and fiction share a substance.'

Clara moved her head. She was intrigued by the wording. 'They share a substance?'

'Yes, something like that. The old debate about the word "homoousion" – whether Christ is of the same substance as God the Father. I've been thinking about that again recently. Can you believe that whether or not the Holy Spirit proceeded from just the Father or from both the Father and Son used to be enough to divide people for centuries? It seems to me a bit of a loss that we argue over who has said the most taboo thing online nowadays – 'taboo' used to be denying the real presence of Christ at the Eucharist. Now it's whether there are enough women on a comedy show.'

'Well, I grew up here,' Clara said. 'My mum could tell you a bit about religious divides. Although I think she'd say that the Parachute Regiment had more to do with it than theology.'

Christina nodded then, her face serious. She sat forward in her chair. 'What age is your mum? Was she there that day?'

Clara looked to the table and turned her notebook over on her leg to hold her place. 'No, she wasn't. She would only have been six or seven, so wouldn't have been allowed anywhere near the city centre on a day like that. My aunt and her went to Donegal for the day with family friends. She said they built sandcastles while wearing woolly hats and buttoned-up winter coats. She always said they had a great day before they heard the news on the car radio coming home. Rose, the woman driving the car, pulled over and wailed into the trees on the side of the road. My mum says she can still hear the sound of it. She only really talks about that sort of thing after a few drinks.'

As she spoke, Clara felt a burst of affection for her mother. She loved telling others about Julie's life before she was born. As she recounted her mother's stories about getting searched before going into shops, getting thrown off an Ulsterbus so the IRA could burn it out, she felt more like her mother's daughter than she did when she was in the same room as her. It was something about the person listening to her tell it: how it made her mother's life seem real and heroic, something worth talking about. Clara told the stories with as much dispassion as she could, leaving room for her listeners to gasp and shake their heads. She didn't want to be seen to be encouraging sympathy, and her matter-of-fact delivery drew it out all the more.

She had a hard time of it, didn't she?

She did some job on her own with you.

Clara didn't like that she used these stories to make herself seem interesting to strangers. When she briefly worked in the boys school in Derry it was something of a relief to realise none of her old stories would impress the students in her classes. Boys who were in possession of much more difficult and tragic family tales, and wouldn't bat an eyelid at Clara's accounts. Back then, she had felt close to her mother, immersed in Julie's context.

When talking about her mother, Clara could see how the unhappy woman who raised her had justifiable explanations. The distance she felt between herself and Julie was also perfectly understandable given the context. Anyone born in the nineties in Belfast or Derry may as well have been born on another planet from their parents. Clara was a child of the Agreement, her mother a child of the Troubles. The implications of this were numerous, varied and hardly spoken of. Julie's child was born into a future considered almost impossible by whole generations of politicians and prisoners, yet Clara was brought up in conditions that to her seemed inevitable. That this resulted in something of a chasm between mother and daughter made sense. And although she would never say as much out loud, Clara almost begrudged her mother her difficult experiences. The satisfaction Clara got out of shocking the English postgrads with her mother's first-hand accounts of soldiers and petrol bombs came with a hollow realisation that in her mouth they would only ever be secondary sources, retellings of some original story. It all meant Clara was proud to talk of her mother and yet frustrated that real life, whatever that meant, had always been lived someplace else. Julie's personality, her ambiguous mix of fierce pride and deep sorrow, was the end of a long chain of cause and effect. There was an authenticity to her unhappiness and something well-earned in her instinctual pessimism about the world. That she often felt just as dissatisfied with life as her mother made Clara jealous of her mother's excuses.

Sometimes on her walk to the coffee shop on a Sunday morning, Clara considered the two women who dominated her thoughts. She recognised that for years she had been distancing herself from the one woman she knew everything about, while pursuing another she would never truly know. The thought, the brutal clarity of it, made Clara hate herself until the coffee-shop came into view.

Christina nodded her head again. 'She sounds like a very interesting woman.'

Clara nodded in return and looked down to her notes. 'I'd like to get back to your thoughts on religion, if we could.'

The women spoke for another few minutes about the overlaps between Christianity and writing. Christina agreed that there was something to Clara's questions, that the relation between a God-figure and his creation had something in common with the author and her novel.

Clara then asked if Christina was ever surprised by her characters and she said it happened every time.

'It does make you wonder about the theologian's commitment to predestination and sovereignty,' Christina said. 'I am in no way sovereign over my own writing, and the surprise of character makes me suspicious of the possibility of a truly omniscient being. The world is much more like a novel than a reliable machine, Clara. Its narratives are interesting, its characters do the most surprising things.' Clara looked into her notebook, satisfied that she'd got a quote for her book.

'I am interested in your idea of character. Rita Mae Brown said somewhere that "character is destiny". I take that to mean that a character's journey may be surprising, but in some way has to have the feel of inevitability to it. That character, whatever it is, must make sense of the arc of a novel.'

Christina relaxed into her seat. She didn't speak for a moment and looked at the cups on the table. 'I think that's right,' she said, looking up then. 'Heraclitus said it first, of course. Authentic characters are those that make sense, even if they are totally crazy. There has to be a coherence to them, again, even if they are incoherent sorts of people. But this all raises questions that have been around for as long as we have. Our theory of character as writers, as readers, betrays our theory of humans, of course. So when we say things like "characters have to be coherent", we are making a huge assumption about the nature of selfhood. I think most people share it, though. No one wants to read a novel where a character does random things for four hundred pages. As an aside, have you ever read *The Dice Man*?'

Clara shook her head as she wrote the name of the novel down.

'An abhorrent book, a bit like the Easton Ellis book everyone talked about. Essentially it's about how a successful man is bored with his beautiful wife, flourishing psychiatric practice and two healthy children and decides to live his life by the roll of a die. His first act is – no, actually . . .' Clara looked up from her notebook as Christina stopped. She had the hint of a smile as she made eye contact with Clara. 'What do you think his first act was?'

Clara shifted in her seat. 'I don't know. Rob a shop? A bank?'

Christina smiled. 'What a high opinion you have of the male sex. No. The first roll of the die decided if he should rape his downstairs neighbour, the wife of his business partner. Now, you have to remember that the dice roll may be random, but the options assigned to each number are entirely drawn up by the protagonist. So he assigned a number to rape. And when that number came up, that's what he did.'

Clara had set her pen into the centre of her notebook as Christina spoke. 'I can't believe that's still out there. I'm surprised I haven't heard of it.'

'Why would you, though? It's read by men who get a thrill out of the radical way of life the book portrays. It's an outlet for frustrated, middle-class professional men. The writer has no interest in people like you. Forgive me, but your kind – bright young women, that is – are the downstairs neighbour.'

Clara went back to writing. She drew an arrow from the book's title and wrote *Option for module on literature and philosophy?* She'd been considering proposed modules for the (hopefully) inevitable job interviews she would sit in the coming months, but pushed all thought of the future from her head and looked up at Christina, who had started to speak again.

'I went off topic with that novel. What I wanted to say was that the only reason a novel like that works is because the randomness of his character's decisions is built into the story itself. If he acted the way he did without ever mentioning the rolling of the die, the novel would be a total disaster. In other words, fiction relies on character being readable, on being, to a certain extent, *guessable* without ever becoming predictable. One of the greatest pleasures of a good novel is thinking you have predicted what a character will do and, when you reach the end, you realise you were wrong for all sorts of good reasons. The ending the writer has provided is exactly right, and you get the impression that you have work to do to improve your own reading. In other words, the pleasure in those situations is realising the answer was lying dormant within the character the whole way through, as though most of an equation had been written and all you had to do as a reader is complete the sum. In these circumstances, getting it wrong as the reader is a pleasure because for one, it reminds you that you are in the hands of an excellent writer and, more importantly, it reminds you that character produces outcomes that are surprising, but also satisfying, even though they may be terribly sad or frightening. Character is destiny, you said? That's what I take that to mean.'

'You also said our approach to character raises philosophical questions.'

'Oh, yes. This arc of coherence that we all take to be a person, or a character. Perhaps the reason we need characters like that is because we spend our days trying to make ourselves exactly *like* that: a coherent arc. I was born here, raised by these people, studied there, got a job here, married this person, had these children, got sick, recovered, retired and died. I've just summed up a decent-sized majority of the population there. But when I find myself writing a character, particularly in those early weeks when I am getting to know them, I always, *always*, get stuck on this exact question: Is the idea of a self an invention or a discovery? Is it something we find ourselves curating to help us get through, or is it a fact of reality that we grow into, that we become more and more aware of? How you answer these questions is crucial but, strangely, it does not impact how you end up writing the character.'

Clara leant in then, drawn by Christina's passion for the subject. Her notebook sat open on her knee, but she hadn't written in it for a long time.

'Because,' Christina continued, her eyes glassed over, 'if you decide that selfhood is an invention we are all engaged in creating for ourselves, then chances are your character is doing the same thing, so they will look just like us. The issue arises for me from another angle, not from living but from writing. When I write a character, is my experience that I am inventing a self for them, or am I discovering the self that they have? And if I am creating one for them, is this in effect the reality we all face every day? Are we all writing our selves, creating them from scraps we find, scraps we were given? I have never quite come up with a satisfactory answer to this. Sorry, I went on. I love that question.'

Christina rubbed her hands together and excused herself. She lifted herself from her chair and walked slowly in the direction of the bathroom.

Outside the coffee shop, the city sprawled like fiction. Beyond the large glass window, a delivery truck had pulled into a parking bay on the opposite side of the road. Its wheels sat beyond the white line and an oncoming bus had to indicate right to get around it, causing beeps from the cars behind. Still further away, a man in an open-necked shirt hit a woman across her cheek with the flat of his hand. She sat down on her sofa, her hand to the red of her face, and he left the house and went to their car. A few streets over, a woman was running towards a hotel, dressed in a white shirt and black trousers. She checked her watch and slowed to a walk when she got to the entrance of the building. Tomorrow, behind the hotel, in a dank alley, there would be a boy smoking the cigarette his friend had rolled for him. They would be wearing school blazers and their mothers would assume they were in class, just like they had the previous Monday.

It would take another three weeks before the principal would phone home and, between them, they would decide on a consequence for the boys. The next day, Tuesday, a man would throw himself in the river at Ormeau Bridge just before dinner, having put the weights he'd bought online into the pockets of his winter coat.

Given Clara would never hear of these things, she would not know to wonder after their meaning. If she ever did hear of the man in the river, she would wonder what had caused it, and feel sad for a few minutes for his family, and for him. Afterwards, she would consider the implications of knowing and not knowing, between invention and reality. What is the difference, she would think, between events she would never hear about and the hosts of things she'd read in novels that she would never forget? At the level of her experience, one set of things was more real than the other. The thought would make her uncomfortable.

There was a silence as Christina settled back into her chair. Clara read over her last question and lifted her head. Before she could speak, Christina asked if Clara would come to her house the following Sunday.

Clara was stunned. 'I'd love to.'

Christina pushed back into her chair and considered Clara. 'Good. I have been in my house for a few years now, and have been working on this book in the upper room since I moved. The troublesome thing is that the stairs are beginning to put me off writing altogether, and I can't have that. I've succumbed to the conclusion that if the stairs are getting tougher, then the mountain will have to come to Muhammed.'

Clara closed her notebook and nodded at Christina. She hated the thought of her getting older, of someone with her mind having to consider ways to ameliorate her own weakening.

'Is that culturally insensitive? I hope not.'

Clara shook her head. 'Do you need some help in moving things?'

'I do. I have an obscene amount of books up there, and an old desk I'd love to bring, but we can see what we can manage between us.' Christina paused and reached into her jacket pocket. She produced a square piece of white paper and held it across to Clara, who took it. 'I intend to cook you a dinner as a thank you. Will you be able to stay for an hour or two? How does that look to you?'

Clara looked down at the paper and read Christina's writing. Her handwriting was not neat, but was beautiful in its shape. The D for 'duck' was a small semi-circle with a long upwards tail moving to the top of the paper before fading into nothing. Some of the individual words only made sense because the words either side were slightly more legible.

Duck Breast, Plum Sauce.

Creamed Potatoes, Buttered Spinach.

'This looks wonderful, Christina.'

'That's very good of you. I'm number twelve on the street opposite. Shall we say five on Sunday? Dinner at seven? Don't bring any wine. My house is coming down with the stuff.'

Clara smiled as she slid the paper into her notebook.

6
Ethical Consumption

'You're a vegetarian, Clara.'

She put the plate she was drying back in the cupboard and turned to face him.

'I know, but I wasn't going to offend her by saying no to the food.'

'You were the one who preached to me about the evils of factory farming.'

'I understand I'm a hypocrite, Daniel.'

'Well, so long as you know, I suppose.'

'Oh, fuck off.'

7
Epistemology of the Closet

As Clara wished to keep the coffee shop solely for her meetings with Christina, she opted to meet Chris in a restaurant. It was unusual for an academic to meet their editor face-to-face, and Clara felt strangely nervous about the dinner, which was something she only recognised as she arrived at the door to the place she'd booked.

She and Daniel had met there on one of their early dates (Sophie said every date until a year was early) and she'd enjoyed the Italian music they played as they had eaten. 'This is how you do it properly,' Clara said, as they shared two pizzas and a carafe of white wine. 'Authentic.' Daniel nodded as he cut his pizza but made no further indication he knew what she was talking about. Clara made a mental note of every café and restaurant that ruined its carefully selected decor and menu with totally unsuitable background music. There was a café on the Lisburn Road fitted with beautiful armchairs, mismatched old wooden tables and a huge wooden counter with built-in display units for the food. They served homemade chickpea rolls and croissants, and, when the shop opened last year, Clara thought she had found a perfect new spot for writing. But by the third visit, the acoustic covers of Britney Spears and Destiny's Child finally tipped her over the edge: Clara had attempted to focus on a Deirdre Madden novel all the while a high-voiced girl was making her way through a torturously slow, guitar-led version of 'Toxic'.

Chris had emailed Clara on Sunday evening to tell her about a talk he was giving at the university on publishing in the academic market. He suggested they meet for a catch-up on the monograph.

I don't usually get the chance to meet my authors, and your project is so interesting.

Clara reserved a table for two at the Italian restaurant near the lecture theatre Chris would be speaking at and replied to tell him the time and place. She made no reference to his new email signature, which read:

Chris Langley

Literary Studies Editor

'Always be true to your shelf.'

When she had left Christina the Sunday before, Clara's head had been swimming. She was going to Christina's house for dinner. Six months ago, she had never spoken to Christina Darnell, and was only faintly aware they had been sharing a city. For years Clara had pored over the woman's books with near-obsession, copying out passages by hand, buying books on literary theory and philosophy solely because they might pair well with one of her novels: *Poetics of Space* for *Promised Land* and its houses; most of Sontag's non-fiction for something to think about alongside Christina's own essays; volumes of Nietzsche for post-religious morality (she'd initially picked him up for the moral philosophy, and stayed for the surprising beauty of the prose – the wiped-away horizon, the spider in the moonlight). She had spent a small fortune following Christina's mind, line by line, book by book. Christina had dictated both Clara's thoughts and her geography, and she had given up every other possible future in order to pursue academia.

Clara would not have considered the decision to commit herself solely to her monograph and teaching as anything other than a clear-minded, obvious choice for a woman like her; but her friends were nurses and social workers now. Sophie had bought a bungalow in Bangor, and Felicity had a son, Pierce. When he was born, Clara bought him a bib that said 'My Mum Loves Henry James', a reference to Felicity's undergraduate dissertation on *The Golden Bowl*. The work was completed too many years ago for the joke to make any sense. But what do babies want? Clara had no idea and her lack of interest in progeny was one of her few lacks that didn't cause her any concern.

The restaurant building was red brick, with a Victorian front it shared with a law firm to its right and a hairdresser's to its left. The white surfaces and sharp lights of the hairdresser's visible through the clean glass looked incongruous within its old brick frame. As Clara walked past there had been a woman leaning over a desk with a phone to her ear. She had striking white-blonde hair cut into a severely precise bob, and Clara thought back to the class she'd audited on semiotics during her first year of her PhD. The undergraduates would have had a field day discussing the various signs the manager had consciously or unconsciously set for display. How the white walls implied a kind of luxurious purity that could be bought, while retaining the clinical sheen of a dental clinic. Clara had the image of the woman she saw inside carefully trimming the straight lines in her hair with a set of nail scissors, her mouth tightened with focus, like a prize gardener training a perennial. Sometimes, when she found herself thinking in such terms, Clara wondered if the world really was coded in a way only cultural theorists would understand, its meaning always just out of reach, like an exhausting game of Pass the Parcel. Or, she thought, was the theory itself a thick emulsion applied to ordinary life, an invented means of making a living for the hyperintelligent but practically hopeless individuals cloistered away in campus offices. Hard to tell, Clara concluded.

On either side of the open door of the restaurant was a glass lantern housing a synthetic flame that jittered and danced as though burning in a breeze. Clara climbed the three small steps up to the open door and then pulled the handle of the inside door and stepped into the restaurant. There was an immediate smell of garlic and fresh herbs, a hiss of something frying. The place was otherwise quiet as Clara stood at the podium, where a sign told her to wait.

A young man, twenty or so, came from behind the bar when he saw her. He was tall and slim, and wore black boots with his black jeans and white shirt. Clara told him her name and he took her to a table by the window, away from the two couples eating at the other end of the room. An accordion was playing over the speakers and Clara took off her jacket and put it on the back of her chair. As she looked over the menu, she made a note of the prices and then considered the etiquette of the meeting she was about to have. Would she have to pay? She had just under £200 in her current account and it was thirteen days until she would be paid for teaching. By now she was used to the countdown to each payday, the text messages from her bank a few days before it arrived to let her know she'd dipped into her overdraft once again. *Precarious* was the word people used on panels about the post-doctoral experience. *Absolute shite* was Clara's preferred term.

Clara had been given a discreet nod by her old PhD supervisor over a three-month research fellowship that could cover her expenses for the summer. And there were always teaching fellowships to apply for: the dreaded one-year posts with a full teaching allocation, no time for research and very little chance of an extension. Until then, though, it would be tight.

She *could* move in with Daniel.

He had offered, and he had the space. She would save a fortune. Clara found again that she could imagine the publication of her monograph with much more solidity and colour than she could ever conceive of a future in which she woke up beside Daniel each morning. She widened her eyes and refocused on the menu. Clara was tired of thinking these same thoughts, in this same order, every day, sometimes twice a day. She forced herself to think about the dinner with Christina in a few days and then looked up from the menu as she heard an English accent.

He was a short man, dark-bearded and dressed in a blue felt blazer over an open-necked white shirt and bottle-green chinos. Clara immediately noted the tension of the buttons at his belly and admired the man's faith in the quality of his clothes. She considered the gender politics implied by a shirt so clearly under stress. For a man, a large stomach could be a mark of distinction, of authority, of expertise, even. It simply *must* be the product of sedentary study, of being holed up in a musty library wrangling with ideas and old manuscripts, of being intelligent, a master of one's discipline. She didn't know a woman in academia who would allow her body to be quite so on display as Chris's was now as he spoke amicably with the young waiter by the podium.

Clara chastised herself then, for making any kind of judgment about another person's appearance, for making universal assumptions about a man who might have a health condition, or simply loved good food and expensive wine. What was wrong with that? And then she considered that it was Chris, after all, who was the enlightened one; that women ought to approach their appearance with the same confidence that he clearly had. All of this happened as she stood to greet him, and before he had uttered a word to her.

'Dr Wilson! How absolutely wonderful to meet you.' He turned to face her and spoke loudly, as though there was no one else in the restaurant. Chris's voice was deeper than she would have guessed, and he approached her with his arms out by his waist, palms facing her. It was, she thought, a powerfully submissive gesture: by showing her his open, empty hands, he put himself at her mercy and she was compelled to take a step towards him.

Clara felt an immediate liking for the man.

'Lovely to meet you,' she said, as he put his arms around her and kissed her on the cheek. 'How was your talk?'

Chris pulled back from her and smiled. He held Clara by the elbows. 'A triumph. They are probably still on their feet in there, clapping.' Clara laughed at the sarcasm. 'I can't believe you're laughing,' Chris said, before laughing himself.

The sound filled the room, bouncing off the walls and causing one of the women to turn to look at the source of the interruption. These were facts that did not seem to concern him.

'Did many come along? Sometimes postgrads can be flaky.'

'I think there were about thirteen there, Clara. And about nine of them listened. I'm just glad I'm not paying for the flights and hotel. Waste of money. And I was about to say "time" as well, but that wouldn't be true, would it?' He gestured to the table and they sat on opposite sides. Chris picked up the drinks' menu from the centre of the table. 'We'll get a glass of wine to start, shall we?'

The same waiter who had welcomed them each in turn came over a few minutes later and took their orders. Chris ordered a wild mushroom risotto and Clara chose the penne arrabbiata.

As the man wrote down the orders, Chris put both his hands on the table and leant towards him. 'Now, what white wine would you recommend?'

The waiter looked up from his notepad to Chris and then Clara. 'I can go and ask what would be best, if you like.'

Chris nodded. 'Fantastic. And no need to come back to check. Whatever they say, just bring us a bottle of that, would you?

We're in your hands.' The waiter agreed and went to the kitchen. 'I think he's new, bless him.'

'I think so. I used to hate when people asked me about wine.'

'You worked in a restaurant?'

'Only for a summer before university. It was a hotel restaurant, so it was always busy. I hated it.'

'Did you? I think I would quite enjoy the constant chatting.'

'That's exactly what I didn't like,' Clara said. 'And then when someone would ask me to make a wine recommendation, I'd freeze. I only drank cider when I was eighteen, so I just used to say "The house red is good." '

Chris smiled at Clara as she spoke. He listed to her intently, and it made her look to the table to break the eye contact.

'What were the chefs like to work with? That's what would put me off.'

'Dicks,' Clara said, and Chris gave another loud laugh. 'They would blame me for any complaints, even if the food *they* made wasn't cooked properly, or they forgot to put the sauce on the side rather than over the chicken or whatever. I used to live in fear of going back in there with a full plate. One of them called me Clara the Klutz because I dropped a tray of glasses on my second shift, and that was all I got for the whole summer.'

The waiter arrived back at their table then. He was holding a bottle and a silver wine cooler which he set in the middle of the table. He opened the bottle and poured into Clara's glass first.

'And what is this?' Chris said, picking up the glass, swirling the wine and winking at Clara.

'It's a New Zealand Sauvignon Blanc. Chef's recommendation for the risotto.'

'Good man,' Chris said, and took a sip from his glass. 'It's lovely.'

'Very good,' the waiter said, and put the bottle inside the cooler, shifting the base around to make room in the ice.

'If you weren't busy, we'd ask you to sit and have a glass with us, but perhaps another time.' Chris smiled at the young man.

'If only. I don't get off until eight. Enjoy your drinks, I'll bring the food over when it's ready.'

Clara watched the interaction while rolling the stem of her wine glass between her fingers.

The waiter left them and went to check on one of the other tables at the back.

'Oh, to be young again,' Chris said, following Clara's eyes to the waiter. 'Years ago, the earring would have been a give-away. Nowadays, it's hard to tell, isn't it? Everyone is wearing everything.' Clara took a drink from her glass. 'It's a good thing, all in all, isn't it?' Clara nodded. 'Shall we talk business?' Chris said and shifted forwards in his seat. 'Tell me everything.'

A tenor was singing an aria in Italian when the risotto and pasta arrived. At the sight of the waiter, Chris poured the remainder of the wine into the two glasses. Clara still had a third of hers left and the top-up filled her glass almost entirely.

'Whoops,' Chris said, laughing to the man and then tapping the bottle. 'We'll have another of these, please.' He put the wine bottle upside down into the cooler and the waiter took it back towards the bar.

Clara had been telling Chris about the structure of the book, of intersecting the typical academic chapters with more informal prose based on the conversations she'd been having with Christina.

He pursed his lips and made small nods with his head as she spoke.

'God, this risotto is perfect, Clara. Do you want to try some?' He nudged the plate an inch towards her.

'I'm OK, thanks. I've got plenty here.'

He pulled the plate back and sifted through the rice with his fork. 'Go on,' he said. 'Tell me about these meetings. Is she friendly? Or is her reputation deserved?'

Clara chewed a mouthful of pasta and looked to the side. She considered the last few months. They must have had about ten or eleven meetings, now. It was a surprising thought, for she still felt a flutter of nerves before each one.

'Well, it started a little colder than it is now,' Clara said. 'She took a few coffees to warm up, to trust me, maybe.'

'I can imagine that,' Chris said, pointing at her with his fork. 'It's only natural she was suspicious of you at first. A career-hungry academic looking to write a career-making book on her. I suppose she was wary of the whole thing. When you emailed saying she was up for it, I'll admit I was surprised.'

Clara felt a little jolt in her stomach, as though she had just read the first email from Christina's agent over again. She had been lying on her bed and had just set aside a new novel about a young woman at university who had fallen for a terrible man. She opened her phone and saw the notification.

> Christina would be pleased to meet with you, Dr Wilson. I am including her personal email here, and you can discuss the arrangements with her. All very best, Madeleine.

Clara thought now about how different her life would be had Christina ignored that inquiry. Writing the same book but without any access to Christina's real voice and opinions. It would have sunk like a stone. Who would want to review a book dedicated solely to Christina Darnell: an author no one had spoken of seriously in years? But with the access Clara had, academics would be falling over themselves to get a proper look at the writer. Clara harboured a hope that it might even return Christina to the critical spotlight.

Clara felt the effects of the wine, the subtle dizziness in her head and the sharpening focus of her eyes, the loss of her peripheral vision.

'I was, too,' she said. 'But I think she's got used to me now. She seems to genuinely enjoy the conversations.'

'I have no doubt about that. Who wouldn't want to be talking to an intelligent young woman every week. Tell me, what do you actually talk about? Do you prepare in advance?'

Clara nodded as she took a sip from her full glass. She had to bring her head towards the surface of the wine and scarcely had to tilt it. 'For the first few meetings I prepared about ten questions, but we never got to them.'

Chris made an approving noise and drank from his glass. 'That's always a good sign, isn't it. Does the conversation flow naturally now?'

'Well, it does. But after a few weeks I realised she was reluctant to talk about her own life. Like, at all. I tried to ask her about the likenesses between her and her characters and she shut it down. I've asked about her parents, what she does between novels. All of it, she manages to dodge. We end up talking about the philosophy of chance, or the virtues of Iris Murdoch, or the problems with contemporary literature. I shouldn't be complaining, though. People would pay a lot of money to listen to Christina Darnell just speak about whatever has her interest.'

As Clara spoke, Chris looked at her. He didn't eat or take a drink from his now half-full glass. 'I am captivated by all this, Clara. It's going to be an amazing piece of work. I feel so lucky you sent me your proposal.'

'Oh, please,' Clara said, and lifted her glass.

'I'm serious. Let's go back to this avoidance of biography. It surprises me.' Chris picked up his fork again.

'What do you mean?'

He opened the bottle cooling in the centre of the table and filled his glass. He drank before continuing. 'Writers. When have you met a writer that didn't want to talk about themselves, prove how interesting or bohemian they are?' He looked at Clara. 'I've never met an artist that wasn't self-obsessed.'

'Really? I think that's true of some art forms far more than others. Singers and actors, yes. Performance artists, absolutely. They are the worst.'

Chris lifted his eyes from his plate then. 'You're right. Because it's all shit.'

Clara laughed, loudly, thinking back to a woman she had studied with, years before, who now received public funds to paint eggs and then break them on the floors of sparsely attended gallery events. Mel was her name. She was a year older than Clara and had studied fine art in Liverpool before moving to Belfast to take up a master's in literature. She had invited Clara to one of her exhibitions, having sat with her for lunch a few times. Clara accepted and took her boyfriend at the time, a history PhD who had no interest in the arts. Philip had laughed at what Clara supposed was meant to be the moment of poignancy: when Mel scooped up the split yokes and smeared them across her chest. The piece was called 'Mothers', and Clara had guided Philip out of the gallery before the wine was opened.

'I can't say I like it much, either,' she said. 'But novelists tend to be quieter, I think. Otherwise they'd do something more obviously public.'

Chris leant back in his chair, his fork still in his hand. 'I think you're being kind, Clara. Artists are narcissists. There's a book to be written on contemporary art, writing, whatever, simply as attention-seeking. Which is to say that art isn't much different to any other behaviour. Anyway, keep going. What's your take on her reluctance? Has she a skeleton in the closet?'

He took a long drink from his glass. It was nearly empty

already, and Clara could see a new freedom in the man's movements, how he had leant back into the chair with no restraint, letting a shot of air out of his nose as his back came into contact with the frame of the chair.

Clara considered the question. It had been her question, too, for months now. Christina certainly had a reason for avoiding talk of her own life. She also – and Clara increasingly returned to this – had a reason for moving to Belfast, swapping London for a place where the bus schedule was strictly advisory and seemingly written as a separate venture entirely from the actual running of buses. Empty shop fronts and abandoned construction sites were common here in a way they just weren't in London. But Belfast did have a charm about it, no doubt. The recovery of the city was remarkable when compared to the version of Belfast people saw on TV. But Clara had gone to London for a conference during her PhD, she'd seen *Wicked* in the West End, drunk white wine in a university courtyard with fellow researchers, learned the subtle socio-economic differences between 'on' and 'in'.

'Where did you grow up, Clara?'

'In an estate in Derry City.'

'Lovely. I grew up on an estate, too.'

Clara loved where she lived, but when she was elsewhere, she did wonder why anyone would opt for Belfast. Coming back from holidays and conferences she would see the small spread of city lights appear below the plane, bordered by the grey of the Irish Sea and hemmed in by the huge green of farms and fields. It couldn't really be like that, could it? On these occasions she felt all her pretensions drop away. She wasn't a cosmopolitan academic dashing between lectures with a takeaway coffee and a busy meeting schedule. No. As her plane touched down in Belfast International, a small building that looked to be made of corrugated iron, a cowshed in the dim of the evening, she recognised she was in an obscure place, relatively speaking, doing an obscure thing. Making the three-minute walk from plane through the airport building to the windy entrance with the other returnees, Clara always considered the cost of a taxi to her flat, inevitably opting to wait the thirty or forty minutes for a bus. That Christina had made that same journey from plane to entrance to her new home was an unsettling fact. There was a mystery in it. She'd have got the taxi, though.

'I don't think there's a big reveal coming or anything,' Clara replied, trying to avoid raising his hopes of a major scoop for the book. 'I think she's very, very private. She wants the work to just be the work, unencumbered by critics picking through the details to make connections with her as the author.' Chris went back to his risotto then. There were only a few forkfuls left. 'She's got me half convinced that literary criticism is a waste of time, you know.'

Chris looked up at Clara. 'Not exactly what your editor wants to hear, Dr Wilson.' He let out a loud laugh that Clara had to join in with due to its length.

'Well, that's the thing. Talking with her has made me less interested in the kind of criticism popular at universities. You know, the kind of articles that all have a short quote from a text, full colon, then a convoluted sentence full of jargon explaining what the article is about. I saw one recently on Sally Rooney. Let me see if I can get this right.' Clara looked down at the table then, her eyes wide with the wine and the effort of memory. '"'Do nothing, say nothing, and love no one': Transgressive Feminism, Climate Disaster and the Transcendent Turn in Sally Rooney's *Beautiful World, Where Are You*". My God. No book deserves that sort of butchering.'

Chris shook his head. 'I've read through your PhD, Clara. I've read your book proposal. You could have written that article on Rooney. You certainly have with Christina, haven't you?'

'Yes, I have. That's the point. I don't know what the purpose of it is. What *value*' – Clara raised her volume on the word as though she had been looking for it and it had suddenly landed in her head – 'do any of these secondary critical pieces add to anything? They are, by definition, "secondary". They just comment on something that someone else has created. And worse, nowadays the critics seem to have less and less interest in the work of interpretation and just want to write biographical or sociological studies of literature. As though it weren't a thing in itself. Can you see I've gone on a bit of a journey, here?'

'I can, I can,' Chris said.

The waiter came to their table then, to take their plates. 'How was everything?'

Chris sat back and assessed the young man. 'It was delicious. It really was,' he said, picking up his glass.

'Excellent.' The waiter stacked their plates and lifted the cutlery. 'Would you like a look at the dessert menu at all?'

Clara rested her hand on her stomach. 'Not for me, I couldn't eat another bite.'

Chris, still looking at the waiter, smiled conspiratorially. 'Having a look wouldn't hurt, would it? She can share whatever I get.'

'Sure.'

Chris watched the waiter as he walked towards the kitchen with their plates. 'Belfast really has it all now, doesn't it,' he said.

'We have supermarkets and central heating too, you know,' Clara replied.

Chris laughed his loudest yet.

Over a tiramisu, Chris set out a proposed schedule for the delivery of the monograph. Clara found it uncanny how seamlessly he could move from loose, near-drunken chatter to the quick efficiency of work talk. He told her there was no rush, that he could wait another six months for a draft.

'But when you do submit the draft, there will be a twelve-week schedule to re-draft, proof, revise, get cover art and quotes and then send to the printers. It's a well-oiled machine, really.'

Clara could feel the excitement of it building in her stomach. Her mother would never get over seeing 'Clara Wilson' written on the spine of a book. She'd show it to her friends. Clara could see her doing it, tilting the book to the side, running her finger across the printed *Wilson*, the thing they had in common. The compliments she would get for raising a writer. Clara pre-empted the feeling of shame she would have at the term. She would never be a writer. Ten years ago, sitting on her childhood bed, she had read the work of a real writer. Her book was only a gloss on the real thing.

'So, what you're saying is that when I submit a draft it should be pretty close to the finished thing?'

'That's right. In terms of substance, nothing should really change from that point. It'll all be typos and references, that sort of thing. But as your book is a little different from the usual monograph, I'd like to read a few chapters over the next month or two, if you would be OK with that?'

Chris smiled at Clara and she smiled back. If someone less affable, less interested had asked to check over her work, Clara would have taken it as a lack of confidence in the writing. But Chris seemed genuinely enthused by the book, and Clara noted how she felt eager to send him some of what she had already written.

'You are very good at your job,' Clara said.

'Why do you say that? I mean, you're right, of course. I just wonder about your reasons.'

Clara joined him in laughing again. 'I actually want to send you the work. Usually I'd put off a deadline for a few weeks, and panic the entire time about how it would be received. My PhD supervisor told me off in my first year for being so nervous about criticism. You've put me at ease.'

'That could also be the wine, Dr Wilson.' Chris winked and then made a gesture to the young man behind the bar. 'This has been delightful, Clara. And it's on me.' The waiter came across with the bill on a side-plate and set it on the table nearer to Chris than Clara.

'That's very kind. Let me take you out for dinner once this book is done,' Clara said.

'And once you get your big job. "Dr Wilson, lecturer in contemporary literature, University of Cambridge." That has a satisfying ring to it, doesn't it?' Chris looked at the bill. 'My God! I see why you like it here. Is this right?' He thrust the bill over to Clara, who ran her eyes down the list.

'That's it.'

'Good God. If we could somehow transport Ronnie Scott's to Belfast, I think I'd move my life here.' Chris paused and looked at Clara. 'By life, I mean cocker spaniel.'

She smiled at the little creases that had formed either side of his eyes. It gave him a childlike look, even as it confirmed his age. 'You have a dog?'

He nodded. 'The most wonderful little guy. He's called Descartes.'

Clara exploded with laughter. 'Are you serious?'

'I am! I didn't name him, though. My ex is a philosopher. Teaches at Kings. He thought it would be funny.' Chris gestured to Clara, who was wiping her mouth with her napkin. 'He was right, clearly.'

'I think it's a brilliant name,' said Clara. 'I think, therefore I am.'

'For him it was more "I fuck my master's students, therefore I am."'

Clara's eyes widened.

'It's a long story.' Chris waved his hand. 'Actually, you've got the gist.' He huffed a small laugh, and Clara could see the hurt in his face as he looked down at the table.

The waiter returned with a card machine. Chris slipped his hand into the blazer on the back of his chair and brought out a black leather wallet. 'The food was spectacular. Compliments to the chef,' he said, fiddling inside the wallet for his card. He tapped the machine.

'Thank you,' the waiter said.

Chris handed the man a note. 'And this is for taking care of us.'

Clara glanced to their hands as the note was exchanged and saw it was a twenty. The waiter did not look down until he had turned away and was walking back to the bar. She saw him almost stop as he saw what he had been given.

Clara and Chris stood up from their table and put on their jackets.

'Clara. It has been a pleasure. I do hope we get another chance to meet rather than just over email.' Chris stepped forward and gave her a hug.

'This was lovely," Clara said.

Chris left the restaurant and, through the window panes on the doors, Clara watched him stop at the bottom of the steps. It was dark outside. Chris looked down towards his phone, tilted it right and then left, turned his head to look up and down Botanic Avenue, and walked towards the centre of town.

8
Pascal

Clara felt like she had been let into a secret; had felt like it since the moment she opened her eyes that morning, in fact. As she passed people in the street, she felt sorry for them that they weren't going where she was going. The air was warm, the sky cloudless.

How many times had she walked past this road; and had she ever absent-mindedly walked past Christina herself on the way to the park, or to go for a coffee? The thought was only tolerable given where she was going now. She and Daniel had eaten at the pizza place opposite the first house on the row last year. She remembered having her back to the window, unaware Christina Darnell was likely writing her final novel just a short walk away as the night came in. Clara pictured her now as she turned onto Christina's street, sitting in a large leather office chair in the top room of her house, writing longhand in thick silence, or perhaps listening to something instrumental, a lone semi-acoustic guitar maybe, a warm lamp illuminating her table, the rest of the large open room in dusky grey light. Clara hadn't given the street a second glance until a few months ago when she first began to meet with Christina, and had had no reason to walk through it until this evening. The light was waning but had a hint of gold about it as it fell through the trees on either side of the road, and Clara walked into her shadow as she neared the gate to number twelve.

The house itself was a tall Victorian terrace that sat back from the wide pavement at the end of an empty tarmac drive and small garden. There were maybe twenty or thirty houses in the row, Clara reckoned, all identical in height and in the position of their windows, the tallest of which overlooked the substantial trees that lined the pavement below. Christina's house was only a matter of metres from the main road, yet the sound of cars and shoppers did not reach her garden, as though there was some sort of invisible separation in place that prevented any seep of noise from elsewhere. It was hard for Clara to imagine people living out their lives in these conditions. She noted how even the quality of the air had seemed to change as she turned off Ormeau onto Christina's street: how it seemed cleaner, more full of light, how the uniformity of the houses suggested affluence to her in a way that the cut-and- paste terraces she grew up in implied difficulty to some of her old university friends. Hedges, well-kept, lush green and straight-lined, separated Christina's garden and drive on either side from the next-door neighbours, and ran along where the garden met the pavement, partially obscuring the front door from view. A crab-apple tree was visible above the height of the hedges and was beginning to bloom soft white against the rust-brick of the house.

Christina's front door, like the others in the row, was set beyond the front wall, so Clara had to take a step through a small archway before she reached it. It was painted plum, in the kind of paint that would always look wet, with a glossy shine that caught the light like the gleam of a clean apple. Two panes of frosted glass sat either side of a black metal door knocker in the shape of a fox, and a black box doorbell with a white button was attached to the right of the door. Clara wondered which method was the least disruptive. The lantern to the left of the door was on, despite the light evening, and was half-heartedly illuminating small patches of brick behind and above it.

Clara tucked the bottle she'd been carrying under her arm and slid a battered book into her jacket pocket. She reached up and lifted the fox, tapped it twice, quickly, on the metal plate below. Then she stood back from the door and waited.

The previous night she and Daniel had debated her bringing a bottle of wine to dinner. He, knowing Christina had already told Clara not to bother, suggested chocolates or flowers instead. But Clara didn't know if Christina preferred milk or dark chocolate (she would have guessed dark) and said she needed to see the inside of her house before knowing which flowers were best, though she knew Christina liked roses from a patterned blouse she often wore to their meetings.

'She's given me the list of what she's making,' Clara said. 'Finding a decent wine to go with it should be easy enough.'

Daniel had shrugged his shoulders and went to finish their teas.

Clara switched on the TV and opened an app. 'Do you want murder or sex?' she called, clicking through the films. She crossed her legs under her on the sofa.

Daniel came back from the kitchen with a bottle of red wine. 'Always sex first.'

Clara sniffed and rolled her eyes as he handed her the bottle. 'This will go with duck. My dad left a few bottles here from his new monthly subscription thing.'

Clara turned it in her hands to read the back. 'It's like you.'

Daniel looked at her with suspicion. 'What do you mean?'

'Precise, focused, richly embroidered.' She held the bottle out to him and Daniel squinted at it as he took it.

He shook his head and Clara took the bottle back. 'It's plummy, apparently.'

'Isn't that what you want?'

'I don't know. It's saved me a tenner, anyway.'

Daniel went back to the kitchen and returned with two mugs. 'Are you staying tonight?' He looked at Clara's bag in the corner of the room. It wasn't the usual overnight bag.

'I don't think so.'

Daniel had a half-smile as he looked at Clara who was looking at the TV. 'What does that mean?'

'No, I don't think I am.' She imagined waking up the next morning in his bed, having to talk to him through breakfast and make her escape after the inevitable coffee. Him wishing her luck for the dinner as she opened the front door to leave. As strange as it seemed, she knew she'd enjoy the prospect of meeting Christina in her home much more if she started the day by herself.

Daniel went back to the kitchen. Clara heard him open a cupboard and then he asked her if she wanted chocolate. Clara said she did and he returned with a large rectangular tin of biscuits.

Clara laughed at the sight. 'You're an old woman,' she said.

'Why?' He sat down beside her.

'Who has boxes of biscuits?'

'My aunt left them last week. She hadn't seen the new place. If you're too good for them, I'll put them away.'

'Oh, give over and open it.' She reached across him to grab the box as he moved it away from her and Clara fell on top of him, her weight on the point of her elbow.

Daniel leant forwards. 'Fuck sake.'

She sat back. 'That was your fault.'

Daniel had his hands between his thighs. 'I hope you don't change your mind about not wanting children,' he said.

Clara said, 'Jesus Christ,' and picked up her mug from the floor. She clicked on the remote and whatever film she'd been on started playing on Daniel's TV.

Now, it crossed Clara's mind that Christina might have

forgotten about their dinner and headed out for the evening. Or that she had tripped and fallen and was lying on the floor of the kitchen listening to someone knock on her door. There was little sign of life about the house. Through the glass in the front door Clara could make out the faint glow of a table lamp and the black and white diamonds of checkerboard floor tiles, but there was no suggestion of movement from inside.

Clara stepped forward and rapped the door again, this time with more force. Clara wondered what she should do next if Christina didn't appear and resolved that she would probably call Daniel and ask him to drive over. A doctor might be just what they needed. She felt bad about only thinking of him when he was useful.

Clara looked up then at the sound of a window sliding up, above her.

'Clara!'

She stepped back to get a proper look and saw Christina's face, framed by the open window.

'If I come down I won't come back up again. The door's open. I told you not to bring wine.'

Clara smiled and waved up at Christina and walked back towards the door.

On stepping inside the house Clara was met with silence, and a set of stairs on her right that led to a brightly lit landing. The landing culminated in a window seat dressed with lilac and blue cushions. The carpet on the stairs was plush and grey and looked new. To her left were two open doors, the first of which led to a beautiful square living room. Clara looked into the room, her eye drawn by the huge rug in the centre. The mat Clara had in her living room was a quarter of the size of this one and had a scratchy, thin feel to its turquoise-coloured threads. Christina's was a deep red in the centre with a multitude of gold Celtic crosses uniformly woven into the silk. Towards the edges the red turned to burnt orange, bordered finally in gold. Clara noticed the rug was at least half an inch thick and looked as though it would cushion her steps if she were to walk across it. It would be impossible to be anxious stepping on a rug like that, she thought. Along the near wall, there was a dark brown leather sofa facing the windows to the garden. Three cushions in varied monochrome patterns were scattered across the seats. A couple of armchairs faced the sofa, backs towards the light, one tub-shaped in expensive black leather, the other a Chesterfield wing-back in deep red. Oxblood, Clara suddenly remembered, having seen the word on sofas advertised online for a local second-hand furniture shop. She calculated that there was comfortable seating for five people in the room, and wondered if there had ever been occasion for all the seats to be occupied at one time. Christina, it seemed to her, lived a solitary life, never speaking about friends or any remaining family. She seemed content, though, solitude being distinct from loneliness.

This was where Clara's thinking always reached when she found herself feeling sad for Christina's quiet way of life, and the thought comforted her, reassured her, that Christina was happy. Clara recognised she needed this to be true, for her own sake.

The coffee table in the centre of the room had a clear glass top set on a strange, abstractly shaped wooden base. The light-coloured wood was thickly cut and had been fashioned into a mixture of smooth curves and angular joins, like a solid, tangible Kandinsky. Clara wondered about the cost of the piece.

She took a few steps forward and looked into a room with a grand dining table dressed in white cloth. A candle burned in a brass holder in the centre of the table. There was a black and white photo sitting on the mantel of the fireplace of a man fishing by the side of a river, his head turned over his shoulder to look at the photographer. The woman beside him was sitting, looking into the water, her back to the camera. She was leaning back on the grass, weight on her hands, her legs bent at the knee.

'Just come straight up,' Christina called from above the landing, and the sound of her voice allowed the house to cast off some of its strangeness. Clara thought of a large dark dog emerging from the sea onto soft sand, pausing briefly to shake the water from its coat before dashing towards the voice calling its name.

Christina's presence, confirmed by sound, also permitted Clara to notice some of the house's imperfections. She could see small fissures of cracked paint above the fireplace in the dining room and, behind her, she was almost certain she'd seen a smudged footprint on the tiles from Christina's muddy shoes.

Clara looked up towards Christina's voice and saw her face leaning over the banister on the second floor, framed by the dark wood of the rail on either side. The sight of her confirmed something for Clara and she felt the beginnings of satisfaction. She could have speculated for days on what colour Christina's tablecloth would be: royal blue, she might have thought, or perhaps a more subtle colour: a pastel pink or yellow. On walks to the university she often found herself choosing music she thought Christina might listen to in her house. Bach or Billie Holiday? Maybe lively big band tunes like Duke Ellington to bring some warmth and noise to the big house, or perhaps something more mournful, like Nina Simone or Chet Baker? In her ostensibly music-focused essays, Christina wrote across genres and gave little indication as to her own preferences. Her essay on Philip Glass in *The Shape of Clouds* moved from piano cross-rhythms to Paul Auster's *The New York Trilogy* to the underlying metaphoric logic of a good novel to the collapse of the Left in England under the then very new New Labour. Clara, having read the essays several times, still had no more of a clue as to what Christina listened to for pleasure as she did when she'd started reading it. Christina would rather those little mysteries persisted, Clara thought. She had wondered in the week leading to the dinner if Christina's hall would be scented with vanilla or lavender or citrus, and further, if Christina even thought of these sorts of things. But on seeing her at the top of her own stairs, the many possible realities imagined by Clara dissolved and settled.

This, Clara thought, was Christina Darnell's home. There was a small reed diffuser on the side table in the hallway that smelled of sea salt and sage and two white dinner plates were on the dining table on either side of the candle. All of Clara's questions would have an answer, she realised, and the warm weight of this accompanied her as she took the stairs towards Christina.

As a girl, Clara did not especially stand out from the other children in her class. She was of average height with sandy-brown, shoulder-length hair. Her reading and mathematical abilities progressed along predictable, steady lines; her teachers considered her handwriting presentable, her spelling in accordance with her age, and she often got a bronze or, on one occasion – when tall Lauren was off with a stomach bug – a silver medal at the sport's day for a solid performance in the Key Stage Two assault course. That afternoon, her mother had clapped her hands quickly, rocking her weight forwards, willing her daughter on, a grin so huge across her face she might well have been in pain. By looking herself, Clara knew it wasn't pain, for if it was, her mother would have had no facial expression at all. She remembered the feeling of giving her mother a reason to smile, the butter-smooth spread of satisfaction inside her chest like a lava lamp splurging into life. It was only later that she would wonder if the distance between them – Clara at the far end of the course, her mother still at the starting line with the other parents – was what gave her mother the freedom to be so visibly proud of her daughter. The image of their separation and her childish desire to run back across the field to her mother came back to Clara often when she'd had a few drinks.

Clara told herself all the time that they were very different people, she and her mother. Julie watched TV, Clara read books; Julie only went out for dinner on birthdays, Clara rarely cooked on consecutive nights; Julie had one friend, Stacey, who she met twice a week for a walk around the two bridges, a pattern they'd unceremoniously maintained for thirty-four years; Clara, by contrast, had lots of friends and had to book nights out with them months in advance, half of which were cancelled on the day. The differences between them were generational, contextual, historical, political and, Clara thought but hated herself for thinking, intellectual. The university degree was the first of its kind in Clara's family. And the master's degree, the PhD, the lecturing and conferences only added to her sense of estrangement from her home and family. Clara and her mother were different – and Clara would have it no other way. When she opened her phone to see who had liked her most recent photo – an ironically captioned picture of her lecture notes (*Lecturing on literature and socialism this morning #girlboss*) – she felt a stab of shame on seeing her mother's sincere comment lodged between the laughing emojis of the other academics. *Good luck, I'm sure they'll love it!*

What a shock it was then, when Clara revisited photos of her mother at Clara's age. They revealed the same half-smile, the mirrored gesture of long hair tucked behind an ear, the nursing of a warm mug in both hands. It confounded Clara, who got by on the illusion of total difference. The similarities of gesture were unlikely to be a fluke, and surely didn't stop at gesture, she thought, though the idea made her uncomfortable. Really, she and her mother were like wildly divergent texts written by the same author, she thought – entirely distinct in genre, plot and structure, yet with a shared syntax any reader would recognise. Recognising herself in her mother made her completely uncomfortable in every situation: in lecture halls and theatres, in the café on the corner by her childhood home, in the pub she used to go to with her school friends. It made her realise there was a reality in family that no amount of reading or travel could ever dissolve.

Christina had talked about character being mysterious and Clara had nodded her head. But it wasn't mysterious at all, Clara realised. It was simple and terrible. Character was inherited, inflicted upon people, entirely unchosen.

Daniel's mother told him she loved him at the end of every phone call. At first, Clara found this endearing, which was an effect that did not last terribly long. She overheard the tail-end of one of their conversations as she came out of the shower a couple of weeks into their relationship and went to ask him how to switch the fan on, for it had not buzzed into life as usual when she pulled the cord for the light. Daniel was making coffee in the kitchen and had his phone set on the counter on loudspeaker as he tipped the beans into the machine his father had bought him for his last birthday. Clara had stood at the door and listened.

'Will you get to the golf course today, do you think?' His mother's voice was bright and fluid and made it easy for Clara to imagine her in her little white room saying "Is it clearer with one or two?" again and again to the apparently never-ending procession of men and women who booked in with Joanna in particular. She was a professional and knew how to ask questions and really listen to the response. Daniel has no idea how lucky he is, she thought, listening to her speak through a crackle of background noise. Imagine a mother who has a well-paid job, a barrister for a husband, a doctor for a son, a solicitor for a daughter and can still hold a conversation on the phone as though it was the only thing on her mind. The woman lived on another planet altogether, Clara reckoned. To Daniel it all seemed fairly standard. He complained about her asking about his love life ('When am I getting my grandkids?') but Clara got him to admit later that in terms of his mother, he had nothing to be sorry for.

Clara had stood at the open door to the kitchen and watched Daniel make his proficient way from coffee machine to fridge to sink, not missing a beat with his mother. Competence ran in the family, Clara recognised, and pulled up her towel.

'OK, Daniel, I will let you go, pet. We have Rachel and Ian round this evening and your father wants to do hake and some lemony potatoes he saw on TV last Saturday. I'm leaving him to it and heading out to look at curtains. Speak soon. Love you.' That Daniel reciprocated without even needing to think, and without any discernible disruption to his movements, confirmed to Clara that there were indeed other sorts of people in the world, people who had no conscious conception of the ease with which they moved through their days.

Clara reasoned that there must be some potential emotional trigger-point that she navigated with no thought, something that Daniel would struggle with, something that would entirely change the course of his day the way a conversation with her mother might for her. There must be something, she thought to herself in the solitude of her own apartment, though, she had to confess, nothing immediately sprang to mind.

Clara's own mother was approaching sixty and there would need to be a party when it happened. The trouble was that Clara could not remember if she was currently fifty-nine or fifty-eight. She reminded herself often enough to scroll through social media to look for photos of her mother's fiftieth and check the year. It had been a small thing then: a meal at the Lodge Inn followed by cake back at Clara's aunt's. It was Ann who had booked the restaurant and told Clara the arrangements. It was Ann who invited Julie's friend, Stacey, and who went to great lengths to ensure Julie's then boyfriend, Stuart, was sober on the day of the meal. Clara made mental notes to do the online search soon, when her mother's upcoming birthday entered her mind, despite having the facility to check there and then. Clara recognised the nonsense of this. Rather than prompting her to go ahead and check for the photos, the realisation she was putting off a simple task led her instead to consider the psychological reasons underneath the procrastination.

Clara reasoned that her irrational behaviour around her mother was because she was never quite sure what her mother thought of her. There was love, yes, but it was a strange kind of strained, incommunicative, love-by-implication kind of love. Sophie said this was just the Irish mother's way of relating to one's children, but Clara had seen Sophie with her mother, had accompanied them for Christmas shopping in Belfast a few years ago. They spoke without awkwardness and didn't rely on Clara for conversation. She had watched them talk and laugh, slightly bemused, and recognised that there really were other ways things could go. The realisation had made Christmas more difficult.

By the time Clara had reached the second landing, Christina was back in her study and Clara had to step over three small piles of books sitting on the floor at the threshold of the room. As she approached the sound of Christina moving what she supposed were more books, she couldn't help but tilt her head to the side to read the spines of some of those on the floor. *We Have Always Lived in the Castle* was piled on top of *The Ballad of the Sad Café* and a thick collection of Flannery O'Connor's letters. Beside them, in one of the other piles, *Gravity and Grace* by Simone Weil was stacked with *Being and Nothingness*, *The Gay Science*, *The Future of an Illusion* and *The Mirror of Simple Souls*. *Swing Time*, *Leaving the Atocha Station*, *The Sense of an Ending* and a collection of Alice Munro stories made up a third stack. It was an eclectic mix, Clara thought, realising she had no idea how these stacks related to one another, for already there was a curious mix of philosophy, psychoanalysis and fiction. Clara made a note of the newish novels Christina had bought.

Clara had often wondered how someone whose life was so steeped in books would actually organise their library. In Clara's apartment, every shelf was full, and the black bookcase with deep shelves she had splurged on last year was already double stacked, with Stephen King, John Grisham and a few Marian Keyes making up the back rows. It was a decision she had agonised over for an entire afternoon. And after putting *Salem's Lot, The Shining, The Stand, The Firm, The Associate, Last Chance Saloon* and *The Grown Ups* behind Cormac McCarthy, Paul Auster and Ali Smith, Clara had cringed. She was becoming a person she didn't like. She had got up from her seat from which she had been appraising her new bookcase and completely removed the two rows. On imagining one of her old PhD colleagues coming over for wine (which had yet to happen), she reasoned that the more literary novels were more likely to be needed for an article or for a quotation, and she put the books back exactly where they had been, this time with a memorised justification.

Clara didn't have the luxury of spare rooms or a study in which to alphabetise or strictly thematise her growing collection. She was only thirty, but already she had enough books to fill her small apartment. At seventy-eight, Christina had about sixty years of book-buying behind her, and a large house in which to keep them. In lieu of the three-story townhouse and the books and the thick rug in the square living room, getting to see how they were all arranged was almost a suitable consolation prize for Clara.

'The absolute state of this place! It's never looked worse. Come in here, dear girl.' Christina straightened up from the cardboard box she had been hunched over and came across the room to give Clara a hug. There was a slight drag in her left leg as she began to walk, almost as though she was pulling it along behind her like a reluctant pet. There was a curved path between the two women among the piles of books, and a mixture of assembled and flatpack boxes. Christina was dressed in black trousers and a blue patterned blouse. She looked relaxed in her more casual clothes.

Clara's eyes widened at the sight of the books. There were thousands of them. Where the ceiling sloped down to meet the wall, Christina had built seven or eight high towers, the tops of which were at Clara's eye level. Large reference books on literary studies, the history of science, world religions and astronomy formed the sturdy foundations of the stacks, which in turn tapered into standard hardbacks and then slim paperbacks at the top.

'Christina, this room is amazing,' Clara said, looking around again. 'It's paradise for a book lover!'

Christina laughed as she put one arm around Clara. 'I'll show you a photo of what it used to look like later. It has been a sort of paradise for a few years, I suppose. Now it's a bomb site.'

Clara handed over the bottle of wine and Christina took it, shaking her head. 'I told you the place is stuffed full of wine. I joined two of those wine clubs they advertise online and they keep sending boxes of twelve bottles every few months. And I don't really drink anymore!' She looked from the bottle to Clara. 'But this is very kind. Thank you, Clara.'

'It's no problem at all. It's actually from one of those monthly clubs. Daniel's dad has just joined.'

'Tell him to cancel. Unless he's a dipsomaniac.' Clara tilted her head. 'Isn't that a nice word. It means alcoholic, but it's a little better. *Alcoholic* is an ugly word. *Dipsomaniac* has that medical ring to it that seems appropriate. He isn't, is he?'

Clara laughed. 'Not as far as I know. His whole family is perfect. They are like what young people would imagine their ideal future might be like. Fancy jobs, nice cars, everyone on good terms all the time.'

'Oh, dear.'

'What do you mean?'

'His dad's having sex with his secretary. Or watches dodgy pornography. There'll be something.'

Christine laughed. 'I hope not.

As much as their perfection freaks me out, I do like them.'

'I'm thinking from a writer's point of view, I suppose. Perfection is terribly dull. Imagine getting stuck into a character like that: the ostensibly perfect father. Oh, you'd take such pleasure in ruining him. I sound terrible, don't I?'

'Not at all.'

Christina clapped her hands together then. 'I spent the morning writing at the dining table downstairs and I have to say, it's given me quite a lift. I have been worried about trying to write anywhere in this house that isn't this room, but this morning has given me a little hope.'

Clara felt a small burst of satisfaction that she knew exactly what this dining table looked like and could now easily imagine Christina sitting at it with her notebook.

'Is this new novel about the destruction of a perfect upper-middle-class family, by any chance?'

Christina smiled. 'Oh, God, no. It's the strangest thing – because I do lean towards the more macabre at times – but this one is quite nice.'

'I can't wait till it's out,' Clara said, putting her hands in her jeans pockets.

'Well, from experience, these things take a lot longer than one would wish.'

Clara remembered the book in her jacket pocket. Her heart lurched a little at what she was about to do. She took out the book and held it in both hands.

Christina saw the book and her face broke into a smile. 'Really? That one?'

Clara laughed and felt colour rising in her face. 'I love it. I've been rereading it and I think it might be my favourite.'

'Oh, Clara. I love to hear that. If a writer's novels are like children, I feel this one never got as much affection as the others. So it heartens me that you've brought it.' Christina took the battered black copy of *Séances* from her hands and held it up to her eyes. 'What *have* you been doing to this poor book, Clara? It's barely a thing anymore.'

Clara laughed. 'It's been read a few times.'

'I love it. I adore a broken-down book. There is nothing more human in all the world.' There was a silence as Christina carefully flicked through the book. She looked up then at Clara. 'I assume you want me to sign it. Or am I being awfully presumptuous?'

Again, Clara laughed. 'If that's OK—?'

Christina went to a bookcase along the far side of the room and took a pen from one of the shelves. She pressed the book against the wall and hovered her pen over the title page. After a moment, she wrote something.

Clara thanked her as she took the book back and put it in her pocket.

Christina gestured to the room. 'Now, look at this shit. We have a job ahead of us. I really do appreciate you giving up your evening. I promise there'll be passable food to look forward to.'

Clara nodded and smiled. Christina had no idea just how many evenings Clara would have given up to work alongside her, packing books, lifting chairs.

Already Clara could sense a much looser quality to the way Christina spoke in her own home. If they had been in the coffee shop, she wouldn't have volunteered any information about her writing project, or admitted to any kind of anxiety about how it was going; but, within her own walls, it seemed like she was more comfortable, that she didn't feel a need to play a role for Clara. Houses did have strange effects on people, Clara recognised. When Daniel was back at his family home, he regressed, in some strangely unappetising ways, to being a teenager. He would let his mother lift his empty mug, sit in the living room while she brought him paracetamol for his sore head, allow her to wash his clothes if he stayed the night. It was as though Clara had a looking glass on these occasions, one that permitted her access to scenes that played out a decade or more before but that, in reality, were happening right before her eyes.

'Get off your arse and wash your cup yourself,' she whispered to Daniel after his mother had taken away the dinner plates and then served the coffee his father had made in a percolator. Daniel glanced over at her with furrowed brow.

'This is her happy place. She loves doing all this.'

When Clara was at home, it usually only took her twenty minutes or so before all the reasons for her swift departure at eighteen came back to her in a quick flood of recognition. The next-door neighbour's music that made the toggle on her bedside light vibrate; her mother's perpetual state of conflict with someone, with anyone; the smallness of their house, not finally due to its size, but because all the things that ever happened in it stayed there – the silences, the arguments, the tears – and meant there was less room for living. Though, if Clara was ever asked to write down the precise events that made her jump at the opportunity of leaving home, she would struggle. It would be like trying to account for the weather, she would think, or the alignment of planets. Her bone-deep need to leave was just the way things were, the reasons so complicated and various they amounted to something simple. The means of escape being the very thing that made returning so difficult, however, was something she didn't consider at the time of the online applications.

Over the next hour, Clara put paperbacks in boxes and then carried them down to a large, light-filled room on the first floor. There was a single bed by the far wall dressed in a floral duvet cover and rose-coloured sheets, and a small desk by the window which overlooked Christina's back garden and the oak tree that sat in its centre.

'I have a man coming to take the bed away next week,' Christina said, shuffling in behind Clara. 'It has never been used and, without it, I think my desk from upstairs could squeeze in. What do you think?'

Clara nodded slowly, looking at the bed. The desk in the study was a long, Edwardian mahogany piece with a curved central lid under which Christina stored pens and thick sheets of paper. The surface of the table was of olive-coloured leather, stitched into the wood above two ornate drawers which Christina had emptied in anticipation of its moving. Clara imagined it in place where the bed now was and nodded again.

'I think it will be lovely there. Or,' she said, turning slightly, 'you could even place it by the window if you could rehouse that desk.'

Christina made a noise of approval. 'We could take that upstairs, couldn't we? It'll not be used now.'

'I could do that, no problem.'

Christina suddenly lifted both her hands towards Clara. 'Unless you'd be able to use it? What am I thinking putting it back into that upstairs room? You would be very welcome to it, if you could get it home.'

Clara smiled and, without choosing to, imagined standing by the desk in her apartment, explaining its provenance to two unidentifiable people holding wine glasses in her living room. 'That's very kind. Are you sure you won't miss it?'

'Clara, I don't even remember buying it. Please, by all means.'

Clara would text Daniel before dinner to ask for a lift later in the evening. She would need to tell him to put down the back seats to make room.

Clara had a ghost of sweat on her forehead by the time she had taken the twenty-first box down the stairs into the spare room. She reckoned she had transported well over two thousand books in the boxes and in the little stacks she'd collected from the floor and taken in her arms down the flight of stairs. By the end, the bed was obscured behind the boxes and Clara wondered how the man was ever going to get it out of the room. She pushed the boxes tight to the walls to create some semblance of a path from door to bed and left it at that.

During the carting of books from top floor to first floor, Christina had stayed in her study, organising the books into specific boxes, swapping one for another, lifting books from the floor to read their blurbs as though she'd never seen them before. When Clara came into the room, Christina would tell her things about the collection, or about individual books. 'This one is signed, so I'm protective of it,' she said, sliding out an old copy of *The Bell* from a shelf at eye-level. 'She was a lovely person.'

Clara's eyes widened. She loved the novel, having read it in her third year alongside *Mrs Dalloway* and *The Blue Flower*. She had even considered writing her essay on Murdoch, but ultimately found Woolf a slightly easier author to write about.

Christina opened the book and held the inscription out for Clara to read.

With much admiration for your writing,
Christina. I hope you enjoy, Iris.

'No way,' Clara said. 'What a thing to have.'

'I do look at it from time to time. She was a genius, that woman.'

'Where did you meet her?'

'Actually, I met her several times. But this was the first one. It was at a reading in Oxford and I queued with my copy of *The Bell*. She'd been reading from *The Message to the Planet* that morning, which is a book I didn't particularly gel with, so I brought along this one. Anyway, I must have waited for a good ten or fifteen minutes in the line and when I got to the front, she called me by my name. Isn't that extraordinary?'

'What year was this?' Clara asked.

'Oh, late eighties. Perhaps '89. Maybe even 1990.'

'So she'd read *Promised Land* then?'

'I think she must have. It was my only novel out at the time, though the second was finished by then, I think. She said that she was intrigued by what I'd do next, that she'd be reading what I published. Isn't that lovely? I shed a little tear outside the lecture room when I saw what she had written.'

Christina had asked Clara to choose a record while she finished cooking, and Clara felt her heart leap in her chest. Books were one thing, but now she was permitted to look through Christina Darnell's record collection unsupervised. It felt oddly personal, like she had been handed her diary.

The player was along the same wall as the door to the dining room – Clara hadn't seen it on her way through the house at first. When Christina led her back down the stairs and into the room, she gestured to the record player, which she'd placed on a long, dark-wood stand. Below, there were six squares in two rows of three into which Christina had packed her collection. A succulent sat on the record player's right, and a candle was burning to its left, a trail of dark smoke rising against the white of the wall behind it. Clara approached the unit slowly, her eyes moving from one square to the next. She noticed the one on the top left was less full. A recording of Vivaldi's *Four Seasons* was first in the row. Clara flipped through the records using her right hand to hold the records her left hand tipped forwards. Mozart's *Piano Concertos Nos. 20 and 21*; Beethoven's *Symphony No. 5*; Mahler's *Symphony No. 2 'Resurrection'*.

Clara didn't know much about classical music. When she was growing up her mother would clean on Saturday mornings and the house would come alive to a Celine Dion compilation album or Dr Hook. Even now Clara couldn't hear 'It's All Coming Back to Me Now' without the smell of Mr Sheen furniture polish returning to her. As she got older, Clara moved from Britney and Christina to Evanescence and then, in a strange leap, to instrumental jazz: Oscar Peterson, Bill Evans, Miles Davis and John Coltrane. She'd had an iPod Shuffle back then that went from 'She Moves in Her Own Way' by The Kooks to 'Flamenco Sketches', and she listened to them all in full almost as a matter of moral principle. On one occasion, Brent, a footballer in her history class, had heard a saxophone playing from her earphones when they were reading in the sixth form study. He saved her number on his phone as Saxy Clara which she thought was terrible, but he invited her round to his empty house at the weekend and went down on her for ages, which meant the nickname became a precursor to something worth remembering. Nowadays, Clara's online playlists were separated strictly by genre and function. *Electronic for reading. Writing jazz. Walking beats. Angry/Sad nostalgia* which meant she rarely had to tolerate silence.

Clara moved on to the other rows of records and found Joni Mitchell's *Chalk Mark in a Rain Storm*, *Blue* and *Turbulent Indigo* side by side with Rickie Lee Jones's *The Magazine* and *Pirates*, which sat beside Stevie Nicks's *Bella Donna* and five Kate Bush albums.

Clara considered *Blue*. It was a safe choice, universally adored, and Clara knew it well enough to hold a conversation about it.

She'd read about Joni's discovery of the dulcimer in the late sixties, and could talk at length about the word 'confessional' as it was applied to *Blue* and the 'confessional' American poets in the same decade. She could argue there was a touch of sexism in it all, reducing women's work to their biographies. But then again, the album was an obvious pick. Clara didn't want to seem as though she were trying intentionally to be interesting and the thought led to a familiar problem: she was making a decision based on how it would look to her from the outside, a vantage point she often found herself in.

Clara changed her mind and took a different record out of its sleeve.

After a moment, Christina came into the room with an open bottle of red wine and set it on the table. 'I love this album,' she said, putting her hands on the back of one of the dining chairs. She stood and listened to quiet percussion give way to a steady falling piano line and then to the voice of a girl.

Clara watched Christina as she closed her eyes until the drums began and Rickie Lee Jones finally sang *we belong together.* Clara dropped her eyes as Christina looked at her.

'I would love to know why you picked this, I haven't heard it in a few years. But first, sit. I have food.'

She moved into the kitchen and returned with the two plates she'd taken from the table. There was steam rising from the sauce which she had poured over thinly sliced meat and drizzled around the edge of the plates in imperfect circles. As she sat the plates down opposite one another, Clara admired the presentation. The duck was arranged delicately on a bed of creamy mashed potatoes and on the far side there was a flurry of green. Clara remembered the little square note and the buttered spinach.

'It looks delicious,' Clara said, still standing. She wasn't sure if Christina sat looking towards the door to the hall or if she would want the seat nearer the kitchen. Christina gestured at both plates.

'Have a seat. Would you like some wine?'

Clara sat at the place nearer the door to the kitchen and nodded. 'Yes, please.'

Christina moved to the far side of the table and poured two half glasses. 'Ludicrous, I know. We'll drink the same amount in the end, but somehow a full glass of wine feels a bit sickening, doesn't it?'

Clara smiled, remembering the perilously full glass she had navigated with Chris a few days earlier. She lifted the glass to her nose. 'It smells lovely.'

'Yours is unopened in there. I had a look and it looks nicer than this one, so I've done the good gospel thing and left the best for last.'

'Didn't they serve the best first?' Clara asked, her mind flitting back to homilies in her mother's chapel.

'That was the custom, yes,' Christina replied, picking up her knife and fork. 'But the whole point was that Christ inverted it when he changed the water into wine and it turned out to be the best stuff they had all night.'

'How do you know all these things?' Clara asked.

Christina looked up from her plate and the record went quiet as 'Living it Up' faded out. 'The Bible is quite an important book, Clara. What else am I supposed to do all day? It pays to know some of the old stories.'

Clara cut a piece of duck and touched it to some of the sauce around the plate. She found the thought of eating meat didn't trouble her at all. She allowed herself to imagine it was Daniel sitting opposite her, which confirmed that it was eating with Christina that gave her conscience permission to avert its eyes for an hour or two.

It was delicious.

'I know,' Clara said, after chewing her first bite. 'But you don't just read the old stories – you can talk about them so well, make connections. I envy it.'

Christina had started to eat, too. 'Yes, Clara, but you are a child by comparison. Or rather, I am ancient. Old age must have some advantages. It can't all be a depressing loss of power until the grave opens. I've found that one of the only gifts of being my age and still relatively with it is that all those books are still in here somewhere.' Christina gestured to her head with her knife. 'I feel like I have absorbed so much. I often only realise it when I sit to write, or sit opposite someone for a proper conversation.' She smiled across the table. 'Now, tell me. Why Rickie Lee Jones?'

Clara had forgotten she'd picked the record and felt her mind whir a little as she prepared herself to answer Christina's question. 'Well, when I was doing my A-levels I started listening to all sorts of stuff. Jazz mainly, like the early modal records. But then from there I got into blues and then some of the session players who played with all those fusion bands in the seventies. Steely Dan was a favourite for ages. But then I found Rickie Lee Jones through "Chuck E.'s In Love" and I adored it. The first album is probably my favourite, but *Pirates* is great too.'

'You're a very interesting person, Clara. Most people your age wouldn't know who she was. I do disagree, though – I think this album is her best. "A Lucky Guy" is her at her most brilliant: sad, melancholy, childlike. She breaks my heart.'

Both women were silent for a few moments as they ate.

'Second albums are meant to be terrible, aren't they?' Clara said then. 'But you're right, this one is perfect.'

'I don't get the second album mythology,' Christina said, shaking her head. 'People say it about books too, especially nowadays, when everyone seems to be offered two-book deals when they have only ever written one manuscript in their lives.

But in my experience, the second book was a dream to write. I had none of the pressure of finding a publisher or reading a first-ever review. I felt so free when I wrote *Séances*, but I guess it was a different time.'

'Did you write it quickly?'

'Oh, I can hardly remember. Memory is a strange thing: it makes up stories, doesn't it? I am not sure I can trust it.'

'It does, but isn't that interesting in itself?' Clara said.

Christina cut another piece of duck. 'Go on.'

'Well, even though what your memory tells you might not be true, it's still valuable in that it is most likely telling you something about how you feel about the past.'

'That's a lovely thought. I think you're right. When I look back at writing that book my memory is that it was written in a blissful three-month period where each day was a rush to get to the writing desk in my little spare room. But that can't be right. The first book came out in, what, '87?' Clara nodded. 'And the second was out in '91. The more likely story is that I had a good writing patch for a few months but that the novel was formed and edited over a year or two. Isn't it funny that I can't remember?'

'I think it's a very human thing not to remember accurately,' Clara said, and reached for her wine glass.

Christina tilted her head slightly and then nodded. 'But I like what you said earlier. Maybe that is what remembering accurately means: the emotional return to a time and place, or an emotional reaction to a time and place you can't fully recall. I think this is what interests me when I write the past within a novel: how a character deals with the failure of their memory to retain detail while they simultaneously experience a sort of full-blooded emotional response. You've hit on something there – that memory might be one of the most obviously human things we have.'

Clara nodded, and took another sip of wine. Inwardly she was ecstatic. She spoke again, a new confidence in her voice. 'I sometimes get frustrated when my body reacts a certain way to a place or a person but I have no logical explanation for it. I think that's something similar, that there is a kind of emotional memory as well as emotional intelligence in our actual bodies, even if our minds don't remember the truth of whatever happened to make us feel that way.'

Christina put down her fork as Clara spoke and rested her chin on her hand. 'What a lovely way of putting it. You're speaking from experience—?'

'I guess so. I get that sort of feeling when I have to go back to Derry, back to my mum's house . . . a sort of gut reaction that makes me want to get a train in the other direction. And there isn't one reason for it, or at least there isn't something that comes immediately to mind. I just don't want to go. I sound like a terrible person, but that is just how it feels.'

'This doesn't make you sound terrible at all. I think it makes you sound honest. Forget fluke weather and reports of apparitions: *mothers* are the strangest things in this world, Clara. I mean that. The only reason they don't appear so unsettling is that they are necessary. I've often thought that in most cases, mothers give their child a wound, or a lack, which they hold the balm for. And in most of those cases, the mother doesn't know she has what the child is looking for, because to her, the child has actually taken something from her, and she wants it back. This all sounds like a horror film, doesn't it? But I think it's true. It might not be sound psychoanalysis, however.'

'I've had to read a lot of Freud and Jung and Kristeva,' Clara said. 'I'm not sure there is any such thing as sound psychoanalysis.'

Christina laughed. 'That's true.'

'What you say sounds so depressing, Christina.' Clara shook her head and cut another piece of meat. She heard herself say

Christina's name out loud and the thought crossed her mind that it might have been the first time she's used it in front of her. 'It sounds so bleak.'

'Doesn't it just. But that is no reason to think that it isn't true. How else do you make sense of your response to going home?'

'I don't make sense of it. I avoid the feelings, go home, and leave at the earliest opportunity.'

'Now, we have both read enough Freud to know that repression is to be avoided.' Christina was smiling then, and took a sip from her glass.

'Repression is unavoidable, though, isn't it?'

'Maybe totally,' Christina said. 'But a lot is probably avoidable, I'd say.'

'But I know so little about you,' Clara said then, unguarded – and felt her stomach drop.

Christina set her glass down and picked up her fork. 'What do you mean? You're writing a book on me. You seem to have read everything I've ever written. You know the way my mind works as well as I do, it seems.'

'Sorry, yes, that is all true. I just mean there is more to a person, to a writer, than what they have written. It was meant more as a compliment.'

'I know. You are right that there is a lot more to a writer than their books. I once met a much-respected American novelist who was totally revered for her erudition and intelligence. I was teaching for a semester in New York and she came to give a lecture. I went along to the dinner and she was such a messy eater, her assistant took her back to the hotel to change ahead of the talk.'

Clara laughed as her mind went into overdrive, trying to guess who it might have been.

'I had read all of her books by then, Clara, and as far as I am concerned, there was not a clue in there that she liked huge amounts of butter on her bread and let crumbs fall from her mouth onto her clothes. This might not have been the kind of mystery you were hinting at, I recognise.'

'When were you in New York?'

'I've been a few times over the years. But I went in the early 2000s to teach a class on fiction writing. It was my first and last time doing something like that, I can tell you.'

'What happened?'

'Nothing major, really,' Christina said.

'What put you off?' Clara asked, keen for Christina to keep talking.

'The students.' She laughed then and Clara joined her. 'It was a terrible few weeks, really. They told me the undergraduates were dying to meet me and learn from my experience. Nonsense. When I arrived to teach the first workshop, there were twelve or thirteen of them and they couldn't have been less interested in genuine fiction if they'd tried. They stared at their shoes when I walked in. I thought Americans were meant to be extroverts.' Clara looked down at her plate then, conscious she had been staring at Christina as she spoke. 'I went round the room to get their names and asked them what they were working on. Seven of them told me they had started work on a memoir. Seven! Over half. I couldn't believe my ears. I said to them once we'd gone round the room that a memoir is typically one of the last things one writes. They just looked at me. We've spoken before about memoirs, haven't we? I think the roots of my aversion are traceable to that class.'

'What did you do with them in the classes?'

'It was my first time teaching writing and, as I said, my last. Writing can't be taught, by the way, but that's another conversation and something I had to find out for myself. But I filled the time by getting them to look very closely at small passages in the sessions and then I'd ask them to read a novel in a couple of days to see what they made of the experience. One of the weeks I got them to read *Housekeeping* on a Wednesday and scheduled a class on the text for Thursday morning. They only had the twenty-four hours. But, fair enough, most of them seemed to read it.'

'And what was the purpose in getting them to read it so quickly?' Clara asked.

She had read the novel, but even though it was so short, it had taken her a couple of weeks as she savoured every line of it. The novel reminded her of Nathan, a fellow undergraduate and potential boyfriend. Something of a sex-obsessive, he had had no time for Clara's reading. He would kiss her neck when she was trying to read about the two orphans and their aunt, move his hands from her hips to her chest as she batted him away with the novel. He had got increasingly frustrated she wasn't in the mood and eventually stopped texting her as she reached the final few pages.

She wondered now what it would be like to read it in one evening. Clara hated book blurbs that said things like, 'I read it all in one breathless sitting.' No one ever does that, she used to think.

Christina chewed on her food for a moment before speaking. 'Well, I wanted them to feel the full cumulative effect of say, one hundred and eighty pages of high-quality fiction all in one go. Students are so used to picking out quotes or, on a good day, a whole paragraph for discussion. I wanted them to feel the wave of a novel crash over them. That is what fiction is about, I said to them all: it's the accumulation of sentences, how they add up, how their meanings adjust to one another, to build towards something; ultimately it's about the formation of a kind of tapestry and not just the individual lines, as beautiful as they may be.'

'And did it work? Did they get something from it?'

'I have no idea. But I did. I read the novel with a glass of white wine in a bar on the university campus. I sat for three hours and did not look up once.' She paused. 'No, that's not true. I couldn't have had just one. I must have ordered another glass.' She smiled at Clara. 'But the effect is amazing, Clara. Have you ever done that? Just read a book from start to finish in one go?'

Clara thought for a moment. 'Never. I read the second half of *Gone Girl* in one day, I think. It was assigned on a contemporary fiction module when I was an undergraduate and the twist in the middle had me hooked. That was the only time, as far as I can remember. Have you ever read it?'

'No, I can't say I have. I saw the film, though. Interesting.'

There was a silence then. Clara imagined Christina buying wine from the girl behind the counter at the cinema, saw her going into the screen, the door closing behind her as she went to find her seat. She would have been a few years younger then, and Clara's mind adjusted Christina's walk accordingly, with a more fluid, effortless movement, her left leg still moving without struggle. Clara's imagination went on past the closed door to the darkness of the theatre, to comfortable dark seats cast in faint green from the exit signs by a door at the front of the screen. She saw Christina sit in the very centre, her silvery-blonde bun just about visible above the back of the seat. There was a stillness in the place, a substantial quiet like that of an empty church. Christina was alone as the light from the booth above was switched on. Clara could see dust orbiting itself in the jet of light, and found it hard to comprehend how that light contained the advertisement for laundry detergent Christina was now watching.

Clara again wondered why, even in her imagined scenarios, Christina was alone. Try as she might, Clara couldn't imagine Christina with a partner. When Clara had first met her, she seemed so passionate about her own life that there was no imaginative space for Clara to invent another person. There was scarcely any room, Clara thought, for Christina seemed so fully realised, so herself, that to imagine another life for her would be insulting to the one she was living, to the one she had chosen. Christina Darnell was a character Christina would have been pleased to have invented.

'You're right,' Clara said then. 'You wouldn't ever think about watching a film in five-minute bits until it was finished. You're meant to see the whole piece in one go. I wonder why we don't do that sort of thing with reading more often.'

'Well, I suppose books are longer,' Christina said. 'A good novel will take a lot longer than the standard film would now. But I take your point. I do try to read in at least one-hour chunks. Usually, I find that if I read for any less than that, I don't enjoy the book: it's almost as though I haven't given the author a fair chance.' Clara nodded as Christina spoke.

'Would that be your preference in terms of how you like to be read? Do you want your readers to read your work for longer periods of time?'

'Well, ideally, yes. I think it's written to be read like that. But then again, the book belongs to them by that point. They can read it backwards if they wish.' Christina put down her fork then and lifted her glass.

The first side of Rickie Lee Jones had finished at some point over the dinner, and it was only then that Clara noticed the absence. She made a gesture towards the record player and Christina said, 'Yes, please. Go ahead.' Clara stood to turn the record.

'I was going to pick a Joni Mitchell album,' she said, retaking her seat.

Christina nodded. 'She is another genius.' She took Clara's plate and placed it on her own. 'You know, something I'll never understand is how Bob Dylan wins awards for literature when someone like her has a dozen albums of poetry.' She sat back in her seat. Her eyes moved down to the tablecloth and she was quiet for a moment. Clara felt her heart rate rise, for it looked like something was wrong. After a moment, Christina spoke.

'There's this stunning set of lines in a Joni song about the trails a plane leaves in the sky and how it looks like the strings on her guitar. That part alone is better than anything Dylan ever wrote.'

'What is it from?' Clara asked

'"Amelia", from *Hejira*. It is the most perfect example of how to write an extended metaphor. The song is about Amelia Earhart and flits between her life as a pilot – distant, removed – and the singer's feeling of dislocation back on the ground. There's this brilliant line, I hope I can get it.'

Clara looked at the floor and readjusted herself on her chair as Christina drummed her fingers lightly on the tablecloth, speaking the line slowly. Watching Christina, Clara could almost see the physical effort of remembering. She spoke with her eyes tightly closed and her right hand beating out some of the syllables of the words on the table as she said them. Clara could glimpse, for a moment, how there could be no real distinction between the mind and the body, for Christina was so clearly accessing something she held inside of her.

'Isn't that just astonishing? As I writer I find it astonishing. Accurate, too.'

'Accurate?' Clara asked. 'What do you mean?' She hadn't listened to the quote and hoped Christina didn't notice.

'The looking down on everything. My only issue with the line is that it might be read as implying superiority, which isn't what she means, I think. But it's a great image of the artistic life. How it feels a lot of the time. That you have to give up something important to get the vantage point from which to work.'

'Do you think that the choice is necessary?' Clara said. 'Does writing have to come at a cost?'

Christina sat forward in her chair and used her fingers to press out a fold in the cloth. 'I'm going to say something very obnoxious, but it's only because I've had a glass of wine.' Clara smiled and took up her own glass. Christina had just topped up both glasses again, which actually meant they were on their second. 'I think if you are a good writer, someone who writes worthwhile, or ambitious things, then it has to come at a cost. At one level that makes me seem very full of myself, I know, but, in another way, it is also a terribly obvious thing to say. Think about it. How can anyone spend a year, two years of their life, writing about people who do not exist, with their own psychologies, motivations, frailties, mothers' – Christina nodded at Clara then, a ghost of a smile forming at the corner of her mouth – 'and so on, without falling a bit out of touch with the people around them who aren't doing the same thing? And it isn't the same as people in other jobs saying things like "Oh, I'm a police officer and that makes me distant from everyone I know who isn't a police officer." That may well be true, but that experience is different to the writer's. It's a difference in kind, not in degree.'

Clara had to concentrate on what Christina was saying. She could feel her mind pick up the words 'degree' and 'kind' like a claw at an amusement arcade and then try to make sense of the sentence by placing them back, once she had reminded herself of their meanings. She did it all without moving her face, nodding slightly as Christina kept speaking.

'The writer feels a necessary dislocation from the world because the world is her source material, it is what she needs to develop an appreciation for as something that is distinct from her, even as she knows that distinction is an illusion. This is what I find so interesting about my own life, Clara: the sheer paradox of it all. When I'm working on a novel, it feels that it is separate from the world, it feels like *I* am separate from the world, even. But, of course, the novel is as much a part of the world as this candle or the wine we are drinking.' Christina gestured to the centre of the table as she spoke and then looked between the bottle and the flicker of flame to Clara. 'Do you understand?'

Clara's mind was racing. She felt conflicted, as one part of her wished the conversation was being recorded for the monograph, and another part felt the absence of a recorder was an important marker for her relationship with Christina. The excuse for meeting her was no longer needed, she thought, and the realisation pleased her. But what Christina had just said would fit so perfectly into a chapter on Christina's essay collection, where she had written her most important, interesting things about art and writing. To combine the essays from 2000 with her thoughts twenty-six years on would be interesting to academics. Clara knew that once the wine had worn off overnight, what Christina had just said would fade to sentiment Clara wouldn't be fit to write down.

'It makes total sense,' Clara said, aware that she hadn't spoken immediately. 'It reminds me of something you wrote in one of the essays in *The Shape of Clouds*. You said something like, "The universe is, as far as we know, a closed box. Everything in it is recycled, reformed, simply returned in new shapes. The artist, trapped along with everything else, is distinct only because she recognises this and her attempt to make something new, is, like everything else, ultimately doomed; but her failure seems to be of the most interesting kind. And surely this explains some of art's attraction: that its failure is self-conscious, that it has given up the illusion that failure can be avoided." I haven't got every word right, but you can tell it left an impression,' Clara said.

Christina had looked at the table when she recognised Clara was about to recite a quotation. She made a movement with her head now, that suggested a reaction. 'I'm impressed with your recall, Clara, I really am.'

‘Four years I spent with your books each and every day,’ Clara said, smiling. ‘Sometimes I thank God you only wrote five!’

‘Me too, actually,’ Christina said. ‘Five decent books. It’s important to know when to stop, or slow down. Anyway, I think I disagree with that quote you just said.’

‘It was your quote. You wrote it,’ Clara said, her voice rising in mock outrage.

‘I know, but haven’t all the atoms in my body been replaced several times since then? It was written by someone else entirely.’ Clara laughed and put her hands up in surrender. ‘So I suppose what I was saying back then is that novelty can never be achieved in the arts because we live in a closed physical system. But I don’t think that’s right. Even at the level of physics, it seems out of date by a long way. The world is much more interesting than we thought – than I thought then, clearly. There are things popping into and out of existence all the time, strange things happening that seem illogical or impossible, radical indeterminacy at the most fundamental levels of reality. It seems rather presumptuous of me to say that the universe is in any way closed. Can you tell I’ve had a subscription to the *New Scientist* for a while, by the way? But I do think that the part about the failure of art is interesting. I probably still subscribe to that. But that’s a human question, not a scientific one, I think.’

‘You think all art is a failure?’ Clara asked.

‘Yes, but not in the negative way your voice makes it sound.’ Clara laughed. ‘You know the old cliché that a piece of art is never finished, only abandoned? It’s trite, of course, but there’s something important in it. Art is always trying to say “It was like this.” Never, ever, does it say “It *was* this.” There’s always a distance between the representation and what is represented. There’s always a failure in that sense. Art is the admission of incapacity, or of the impossibility of crossing a distance. Writing, painting, sculpture, film, theatre. They all share an ancestor in the first simile.'

Those lines ought to be in the book, Clara thought, and considered typing it into a note on her phone, but stopped herself from reaching to her pocket. It would rupture the mood. Clara looked at the woman opposite her. She was still adjusting to the idea that every moment she had been alive, somewhere, in some room or in some place, Christina Darnell was drinking, or reading, or eating, or speaking. That her 'now' included Christina's writing of *The Hiding* and *The Shape of Clouds* was still a strangely thrilling thought. As Clara was practising her papers for the transfer test, age eleven, Christina was somewhere hand-writing the final pages of her fourth book; and, on one afternoon as Clara was swinging on the monkey bars at the park, or, perhaps when she was with her father for one of the few fishing trips he ever took her on before disappearing completely, Christina was posting off the manuscript to her editor and agent and then returning to her home, feeling whatever it was she was feeling. Coexistence was a strange idea, Clara thought.

'Do you know what I hate?'

Clara looked from her hands on the table to Christina as she spoke. 'And I think you'll back me up on this, too.'

'What?' Clara felt another spike in her heartbeat. She values my opinion, she thought.

'Book reviews that refer to a character as *unlikeable*. When did that become an acceptable thing to say when discussing a book's quality?' Clara went to speak but Christina continued. 'How likeable a character is should have no part to play in a review. It's like downgrading a starred review of a book because the sideboard in the protagonist's living room was oak rather than pine. No?'

'Oh, I totally agree,' Clara said. 'I think it's quite a recent thing, though.'

'I suspect you're right. Probably as more and more people think the only way to get people to read books is to talk about personality rather than literature. That probably explains the obsession over author interviews and social media and all the rest of it. I was thinking about all this today after I finished writing. Maybe this new book's reception was on my mind or something. But I realised that it says two things about the reviewer. First, it shows a misunderstanding of what fiction is about. Whether a novel "works" or not will never be down to if the writer has managed to write a "likeable" character.' Christina created air quotes around the words with her fingers. It was the second time she'd used the gesture and Clara considered it a result of feeling more comfortable in her company. Or it was the wine. 'And also – and I think this is the key thing – reducing a book to the likeability or unlikeability of its protagonist shows a remarkably atrophied sense of empathy on the part of the reviewer. What they are really saying is, "My moral imagination is so shallow, so inhuman, that I cannot *like* this character," forgetting, of course, that this shows *them* up rather than the writer. In the course of good, even decent, fiction, the writer knows a lot more about their character, about their reasons for writing the novel, than the reviewer. A little faith in writers wouldn't go amiss, I think. People, after all, are often unlikeable, until you discover that most people, if you really try to see, have every reason to be the way they are. And behind that, there's a whole teeming mystery called a person – a soul, even.'

Clara leant back in her chair and breathed in.

'I often worry I'm unlikeable,' Clara said then. 'That I'm too distant, or cold or something.'

Christina sat back, mirroring Clara's movements. She clasped her hands together on the edge of the table. 'Yes,' she said, smiling. 'You really are beyond saving.'

When Professor Stewart returned to his office, he was breathing hard. The response had been extreme and now his body was reacting to its initial reaction, trying to make sense of what had happened. It had only been the mention of Edward's name. The glances he felt could well have been imagined, although the colour that rose in his neck and face was not, he feared.

He began to read the spines of the books on the shelf opposite him, tilting his head slightly to the right to see the words. Anything, he thought, to give his mind an anchor, which, he felt, was in danger of spinning out of his grasp entirely.

Tillich's *Systematic Theology*

Gerstenberger's *Theologies in the Old Testament*

The Silent Cry: Mysticism and Resistance by Dorothy Sölle

The books were a comfort to him; even the volumes in which he had scribbled copious objections and comments, irritated question marks underlined in black ink. Perhaps those were the most precious books he owned, he thought then, his heart calming against his chest. The marginalia was evidence of a conversation, he decided, of some sort of company over a long loneliness. He often wondered to himself if his passionate beliefs, inscribed and implied in the white spaces of books he might never open again, were not just beliefs that came to him *ex nihilo*, but, rather, symptoms of a deeper need; one that had never really been met, or brought to light.

Our heart is restless until it finds rest in you.

Augustine's famous line in *Confessions* sat framed above his desk on the far side of the room. His uncle, a minister in the same denomination, had had it made in needlepoint by one of the older ladies in his congregation. As a student, away from home for the first time, it had kept him searching, convinced that the absence of peace meant his journey hadn't quite finished. Now, as he read Augustine's statement again in the clarity of his panic, he saw how it was unfalsifiable, how a statement of its kind could never really be settled as true or false. The line between divine truth and unverifiable nonsense was thin, porous, perhaps, and Professor Stewart, with his back flat to his study wall breathed out, and for the first time felt his restlessness as a companion.

'"And for the first time felt his restlessness as a companion."'

Christina glanced up as Clara spoke. 'What did you say?'

'"And for the first time felt his restlessness as a companion." It just came to me, that line. I have it underlined in my copy. I really love that sentence.'

'Oh, you do? It's an odd one to hold on to, Clara.' Christina laughed a little.

'Do you think so? It is one of those quotes that lands in my head every now and then. It's a moving moment in that novel, too.'

Christina set down her glass. 'One of the strangest things in the world is hearing something you wrote quoted by someone else,' she said, colour rising in her cheeks. 'It never gets less strange. It's the other person's voice, the rhythm they say the sentence – it feels foreign. It makes it feel real. Solid. As though you haven't wasted your time, or that someone else is sharing in your peculiar delusion, perhaps.'

'Does a novel feel slightly unreal until it's published?' Clara asked.

'Well, by definition it is pretty much unreal until then, but I know what you mean.' She paused, her eyes moving down and to the left. 'I think yes, a work of fiction will always feel unreal, or like a fantasy. When I take delivery of the first copies of my new book, I always, and I mean always, have a slight panic when I look at them.' She smiled. 'Even thinking about it now, I can feel my heart.'

Clara laughed. 'Why is that?'

'Well, because the whole world you have lived in for a year, two years, is now sitting, unfixable and final between two covers. The whole limitless possibility of the thing you could have created is now reduced, finite, into a pile of paper. It sits there in my hallway or dining table like the fucking block universe, unchangeable and stubborn. Oh, I hate that part, Clara, I really do. It feels like a sort of death, all the endings that could have been written, all the characters that got cut, all gone, forever.'

'Has it always felt that way?'

'Good question.' Christina leant forward. 'No. It hasn't. When I received my ten copies of *Promised Land* back then, I couldn't stop picking them up and flicking through them, smelling them. It was like I'd won the lottery.'

'And what has changed?'

'Well, you can only have one first novel, for a start. And after the first one or two, you get wise to the reviews and the critics, and you want to skip the bit that should be happy, the getting the copies and celebrating, because now you're braced for how it will be received. It's the most tense feeling, Clara. I know I don't come across as a terribly anxious person, but for the day or two around getting the first copies of a new book, I am unbearable. Pacing, trying to avoid going back to smoking. When *The Hiding* was published, I put my copies in a cupboard in the kitchen until they were being sold in bookshops. It had been a few years since I'd put out a book, so I was even more nervous than usual. It's lucky I live alone, Clara, honestly.'

Clara felt a small jump in her stomach as Christina finished speaking. The comment hung in the air and Clara felt caught between changing the subject and following Christina where she had led her. While the wine had certainly made Christina more open, less guarded about the details of her life – even her gestures were looser, the way she shook her head or used her hands as she spoke was more expressive than Clara had ever seen her – she hadn't expected Christina to broach that subject on her own, unprompted. She suddenly became aware of how dark it had become outside the house. The small window to the back garden showed less and less detail as the night closed in, and the lamp behind Christina outlined her silhouette in thin gold light. The wine had made Clara unusually present, and she hadn't noticed how hard it was getting to see Christina's mouth move as she spoke. The candlelight that flickered in the small movements of air from napkins and sleeves fell across her face intermittently, giving her features an unreal appearance, wax-like, inhuman.

Slowly, Christina got to her feet, both hands pressed flat against the table as she stood. 'If you'll excuse me, I'll be back in a moment.'

'What were you getting at with that line about restlessness?' Clara asked Christina this question when she had only just re-entered the room, after counting her slow steps on the stairs, breathing out slightly when she heard her shoes reach the entrance to the dining room.

While Christina had been upstairs, Clara texted Daniel to ask for a lift.

Sure. What time?

Dunno yet. Can you put seats down for a desk? I'm getting a desk!

OK no worries. Text me later x

Thanks! X

She also made some notes on her phone, phrases Christina had said, though she knew that already she had forgotten her exact wording, and the notes would be useless. She typed a few more sentences and put her phone away when she heard a door close upstairs.

Alcohol made Clara hasty with the question, and the part of her mind unaffected by the alcohol was grateful for the looseness that had settled between them.

'In the first part of *The Hiding*?' Christina asked, as she passed Clara's chair.

'Yes. It's one of those lines that passed me by the first few times I read the novel. But a year or two ago, it hit me over the head.'

Christina laughed, full-throated, and a speckle of colour came into her cheeks again and it made her look pleased. 'Isn't that an interesting thing,' she said. 'How a book greets you at different stages of life. I had almost the opposite experience with *Walden* by Thoreau. When I first read it, I was a young woman, maybe nineteen or twenty, and it blew me away. I was ready to move into our local woods in Cambridge and forage for the year. I asked my mother for a tent and she put her hand on my forehead to check my temperature. Anyway, I picked it up again when I moved here and was stacking the bookcases that we just spent an evening unstacking again. I sat down and flicked through it for an hour, maybe more, and was shocked at how much I hated it. Appalled at myself for ever liking it!'

Clara looked away and smiled. It had been assigned to her on 'American Beginnings', a module that went from the transcendentalists and slave narratives of Douglass and Jacobs to Robert Frost, Elizabeth Bishop and Richard Wright. She was taught by a man in his late forties with a small amount of thin hair he appeared to be holding hostage on his head, brushed forwards and spiked with what Clara imagined was mousse. He was enthusiastic about the book, joking with the students in the front row that their expensive university fees were a waste of money, that they ought to go and live in the wild and learn in the University of Nature. That these same fees funded his research trips to Connecticut and Massachusetts was not mentioned. Between classes, Dr Barnes was sarcastic and unpleasant, and the students recounted the latest replies they'd received to reasonable questions as they sat in tutorial groups chaired by the man's weary-looking PhD students.

> As noted in the lecture, this question is answered in the module handbook.
>
> I would advise waiting to write about Whitman until you have something worth saying. He is one of the greatest poets of the nineteenth century. He doesn't deserve an essay so half-considered.
>
> Go back and read the poem. My job isn't to read it on your behalf.

After reading week, Dr Barnes had stopped his lecture on Bishop's 'At the Fishhouses' and stared at two students in the third row, who were whispering about something.

'You know I'm not on TV, right?' he said. 'I can see and hear you, which means everyone else can see and hear you too.' He had stood at the front, unmoving and calm, for what had felt to Clara like a full minute.

She was put off *Walden* by the man. In theory, it was a book she should have liked: solitude, self-sufficiency, nature. But because Dr Barnes loved it, she felt compelled to find fault with it. 'It's too long,' she found herself saying to Henry, the teaching assistant who took her seminars. He rolled his eyes and asked another question to the group about the connections between Thoreau and Emerson.

Clara was pleased to hear Christina also didn't like the book. 'I agree with you,' she said. 'It is a dreadfully boring book.'

Christina's eyes lit up. 'Isn't it? And so manly. The lone pioneer in the woods discovering God in the details of his new monkish life. The house he lived in was given to him for the two years he was there. Ralph Waldo Emerson owned it and put him up. Thoreau didn't tell us that, though. It took me a long time to see just how much fortune and privilege there has to be to write a book like *Walden*. I know that's something coming from me'– Christina gestured with both hands at her own house – 'but at least I don't pretend to be some poor soul struggling after some divine truth in a forest.'

Clara smiled. She felt a warm satisfaction in hearing her views expressed by Christina. She also couldn't help imagining her mother overhearing the conversation she was having: the raised eyebrow and shake of her head. *Not a word. I don't understand a word.*

'You were going to tell me about that line from your book,' Clara said then.

'I was. Would you put another record on, Clara? It's quite a novelty for me to have music playing that I haven't chosen.'

Clara pushed her chair back and turned to the stand. She knelt down and began flicking through the records on the bottom right of the storage unit.

'I was very much taken with Augustine's line about our hearts being restless. Grammatically it is all over the place. "Our heart" is restless. Shouldn't it be "our hearts"? I thought when I read it. As it turned out, there are different translations, with some saying "hearts are" and others saying "heart is". But that was my way in – the grammar.'

Clara laughed a little as she listened.

'But anyway, it is a beautiful line, regardless, and seemed to me to capture something that theologians never typically get about the human experience. They are always talking about our sinful natures, or our wanton desires, but "restlessness" seemed to me to capture my own experience of myself much more satisfyingly. It's an evocative description, isn't it? For me it's the image of a child who can't sit still in a classroom, or the feeling of anxiety in the pit of your stomach that won't let you settle to read or write. Restlessness is one of those words that seems so much more humane than the usual words those sorts of men use to talk about people. It implies a desire for something good – 'rest' – and not, as is more typical in these sorts of discussions, a wilful desire to do something bad. People just aren't bad, Clara. This is my conclusion after fifty years of watching people, of inventing people. They aren't "bad". They are restless. And I mean that in the truest, most literal sense of the term. They are "without rest", avoiding something, stuck in an invisible cycle, seeking an easier way to live, perhaps by blaming the wrong people for their lot. Augustine talks about finding rest in God, and for some people that might feel like it works. But in my experience, that's too neat. It exports the solution outside ourselves, which is just too easy – it makes for bad novels. Finding rest is up to us, I think. And, in my experience, Clara, most people are one brave conversation away from coming home to themselves. That's what that novel is about, I suppose.'

Clara paused, her back to Christina. She took the record from the cardboard sleeve.

Billie Holiday was making her sad way through 'I'll Be Seeing You' when Christina stood and walked through to the kitchen.

They had been talking about Clara's job prospects during 'Yesterdays' and then about Christina's job as a housekeeper when she was writing her first book. 'I haven't had a normal job since,' she said, and Clara felt a familiar sense of loss come over as Christina left her alone.

She heard the click of a lock and then felt a cool air enter the dining room.

'Oh, the moon, Clara. Come here.'

Clara stood and walked towards the open door where Christina was standing, her right hand gripping a handrail that had been fastened to the outside wall. The older woman was silhouetted black against the milk light that was pooling over the back garden. Clara looked over Christina's shoulder to the huge oak tree. Its branches were like a nest of veins against the sky, which had become blue and dark, the moon a white orb, distinct and shining.

'Isn't that a stunning moon? You can see to the bottom of the garden.'

Clara looked past the tree to the hedges and fence. She could make out a bird feeder and bird bath, their shape suggested by the path the moonlight had to take around them.

'A full moon always scared me as a child,' Clara said. 'It was when I learned about the word "loon". I thought it made people mad, and my mum told me more crimes are committed under a full moon than at any other time.'

Christina made a small laughing sound. 'I think every child is told that. I was, too. It's not true, by the way. The moon doesn't cause madness. I think it's more likely that people take walks on a well-lit night and more things happen, or more things are seen than otherwise would be. Clara, would you pass me those cigarettes from the counter, please?'

Clara was surprised at the request. She hadn't once detected the smell of smoke on Christina, and her hands had no signs of nicotine stains. The packet was sitting beside a beige-coloured kettle and she held them towards her.

'Thank you. I know it's terrible. I used to smoke when I was your age and then not for about thirty or so years. I have the occasional one now. Especially after a good day's writing, or when it's a pleasant evening like this. Would you like one?' She reached the packet out a little.

Clara hadn't had a cigarette since she was nineteen. Then she'd been drunk with Sophie and they'd both joined in with two men who had bought them a drink in Thomsons. She woke up the next morning with an unpleasant sandpapery feeling in her mouth and a bad taste on her tongue. She had used peppermint mouthwash twice before breakfast.

'Yes, please,' Clara said, and moved past Christina and down the step onto the grass. Christina pulled one out slightly from the packet and held her hand out towards Clara, who took it. She stood with it dumbly between her fingers, not sure what to do with her hands. Christina produced a lighter from her trouser pocket and lit the cigarette she had between her lips, then she reached the lighter to Clara.

After a few moments, Clara felt the nicotine fill her legs and arms, felt it lighten her head and soften her vision. Behind her, Christina made a satisfied sound. 'I know it kills people, but, God, blowing smoke into the night sky is one of life's pleasures. I don't think I'll ever tire of it, Clara, and that's the truth.' Christina took another long drag of her cigarette and blew a trail of smoke that caught the light and faded into the wind. 'I wrote well today,' she said, after a moment, and Clara felt a flutter in her chest.

'Can you talk about it. Or is it too private?' She took a small puff of her own cigarette and breathed out.

Christina looked towards the end of the garden. 'I wrote the last page today. I know that much.'

'Does that mean you're finished? That's exciting.'

'No, not quite finished yet. I think there's probably about two or three thousand words missing from where I left it, and this last page. But I know how it ends, and that's something.'

'Is that typical for you?' Clara asked. 'That you have an ending and have to write towards it?'

'No, I've never had a definite last page until I finish a novel. Usually, I have a vague idea of a last line perhaps, or a movement towards a close. But this time I have how it ends set in stone. I've known for some time, I think. It changes things. It'll make each word that goes before it all the more significant. For a change, I think I've written something of a happy ending.'

Christina looked behind Clara then and Clara turned her head. A small black and white cat was bounding from the tree towards the open door, its tail a bouncing question mark pointed in Christina's direction. 'Here he comes now,' she said, blowing smoke. 'This is Pascal. He won't stop to say hello. He's heard us talking, I bet.' Clara turned back to Christina, whose face was lit up with a smile. She stooped a little as the cat approached her, and Clara could see she wanted to bend her knees further but thought better of it. Christina held her hand down and Pascal rubbed his cheek off her thumb and trotted into the house.

'He's beautiful,' Clara said.

'He's a wonderful cat. He found me, I think. He pawed at this door every morning while I was making breakfast. I gave him the usual little bits of ham and a bowl of water. After a month he was called Pascal and he was mine. You want to hear him purr, Clara. He's a little engine.'

'Have you ever had a pet before?' Clara wondered how the cat had never come up in their conversations.

Christina stood up to her full height again and took a drag of her cigarette. 'I have, I suppose. There was a dog once. A little spaniel called Alfie. He wasn't mine technically. He belonged to the woman I was with then. He was a beauty. So clever. They can be so clever, can't they?'

'They can. I love dogs,' Clara said. 'What happened him? Did he pass away?'

'I suppose he did. By now, I mean. She left and took him with her. I have been alone since.' Clara couldn't look at Christina as she spoke, and Christina looked into the air. 'Well, I was until Pascal pawed at the door.'

Clara looked from Christina to the garden.

'He makes an appearance in my novel, you know. That's what I wrote today.'

'Pascal, you mean?'

'Yes, although it's not really him. Inspired by him, though.'

'I can't wait to read it.'

There was a silence then. Christina blew her final stream of smoke in the air and Clara looked at her, the stoop in her back, her hand gripped around the rail. Clara had more questions and was thinking of which to ask when Christina, still looking at the moon, spoke into the silence.

'You know, I've been reflecting a lot recently, given this is my last novel. And a thought came to me this afternoon, a bolt out of the blue. It struck me as important and I want to say it to you. I don't know if you'll understand it. But as I look back on a life of solitude, which is what mine has really been, I have never been lonely. Never. Clara, what a gift that has been. I am so grateful. I just want more of it.'

9
Affect Theory

The next morning, Clara woke up with one of Christina's essays on her mind. It was a bright Monday morning, and as she had slept with the curtains open – too tipsy to care about the next day, and too tired after she insisted on carrying the desk into the apartment building on her own – her room was already bathed in pale morning light when she opened her eyes. The radiator beside the bookcase had groaned and clanked into life and woken her up, though it might well have been the growing light. She thought immediately about the night before and stretched out with a feeling of pleasure. She had spent the evening with Christina Darnell. They had talked for hours, shared cigarettes, asked one another questions, listened to records. Clara thought back to the first email from Christina's agent, of how elated she'd felt with even the suggestion she might get to meet the woman behind the fiction. Now, she might even go as far to say they were friends.

Simultaneous to the satisfaction, a feeling of ghostly unreality hung around her memories of the conversations over dinner, and the moving of books felt more like invention than something she had done twelve hours previously. The wine she and Christina drank had settled into a sharp pain in the right side of Clara's head and was accompanied with a bodily tiredness that meant she was pleasurably aware of each part of her that was touching the mattress and duvet. She shifted her legs and turned her weight onto her right side to look out of the window. The sky was a light blue and the sun was beginning to appear above the row of houses opposite the apartment. It was going to be a nice day, and Clara felt the morning open up as she lay still.

She remembered asking Christina about her essays and felt compelled to leave her bed to retrieve *The Shape of Clouds* from the bookshelf. On standing, she became aware of a bad taste in her mouth, and went to the bathroom. As she returned, her mouth tasting of peppermint, she lifted the hardback book from the shelf and turned on the radio on the dresser. It played classical music that Clara did not recognise. Daniel would have been able to tell her the composer and the key – the benefit of a childhood in his mother's car after rugby practice. Clara took the book to bed and opened it to the third essay.

The spine had come loose from the binding in places, and moved from side to side as she shifted the book in her hands. On the page she was looking for there were underlines in black scattered across the first few paragraphs, and, as she flicked on, a few bright blocks made with a yellow highlighter. She'd read the essay many times during her PhD, quoted it several times across the thesis, and now, sitting on her bed with her sore head, Clara read it for comfort.

On What We Are: An Essay Concerning Persons

It astounds me that despite endless talk of economic organisation, war, scandal and disaster, we seem to spend comparatively little time with the more fundamental question of what exactly constitutes a person. A person, that is, being the only common feature in the list of things I have just given. How can we do anything other than think of this question? It is incredible to me that we debate theories and ideas that necessarily rely on some notion of what a person is without ever really opening that question for ourselves. 'Window dressing' is the term that springs to mind. For without knowing what we are, any other talk of how we organise ourselves will be, at best, naive and wishful and, at worst – as we have seen over the millennia – a disastrous experiment in wilful ignorance. I am compelled to attempt an answer to this question, not as some final attempt at the truth, but to add my own lines to a discussion that ought to be vigorous; as vigorous, that is, as any discussion of first principles ought to be.

What is man, that thou art mindful of him? the Psalmist asks. What is it in us we have thought worthy of the attention of God? We have considered ourselves in such terms for a very long time. Even Gilgamesh tells of a profound connection between man and the gods, though its gods are more human and capricious than Yahweh or Jehovah, if only by a small margin. We can take it as a given, nevertheless, that human nature has been the concern of writers for as long as there have been writers, and, crucially, that the estimation made of human persons has, traditionally speaking, been as high as logically and theologically possible. What is man, that thou art mindful of him? The answer in the Hebrew scriptures if, of course, that man is made in the image of God. A more elevated anthropological statement surely cannot be imagined. The story goes that God himself then becomes incarnate, dying in a state-sanctioned killing simply to share his creation's experience in the fullest manner possible. Christianity, a religion for which I still have some affection, has possibly the most strangely beautiful anthropological vision I have ever encountered. It is possible to become numb to its implications, of course, yet as I have got older, the ancient stories have become strange to me, and I have had the gift of rediscovering them in something that must be like their

> original strangeness. It is the value those old stories put on persons that now seems rather poignant to me. I can almost entirely take or leave the narrow questions of historical verifiability that seem so pressing now and appreciate them in their original form, as story. This seems right, appropriate, even, in our current climate.

Clara flicked forward a few pages in the essay until she reached a familiar block of yellow. The page was still folded down, its large triangular corner obscuring the first third of the text. She'd read the highlighted paragraph many times.

> That literature in particular, and art in general, may not be simply an enrichment of life, but rather a way into what life might actually be is an idea I have sat with for a considerable amount of time now. Writing is often seen as a pastime, a distraction from reality. I cannot say with enough force how wrong this notion is. Speaking as a writer, I have found that through the writing of novels I have been introduced to the substance of people. People, after all, ought to be an illusion. We fly through time with no justification or satisfactory explanation for how we remain coherent things. There is no good scientific argument, as far as I can tell, for our sense of ourselves as recognisable souls. The writer, though, knows that people cannot tolerate the impersonality of time, and that the creation of story is inevitable when the alternatives are considered. Artists of all sorts are, above all then, students of memory. This is where they learn about the writing of fiction and the invention of story: from how their own mind writes fiction and invents story. Story is a response to the threat of time, we might say, and we rise to meet it, again and again. A philosopher once said that a story is 'humanised time', and I like that. We are a gathering of stories. For me, seeing a person in this light makes sense of how we move through a world

that, without us, would be unstitched, would pull apart in the absence of narrative. There may be other ways to answer the question I posed myself at the outset, certainly more rigorous or testable hypotheses, but this one is mine. *What is man, that thou art mindful of him?* Man is fiction.

Clara's phone vibrated from the bedside table. She picked it up and saw it was from Lauren, the PhD student who took the tutorials for 'Introduction to Contemporary Fiction'.

Hey Clara, I've been in bed all weekend with a head cold. Thought I'd be much better than I am today. Should I cancel the tutorial? I can rearrange it if we need! Sorry again.

Clara groaned and pushed her head back into the centre of the pillow. She pushed until the sides came up to her ears and she couldn't hear the radio. After a moment, she opened her eyes, looked at the white ceiling and opened her phone.

So sorry to hear you're not well, Lauren. Rest up. I'll cover you today. Rearranging can be more trouble than it's worth. Speak soon x.

I am a good person, Clara thought, as she rose from her bed and grabbed her towel. I am a good, good person.

Clara needed her phone when she arrived in the foyer of the lecture building. The walk from her apartment had passed her by entirely and she found she couldn't recall leaving her front door and turning left towards the university. She hadn't needed to rush, but, because she hadn't anticipated teaching, her mind was in a flurry as she navigated the Lisburn Road, Elmwood Avenue and walked finally through the open doors of Lanyon Building. She hadn't any notes to go on, had made no handouts or presentation slides from which to base a discussion. To make matters worse, she thought, the lecture last week had almost been a tutorial itself, with all the group work and freewheeling discussion she had organised. She would have to improvise her way through the hour, she realised.

When she arrived the building was quiet, Monday afternoon being a time of markedly less student enthusiasm. A young woman walked past Clara with a large book clutched to her chest. Clara glanced at the title, *The Affect Theory Reader*, and realised she was probably one of hers. She considered following her as she disappeared through double doors to the stairwell, but thought better of it. She could be heading anywhere. Clara brought out her phone. The module schedule was somewhere in her sent box, for she had forwarded it to many students who hadn't made it to the first lecture in late January. Please find attached the module overview with times and room numbers. Remember that attendance at lectures is a requirement. She found one of the passive-aggressive emails and opened the pdf. Monday's tutorial was on the first floor, in one of the smaller rooms.

Clara glanced at the time and saw she had ten minutes to spare and went to join the queue for a coffee. In the line, she found herself considering her senses. For whether it was the slight hangover from the wine at Christina's table or the unexpected rush to teach a class she hadn't prepared for, she felt, as she stood with one hand in her jeans pocket, that her sense of things wasn't quite right; that there was a kind of unreality to her perception. The colours and sounds in the lecture building seemed created, curated even, that she was outside the experience while having it. It was a necessary evil of being an academic, she often thought: the moment to momentness of life was the stuff of analysis, which made it near impossible to stay present. The green exit sign by the double doors was decodable by Saussure, the sickly sweet pop music piped in from the speakers above was evidence of the homogenisation of mass culture, the clothes the undergraduates were wearing were class signifiers, or expressions of gender politics.

Clara had tried meditating once, her legs crossed on her bedroom floor. *Bring your mind back to stillness* the podcast host said. After four minutes (Clara had set a timer for twenty) she gave up, frightened at the sheer speed of her unbidden thoughts.

She remembered having similar feelings when she was a child off sick from school with a high temperature. In those moments she would lie on her mother's sofa and watch children's TV programmes, wondering why they were on when all the children were meant to be at school. Auntie Mabel and her dog Pippin. She recalled they went to a toothpaste factory on one occasion, with Auntie Mabel making the usual flight in her tiny plane. Clara's elevated temperature made it all feel like she was watching herself watch the TV, that her watching the TV was just as fabricated as the programme itself, that she really existed in some place external to the experience. She spun into an infinite regress of versions of herself watching the versions of herself watch herself. Where am I? Clara wondered then, aged eight. Where am *I*?

Clara considered revisiting meditation as she reached the front of the queue. There must be something to it, she thought, before her mind spiralled into the ethical questions raised by the wellness industry.

The muted roar of the coffee machine brought her back closer to her body and she flicked her phone on to pay at the small white card machine displayed on a swivellable plinth. Christina would have no time for solipsism, Clara thought, thinking back to the previous evening. She had been surprised at how passionately Christina had spoken about music, how even when she was criticising other writers, it was for their lack of sincerity and warmth. Solipsism, Clara knew by instinct now, would be alien to Christina's way of moving through the world. She would probably say something along the lines of *As I feel a character form, the slightest intrusion on my part will make them suddenly inauthentic, unbelievable, something obviously constructed. You would be able to tell, Clara, if people were not real. Any good reader could work it out.* She was pleased at what she had imagined Christina might say, how she was able to hear the rise and fall of her voice in her mind, so clear and fluent that she may as well have said it.

The man returned to the counter with a lidless cup of black coffee and pushed it towards her, an implausible number of brown bubbles communicating on the surface like alien eyes, or frogspawn. Clara's thoughts turned to Daniel. As she stood near the door to the stairs, blowing on her coffee, he would be making his proficient way down a corridor, she reckoned, baggy blue hospital shirt making his actual body seem unlikely, though she knew what it looked like, had felt every flex of muscle in his back. He would be on his way to speak with someone senior, perhaps with a note in his hand, feeling no nerves because they liked him and because it was an opportunity to network. And why wouldn't they like him? He made few mistakes, joined in with their jokes, respected hospital hierarchy, had a father who belonged to a similar societal echelon. Clara felt a little flutter of pride that she knew him in a way they never would; as hungry for her, as an animal, insatiable, eager.

As Clara walked towards the stairs, she thought for the first time about how Daniel would have been at school. *Insufferable* was the first word that came. Certainly someone like him wouldn't have looked twice at someone like her. He was a star on the rugby field and a hard worker when it came to his studies. Natural charisma covered just how hard he had worked at home for his exams and coursework. He'd said so himself. Clara often thought of him in terms of the apparently serene passage of a duck moving through water – how its appearance was at odds with the frantic work going on under the surface. It was a small price to pay for perfection, Clara thought, a bitterness rising up in her then. What do *I* get for being good at what I do? I have no stable job, a decent draft of a book manuscript that will do well to sell more than one hundred copies to libraries, no secure income, and a mind full of interesting ideas that have no practical use in the world. What do I get?

This, a voice inside her said. What just happened to me. What happens a few times a week, now. The feeling of fiction, of being my own double, of seeing through to the other side of everything. That's what I get. Well, good for me, Clara thought as her seminar room came into view. She nodded at the three students who were waiting outside and they took this as permission to enter. The last of them was the girl with the affect theory book.

Clara found herself hoping she would lose herself in the next hour.

On entering the room, she saw that the three students were all seated in the second row of seats, and faced the front as though at another lecture. Clara was puzzled. She had told Lauren to do tutorials in a circle. 'It is a more natural setting for discussion,' she'd said. Clearly, Lauren let the students sit where they wanted.

'Sorry, before we start, I'll need your help rearranging these,' Clara said, and began lifting and moving chairs, pushing others to the back of the room. She wasn't sure how many to expect, but in the end settled for nine seats, and took the one nearest the door for herself. 'Much better, isn't it?' she said, setting her bag down to her left.

The woman with the affect theory book smiled thinly at her and nodded her head. The other two students were male, which surprised Clara. In her experience, men made up no more than 10 per cent of any literature module. She worried about trying to get discussion going with this group, but as she was about to begin, the door to the seminar room opened and in came two young women: one of them Aithne, who had stayed behind after the lecture. They were both smiling similar smiles, so Clara reasoned they were friends and had been sharing a story before they opened the door. She felt relieved. They might carry this, she thought.

Clara took a notebook from her open bag and clicked her pen against its cover.

'You're stuck with me this morning. Lauren isn't well, but she should be back next week. I know some of you from the lectures,' she said then, looking around the circle. 'But let's start with names and your favourite novel on the module so far.' Clara paused. 'I should start, shouldn't I? My name is Clara, and if I was forced to pick a text from our list of ten, I'd probably go with *Lincoln in the Bardo*. It is funny, surprising, and Saunders has only written one novel and it wins one of the biggest literary prizes. How is that possible? So that's my choice. Who's next?'

Aithne chose *The Gathering*. Anne Enright was her favourite writer to listen to in interviews, she said. 'She's so intelligent and takes no shit. I wouldn't want to get on the wrong side of her.' All of the students laughed a little.

Aithne's friend, Katie, chose *Shuggie Bain*. 'It was a gritty portrayal of working-class life,' she said.

Clara detected the rounded hints of a North Down accent that suggested the novel might well have been Katie's first encounter with such a setting.

'I loved *Shuggie Bain*, too,' Adam said. He was the taller of the two men and spoke in a thick Belfast accent. 'It was rough round the edges. Reminded me of Belfast a bit, the way the city was described. I want to write my essay on it anyway.'

The shorter man spoke next. 'Hi, my name is Darren.'

'Hi, Darren,' Clara said, writing his name down with the others.

'I know this is maybe cheating as we haven't covered it yet, but I love *Snowflake*. I read it in the summer before university. A friend who's already at college recommended it and I read it so quickly. It was funny, and not many books from here do that very well. So I'd say that one. I think I'll write on it, if I can figure out what question to do.'

The final woman, Laura, sitting to Clara's right with her textbook under her chair, said she was disappointed Bernardine Evaristo wasn't on the reading list. 'I loved *Girl, Woman, Other*,' she said.

'It's a difficult thing to pick only ten books on a module as wide as this one,' Clara said. 'In my defence, I didn't pick most of them. The module hasn't been reshaped in a few years and I was handed it already made. All complaints must go above my head.' Clara smiled at the woman.

'It's a really good book, if anyone hasn't read it. But if we're going with just the ones on the list, I'll go for last week's one. *The Little Stranger*, was it called? I quite liked the atmosphere the writer created. I love horror films. *Insidious*, *The Exorcist*. So I enjoyed that one.'

Clara looked up from her notebook and smiled at the students gathered in the circle. 'Thank you, everyone. It's really nice to get a chance to talk with you all up close rather than from the front of the lecture room. I want this hour to be useful to you, of course. We can talk about essays and assessment near the end, but can we devote some time to getting stuck into the heart of the module? I want to hear your thoughts on what we've covered over the weeks. Hopefully by forgetting about our essay questions for a while, we will all be a bit refreshed and learn something from one another.'

The students looked at Clara.

'Sound good?' Clara said, forcing them to nod their heads and shift in their seats. On the walk, Clara had decided to start the seminar with broad questions, low-stakes stuff to encourage them to talk to her.

She sat forward in her chair and clasped her hands together. 'The module is meant to be an introduction to contemporary fiction. Let's start with that. For fiction to be contemporary, it needs to have been written relatively recently, doesn't it? Maybe within the last twenty, thirty years. That's obvious enough. But let me ask you this: what makes contemporary fiction "contemporary"? Aside from its publication date, is there anything else? Draw from your experience of our module, if you can.'

There was a few moments of silence that Clara relaxed into. She had her pen resting on the notebook, poised to write something, should anyone speak. It was a gesture she'd seen one of her old lecturers perform to great effect. It showed the students she was prepared to commit their thoughts to paper.

Aithne spoke first. 'I suppose the label "contemporary" might suggest that the novel in some way engages with questions and ideas that have relevance now. You know, that it reflects what we are talking about in culture. Identity, injustice, what it is like to be alive at the moment.'

Clara smiled at Aithne. 'Thank you. Are you saying that one of the requirements of contemporary fiction is that it touches on the live debates we, as a society, are having?'

Aithne bit her bottom lip. 'No, I think "requirement" is too strong. Like, for example, a historical novel set in, I don't know, Edwardian England could be published tomorrow. It wouldn't be about our society, at least not explicitly. But is it a contemporary novel? I guess it is because it's just been written. But it is so far removed from contemporary life that it feels like a stretch to call it that? Oh, I don't know. I'm talking in circles.'

'No, you're not at all. See, this is why I asked the question. The module title is a bit of a lie, isn't it? If you look at the texts chosen for "Introduction to Contemporary Fiction', you'll see that it is really an introduction to recent literary fiction. Isn't it?'

Adam nodded his head and sat forward. 'I thought that. When I signed up for the module I thought we'd be doing crime novels, sci-fi, fantasy as well as the usual uni books. Sorry, I mean the sorts of books lecturers pick.'

'Yes,' Clara said. 'There is a massive bias within English departments towards literary fiction. Why do we think that is?'

Katie shifted in her seat and Clara braced herself for the accent. 'I suppose because with sci-fi and fantasy and those sorts of more genre-based books, there is sometimes less to talk about. Literary fiction tends to have more ideas in it. Like even the book this week. You could call it a horror novel but it is at least a literary horror novel in that it is interested in more than just scaring the reader. There are all sorts of ideas in it that make it more than just one thing. I think that's why university lecturers pick it: they can get stuck into the meatier things.'

Clara stopped writing and looked up. 'And what are these meatier things for contemporary fiction? What are the ideas that we find again and again in the novels coming out these days?'

Aithne raised her hand slightly before speaking. 'There is way more stuff now by writers of colour, queer writers and so on. Publishing is getting more diverse, more open to everyone, and this seems to me to be a feature of contemporary literature. I guess the opposite of contemporary literature – what, classics? Canonical texts? – they tend to be written by white men, don't they? Dickens, Tolstoy, Joyce, Nabokov, Foster Wallace. You could list for hours and not land on a woman or someone who wasn't white. I guess one of the hallmarks of contemporary literature is that the names that immediately come out of people's mouths now are Zadie Smith, Bernardine Evaristo, Ocean Vuong, Hanya Yanagihara. That's a really positive shift, I think. I want to have an exciting bookshelf to choose from, not a list of dead white males.'

'I see what you mean,' Clara said. 'The contemporary-ness of contemporary fiction has that edge to it, that it isn't a replication of a stale literary tradition. Well said. Anyone want to add to that?'

Katie nodded. 'Yeah, I mean, I totally agree. I think if I was born, like, twenty, thirty years ago, I wouldn't have read anywhere near as much as I do now. The reason being there was nothing then that reflected who I am, what my experience of the world might be. Now, I can walk into a bookshop and pick up a dozen books that speak directly to my own experience.'

'And is that the goal, Katie? Everyone? Is that what you want from a bookshop: that it offers you novels that reflect your own life?'

Katie went on. 'Speaking as a woman: yes. For so long women had to be OK with reading men writing women characters. With men being the hero all the time. What I want is to buy books that say something about what it means to be someone like me in a place something like this one. I don't think that's too much to ask.'

'Interesting thoughts,' Clara said, smiling at Katie, who looked down at the floor.

Adam spoke then. 'I understand what Katie is saying about seeing yourself reflected in books. But sometimes I also want something to take me way out of what I know. I don't mean escapism. That's probably a shite word.' Adam ducked his head involuntarily as he said the word. 'I mean I want to learn about other people's experiences, or maybe other places in the world. I don't just want my own life in every book I read.'

'But that shows you are just so used to being at the centre of a story, though, as a man, I mean.' Katie was looking directly at Adam. It was the first comment not directed towards Clara. Usually this was a good sign, evidence that conversation was taking off in the room.

Adam nodded at Katie as she spoke, and Clara liked him for it.

'No, I don't think so,' he said, once Katie had finished. 'I don't think I am at the centre of many stories.'

Katie laughed. 'What? Are you serious?'

'I am. There was a book published a year or two ago that had a main character who was a young fella from my area of Belfast, but apart from that I find it hard to see myself in most of the novels I read.'

'But as a man you will automatically have much more to identify with in literature,' Katie said. 'It used to be primarily written by men, featuring men doing heroic things.'

Again, Adam nodded. 'I'm not disagreeing with you. I'm just saying your argument is very simple. Just because I'm a man doesn't mean I always find myself in those books. There aren't many books about West Belfast Catholics from single-parent families, you know? I could as well sav that anyone from money finds themselves reflected in most books. You've just chosen to focus on gender. What about class?'

'I just think that gender has been one of those classic divides in human history. And women were second-class citizens for so long that literature can definitely be understood as an expression of patriarchy.'

'Of course,' Adam said. 'And patriarchy is also a class system. And, aye, middle- and upper-class men have had power for ages. But that doesn't mean *all* men are powerful or are patriarchal or whatever. The working classes were, are, subjugated. It's too simple to make the whole thing about one binary when there are loads. What about disability or sexual orientation, or race? Surely all those things are key too.'

Katie went to speak again but Clara got in first. 'What we are talking about here is intersectionality, isn't it? The idea that one's identity is not a static fact, or reducible to one facet or fact. Each of us in this room is the meeting point of lots of factors, the ones Adam has just listed. We could list another few dozen, I'm sure. But the idea is that we can't talk well about things like literature, identity, politics, etcetera if we aren't prepared to be nuanced and open to the reality that most things, including people, are multifactorial.'

A silence followed Clara's interjection. She felt bad about clearly siding with Adam, and she recognised the discussion between the two of them had hit a nerve. In her couple of years teaching in universities, Clara was increasingly sensitive to the invisibility of class to many college students. Most of them had gone to grammar schools and mixed with people of the same level of privilege and the result, Clara thought, was someone like Katie. Clara felt like a hypocrite, however, in defending her own background in terms her mother wouldn't understand at all. She looked down at her notebook. 'Let's keep this going. Keep talking to me about features of contemporary literature. Anything else spring to mind?'

There was a silence and Clara let it happen.

'Sad young women in Irish cities.'

Clara looked at Laura. It was the first time she had spoken since introducing herself and Clara laughed out loud. 'Go on, please.'

'Well, if we're talking about tropes, surely the biggest one right now is the rise of the sad woman in her early or mid-twenties who gets drunk most nights of the week, takes recreational drugs, has lots of miserable sex and thinks deep thoughts about politics and literature in between all of those things. Bookshops are coming down with them, now. Don't get me wrong, I'll read every last one of them, and enjoy every sentence, but in terms of recognisable tropes, that's the big one for me.'

'You have a future as a book reviewer, Laura,' Clara said, giving her a wide smile. 'Let's talk about this. Why do we think this figure – the "sad, young Irish woman" as you call her – is on the rise in fiction?'

'I know it's the obvious answer,' Laura said, 'but I think there are lots of sad young Irish women in Ireland. Not just Ireland, but you know what I mean.' There were laughs around the circle and Laura continued, staring into the empty space in the centre. 'It's not a new thing, the sad Irish woman – in real life, I mean. It's not like we invented sad women in the last fifteen years. It comes back to what Katie was saying. Now that women my age are getting publishing deals, they are free to write about an experience that is wholly theirs. It's sad that so many of us buy these books because we see ourselves in them. But there are loads of women who are clever, articulate, socially disastrous, always in and out of pubs near a university campus, having terrible hookups or short stints with someone. It's the contrast I think that has helped those books do well.'

'What contrast do you mean?' Clara said, quietly, so as not to throw Laura off her train of thought or disturb what looked like a fragile confidence.

'The contrast, or apparent contrast maybe, between how intelligent, politically engaged and analytical the women in those books are and the absolute shit-show of their friendships and love lives. It makes for really interesting reading, even if you're not someone who resembles them, I imagine anyway.'

Darren had been nodding his head throughout Laura's contribution and spoke. 'I totally agree. I think I've read all of those books that Laura is talking about. I haven't read anything with as much sheer enjoyment since *Twilight* came out, when I was, like, twelve. Different times, different books, I know. But the point is that these new books have hit a nerve that must be so common across our sort of generation. I'm not a woman, obviously, but I like to think I am intelligent and analytical, or whatever it was you said, Laura. And I also can't hold down a relationship for more than a week or two. Maybe the problem is the men. Not us protagonists.'

Darren looked at Clara with a smile as everyone in the group laughed.

'Let me ask you another question,' Clara said. 'What is it this generation, as we are calling it, seems to be looking for in these books? *Is* it as simple as reflection of their own experience? Literature, in another rendering, is about the transformation of experience, of a person's journey from a recognisably sad and lonely existence to a much fuller life. But that's not what you're saying is in these sorts of books. What is it that makes them sell so well, then?'

There was a silence for a moment. Clara found herself feeling slightly relieved for the pause in the discussion, for in a more talkative group like this, silence implied they were actually thinking about her question and not thinking up new ways to avoid eye contact.

After another few seconds, Adam spoke. 'Not to put too fine a point on it, but that version of literature – the idea that life can get better, the hero's journey or whatever – just doesn't wash now. Unless you're writing fantasy or sci-fi or something. Then the reader can go along with it as it's so clearly made up. But literary fiction, if that's what we're talking about, can't do that with a straight face. The author knows her or his readers won't go along with it.'

'And why do you think that is?'

'Because we're all fucked,' Adam said. 'Sorry for the language, but it's true. We are the first generation in ages who probably won't have better living standards than our parents. There are wars kicking off, the government can't control the price of things, there's the rise of the far-right everywhere, none of us will ever buy a house and the climate is falling apart. So, imagine you're trying to write a novel about being a young adult in Ireland or the UK. How can you write something hopeful while still making it believable?'

Katie tilted her head and nodded. 'I pretty much agree,' she said. 'But I think if you look a little closer at the new literature in Ireland, there is a real subversive sort of hope in some of the novels. This hope is buried a little, as the characters are, as Adam rightly said, struggling with so much going wrong in the world at once. But I can think of a few texts that actually find a little light amongst the dark. A lot of people found Sally Rooney's third book quite depressing. But they didn't read it closely enough. The end of that novel has a surprising moment of contentment. It was such a brave novel, given how much was riding on it for the writer.'

'This is good stuff,' Clara said. 'Here's another question. Does contemporary fiction – and let's keep it restricted to Irish contemporary fiction, British if you need to – exist to educate, challenge, comfort, entertain? What is its purpose, its function, if you can reduce it that simply.'

Clara sat back in her seat. It wasn't a very academic question, but she asked it because she was genuinely interested in what the group would say. For Clara, fiction was not really entertainment. She read Christina Darnell to be shocked, challenged, impressed. She massively enjoyed reading her novels, but she realised that the enjoyment was in feeling shocked, challenged and impressed, not as an end in itself.

Laura and Aithne began to speak at the same time, and Laura stopped to let Aithne continue.

'Sorry, what I was going to say was that I don't think there's much of a distinction between those ideas. Surely when you're reading, it's always to be entertained?'

Clara nodded to show she was taking it in and then nodded to Laura.

'I was actually going to say the opposite. I rarely read for entertainment. Maybe enjoyment, but I think those things are very different. I think I read certain books because I am interested in learning about a new idea or perspective, or I am intrigued by the setting. But all of these new Irish books we were talking about, I read them because I really like the reassurance they offer. Makes me sound like a sad case, but it's true.'

Darren laughed. 'Maybe I'm sad too, but I agree. I don't read them for entertainment necessarily; it's because they are so relatable that I just fly through them. Maybe I'm just a narcissist, though, who can only read stuff he finds relatable.'

'And what exactly is so relatable about those books? I've read a few of them and really enjoyed them. But I wouldn't say they're classics,' Clara said.

Darren came right back. 'Maybe they aren't. But do you think the reason we gobble them up is because you are slightly beyond the experiences they are about? Not to overstep but, you have your PhD, a job, a way to use your intelligence. You aren't some sad Irish woman in a novel. Unlike the narrators or protagonists in those books, you actually have an idea of what you're doing with your life.'

The group all turned to look at Clara.

Clara laughed, tried to speak and then laughed again.

10
The Death of the Author (2)

Clara's granda died the year before she was born, and his wife, Margaret, Clara's mother's step-mother, died the following month. It was sudden, Clara had heard – she just went in her sleep. 'It was heartbreak,' Julie often said. 'The woman died of heartbreak.' This all meant that Clara was born at a difficult time, to a woman who had lost her father, her mother and the woman who had stood in for her mother for the previous seven years. Clara often wondered if the loss and grief had been transmitted to her in the womb, so that when she was born, she felt relieved to be set free from the sorrow she'd been stored in. She wondered if she associated her mother, on some primordial, preconscious level of her mind, with grief, and if that might go some way to explaining how she often felt like the carer when she was with her.

That all this loss had happened before Clara arrived meant that she had never experienced the death of someone close to her, so when Madeline emailed Clara to let her know of Christina's passing, she was unrehearsed.

Christina had sent her a short email the week before, late on Saturday evening. Clara had been out for dinner with Daniel and checked her phone as he got up to pay for their pizzas.

Sorry, Clara, I won't make tomorrow morning. Speak soon, CD

Clara had been disappointed, but felt the restriction on her evening disappear. With nothing to rise early for, she suggested to Daniel they go to a bar. He smiled at her, a little confused, for he knew Sundays had become work days for her, and then led her out of the restaurant.

Clara had felt a pull of longing for him in her stomach as he grabbed her hand in the street. She paused outside the restaurant and pulled out her phone.

No worries at all. Looking forward to seeing you soon x

Clara thought nothing more about the message until the next morning, when Daniel left the bed. He had been naked beside her, she realised. Both of them were too drunk when they got back to do anything other than sleep, and when she looked at the clock she saw it was already after ten. She would have finished her coffee with Christina already by now, and Clara instinctually picked up her phone. No messages, just a notification to say that Sophie had liked a photo she had put up. Clara unlocked her phone and looked at the image. Daniel was kissing her on the cheek as Clara took the photo. She had no memory of it at all, but could recognise the bar from the lights behind her head. As she looked up from her phone, Daniel was in the doorway, leaning with one hand on the frame and the other arm hanging across his navel, his hand obscuring his cock from view. Clara put her phone back on the bedside table and slid off her underwear. Daniel caught the movement and walked towards her. In the four or five steps it took for him to be by her side of the bed, he was hard. Clara's pupils had dilated, black, unblinking, and her lips parted as her breath quickened. She had slept without a

T-shirt, and Daniel peeled the duvet back and down, letting it rest across her waist. He traced his finger on her breast, and they both observed goosebumps rise. He smirked down at her and Clara lifted her head from the pillow to take him in her mouth, gripping him in her left hand. Daniel made a shocked sound, a small exhalation of breath, and then stroked her hair. Clara traced the trail of hair up Daniel's stomach and back down. She moved her head away for a second and he gently moved her back onto the bed, lifting the duvet and parting her legs. By now he could kiss her and slide inside her at the same time, and Clara made a sound against his mouth as he pushed himself all the way in. They stayed like that for a moment, their mouths pressed together, Clara's legs drawn up either side of his hips, the muscles in his back taut, primed. She loved this part: the waiting before he started to move. When they had first had sex there had been little waiting at all. Then, he had slid inside her and immediately started to move against her. She ran her hands down his back, slick with sweat already. She'd grabbed his ass that night, forced him deeper and he'd come within seconds of being touched. Since then, they'd grown accustomed to one another. She'd taught him how to make her climax, and he'd learned she liked to be made to wait, to have her neck kissed gently. Clara had learned he liked it when she took control, felt him swell as she sat on him, when she allowed him to come inside her, when she came while he was behind her. She could feel herself adjusting to him then, could feel the fullness of him, the way he tensed and released inside her as they kissed.

She had to force herself not to move against him, knowing it was worth waiting for.

The sex they had was surprisingly good, Clara thought. Initially she'd been sceptical that doctors could be good in bed, that their interest in medicine probably meant they would all be against improvisation and instinct, that they would be overly cerebral in how they approached the whole thing. But Daniel was neither clinical nor overly male about sex. On most occasions, she would come first, the only exceptions being when she told him that she wanted him to, and gripped him hard as he thrust in and out of her. When that happened, she knew she would have something to think about when she was alone. Sex, she had decided long before Daniel, was like the writing of a story. It was a journey to a determined endpoint, but, ultimately, like a story, the end wasn't really the goal. Only after, with her breath slowing and sweat cooling, could she see that the end was just one event among many, and rarely was it the one she remembered about the whole thing the next day.

Dear Dr Wilson,

I am so sorry to be sending this email, but I know you were probably to be meeting Christina this Sunday. It is with deep regret that I must tell you that Christina passed away yesterday. She hadn't been well for some time. I know this will probably be a huge shock.

She spoke very highly of you, Clara, and I know she got a lot out of her meetings with you. I'll be in touch again, but I just wanted to let you know in advance of Sunday. I am so very sorry for your loss. For our loss.

Madeline

Clara had once heard a novelist say that realist novels often have disappointing endings. During the Q&A, one of the master's students in attendance had asked him if he wrote his books with an ending in mind. He'd thought for a moment, crossing his legs opposite a twitchy interviewer who looked concerned he might not say anything at all.

'Sometimes I know where I am going,' he said, eventually, in a quiet voice. 'But oftentimes I have no idea or, if I do, it inevitably changes in the course of writing. But endings don't really matter as much as people think. Perhaps they do in thrillers or a murder mystery, but for the realist writer, an ending is often an arbitrary decision to stop a story here and not there.' He gestured with his hands, cutting the air to his left and then right. 'Real life, save for death, tends not to have satisfying or conclusive endings. So I don't worry about writing a perfect conclusion. Most people just keep getting on with things. It's not exactly the discovery of a long-lost daughter or the revelation of some huge secret, most of the time. Life just tumbles along, doesn't it?' He looked to the interviewer for a second and crossed his legs in the other direction. 'It would be a mistake to judge a realist novel on how it ends.'

The interviewer leant in then. 'Endings aren't all that important to you?'

The writer shook his head. 'Of course they are. They just aren't any more significant than beginnings or middles.'

'This is your commitment to realism.'

'Yes, but realism is a trick,' he'd replied, animated. 'Just like everything else. It's still an invention. So many people think a realist novel has to end in harsh circumstances, as if that is the only realistic way to conclude a story. But best-case scenarios are just as likely as worst-case scenarios. We are encouraged out of this kind of thinking, nowadays. So many writers think a pleasant conclusion to a book is too unbelievable, that somehow it isn't chic to write happiness. This cuts out so much of life. So much of life is pleasant. Death is the end of every story, I suppose, and we allow this to colour our interpretation of what led to it. As a writer I get to choose when and where my book ends. It's one of the pleasures of the job. By choosing a moment of happiness as my arbitrary ending, I write a happy novel. There's nothing much wrong with that.'

11
On Existence and Non-existence

Language, as soon as it helps us acquire means of reproduction, food and shelter, becomes, almost by definition, gratuitous. Beyond survival, what else do we need? Language may have emerged in us to satisfy a will to continue, to ensure survival of ourselves and our kind, but everything else it does: the poetry, myth and story of humankind, is more than is necessary. Except we find that isn't true, is it? In fact, these things have proven themselves to be just as necessary as physical sustenance. As a writer I have a bias, of course, but I tend to think language might well be the phenomenon that tells us most about who we are, beyond the narrowest of biological definitions of our species. Who, after all, recognises themselves in the sorts of discussions that reduce humans to beasts engineered in ancient patterns to simply procreate, defend and hunt? There are some thinkers who talk about art as if it were evolutionary in the most obvious sense – *In Search of Lost Time* as a supreme mating dance. For what it's worth, I don't think so. That Proust had no interest in mating in the biological sense should be enough reason to pause and rethink these purely biological classifications of art. The nature, quality and content of his writing might be another.

You see, language, while often being gratuitous, is also ephemeral, even the most important sentences. 'All human beings are born free and equal in dignity and rights. They are endowed with reason and conscience and should act towards one another in a spirit of brotherhood.' A more beautiful, crucial set of words we could scarcely imagine. And that's the point. We cannot imagine a more powerful set of words, just as we cannot imagine the time or the people who look back on these words as the work of an immature, underdeveloped culture. Imagination and its limits generate the borders of what is thinkable and sayable. It is typically only the prophets who can truly say anything new, refugees from a place no one has yet seen.

All of this talk of language is really talk about the ephemeral, which includes not just language but most things, depending on the temporal viewpoint we take. Fruit flies and mountain ranges have similar life spans if we really zoom out, after all. You see, I plan on dying one day, just as this essay will end and the tree in my mother's back garden was cut down and taken away after she died. It's meant to be avoided, death. That's what our culture reflects back at us: dying is a terrible thing. But I am not sure I understand the wisdom in this. I can say that, having brought long works of fiction to a close, I have somewhat made my peace with the thought, no, the necessity of endings. The mystics in every tradition say that death is a re-entry into what always was: that the Whole receives another of its parts. There's a real comfort in that thought, and in the consistency with which it is asserted by traditions across time and space. The idea of being welcomed back into where we came from, free from doubt, worry, the need to insist.

But I'll miss writing.

And every mystic in the world would say, this is a wrong-headed thing to think, for there will be no 'I' to miss writing. Nor, they might say, was there an 'I' that did the writing in the first place. And while I can just about assent intellectually to these traditions, I seem to know in my body that I will miss sitting at my desk.

In the autumn, at about eleven o'clock in the morning, there is a stream of gilded light that finds my window and fills the room I write in. Sometimes I find myself writing in anticipation of that light; other times, I come back to myself having written all morning to find I am in it, my face and hands warmed. It is the particularity of this that I will miss, how it makes the desk seems more wooden, the rug more full of colour. It is precisely those mornings that 'I', after death, whatever that may mean, will miss.

12
Time Passes

Clara was surrounded by beauty in the days that followed. That's how she would remember it, anyway: that roses greeted her in the university quad, heads lolling in the warm breeze, petals seeming to turn like a house cat's cheek towards sunlight. The sun itself was more present, too, it seemed, less an idea now than a presence, a constituent of experience. Her grief was too abstract for her mother to understand, she thought: Christina synonymous with the mysterious life Clara had abandoned home for. But she did text her daughter, offered her a home-cooked meal and a bottle of wine back in Derry. Clara, however, sought solitude and found her eyes alive to peripheral things, the sorts of objects that usually went unnoticed: vases, cigarette butts, coffee cup rings on a wooden table. The absence of Christina meant she consciously entered into aesthetic experience in an effort to find her, or to feel closer to her, or to forget about herself. She found herself thinking in similes as she went from apartment to class, from class to apartment. The warmth of the early summer was like something, everything was *like* something, she thought, as she looked down at a square of light on the blue carpet of the seminar room.

Looking back later, Clara recognised she had slipped out of the typical flow of time for the period following Christina's death. The experience was not, as most might presume, characterised by numbness, by a bluntness to the world; instead, Clara experienced a sense that the moment in which she found herself was already safely in the past and, as such, was of no risk to her, its potential spent. She wasn't at all in the present, but slightly ahead of herself looking over her own shoulder. And there was a sort of peace in it.

Having no belief in God had its drawbacks. For Clara it meant there was no divine goodness, illusory or otherwise, to rely on, to take refuge in, to hide in. There was therefore no promise of another meeting, or of a swift cosmic justice that would ensure that what ought to happen would indeed happen. Despite this, Clara was surprised to find herself feeling relieved in the weeks that followed Christina's death. The loss was private, for no one she knew had also lost Christina Darnell, and this meant that the pain Clara felt during this time – which was considerable and sharp – was her own. As a result, she felt that she had been unharnessed and had the feeling of plummeting. It was thrilling, and she found herself occasionally sighing loudly as she did the washing up. What she was feeling was the worst of it, and she was still here. It had happened. The veil that separated her from the people she walked past in Botanic Gardens was removed during this time, for she was experiencing something generally shared, though its particularities – the soft pink of roses and the smell of coffee – made it seem unique. Nevertheless, Clara felt a debilitating compassion for strangers. Her eyes would drift from *The Sea, The Sea* to the grandmother with a toddler on her knee, anticipating his inevitable loss now that she was familiar with it.

Clara found books surprisingly pleasurable during this time, and spent days reading her way through novels she had owned for years and never opened. Walker Percy, Jonathan Franzen, Edna O'Brien. This sudden upsurge in reading came at the expense of writing the monograph, and her new desk went largely unused. Sometimes Clara would stand in her living room and look at it sitting square to her window. She would imagine Christina writing at it, hunched over, words coming slowly and then quickly. It was a fantasy, of course, for Christina had never used the desk for her novels, but Clara's imagination invented stories she thought in retrospect she might well have needed. Her copy of *Séances* sat in the centre of the desk and Clara occasionally went over to leaf through it and smell its pages and turn to the title page, with its untidy black ink.

For my friend, Clara.

Thank you for the coffees.

What does a life amount to? It was a question Clara returned to often during that time, both by choice and some internal compulsion. There was a desperate void between the two possible answers and Clara found her mind panicked between them. Christina's life either mattered or it didn't. It was either a substantial thing in itself or it wasn't. The notable events of her life were recounted by a priest in Cambridge. Clara could have done it herself. Her birth, her parents, the first novel, the prizes, the reviews. Clara sat at the back and counted eighty-three people. She recognised no one.

On the plane back to Belfast Clara looked out at the nothingness below her – the Irish Sea, she presumed, though it looked like an absence at night. The things the priest mentioned were not Christina's life. They were the details in brackets that her actual life happened around and between. Clara's forehead pressed against the cool of the plane window. She looked at the black of the sea through her own reflection. Life, when it is done, amounts to very little, she thought. It is intangible, made up of indeterminate, shifting things. Memories and stories. Christina's fiction had taught her that. Plot is what is left behind after everything important has happened.

She remembered one of her second-year professors quoting Alan Bennett. Professor Walton had asked her students if the dominant conception of history in a culture impacted the writing of novels. 'If history is just one thing after another,' she said, 'then there is no inherent narrative to the movement of time. Things just happen. Think about the inside of your own mind. You do not choose your own thoughts, it's just one thing after another, isn't it? Enter, then, Virginia Woolf.' The memory returned to Clara as the seatbelt sign came on and the lights of Belfast appeared ahead of the plane. What is true of history must be true of individuals, she thought. Was Christina's life just a series of disconnected events? Did the priest impose a story on her that afternoon?

Clara thought not.

It was an instinctual reaction, like when a child's arms go out to break its fall. To think that Christina's life was simply an imaginary continuity within chaos just wasn't right. Clara's reaction wasn't a rational thought, a position reached through careful debate and calculation. Her belief in the significance of things was something alive inside her, something she hadn't chosen, something she was grateful for. The relief she felt accompanied the sad realisation that if Christina's life hadn't mattered, so much of her own never would either. And that was it. Clara wanted it to be true, so it was.

The plane touched down with the smallest of bumps and within ten minutes Clara was queuing for the bus. She opened her phone, turned on her headphones and played the latest episode of *Rescuing Rapunzel*. The time stamp remained where she had last left it.

... from exciting debuts to some sad literary news. Christina Darnell, the author of *Promised Land*, one of those classic contemporary novels so many of us read at university, died last week. She was a writer much admired in the literary world for her fine, sophisticated writing and her sharp mind. I wanted to take a few moments to discuss her work with our two guests. Dr Robertson, you must have taught Darnell's work over the years—?

I have, I have. Darnell was one of those rare writers that seems to come about only once in a generation. She was a writer and thinker of quiet brilliance. I taught her first novel *Promised Land* to our undergraduates for years. It was a reliable book for a university lecturer, as the students always had something to say about it. It was one of those books that young women, in particular, latched on to for its nuanced examination of female identity formation. She will be very much missed by a host of readers, and by academics who have spent considerable amounts of time with her work.

And Professor McAdams, I know her work doesn't fall into your research interest, but I'm sure you've read Christina Darnell over the years.

I'm embarrassed to admit I've never read any of her novels. I think I'll have to, having seen some of the articles writers have put together about her influence on them. She seems like a remarkable figure. That said, I did read a piece she wrote a handful of years ago in the *New Yorker*. It was about how a culture relies on mythology to sustain its foreign policy. It was excellent, from memory. I think it was Christina Darnell, anyway.

Dr Robertson, when it comes to summing up a writer's contribution to culture, to thinking and writing more specifically, how would you begin with Christina Darnell?

Well, we could never accuse Darnell of forcing herself on anyone, that's for sure. She wrote four novels and one collection of essays in the forty-plus years she was active. A fifth novel was due to come out, I hear, so we will wait to see what state it was left in, whether we get to read it as a finished piece or not. But to answer your question, I think there are a few ways to approach Darnell's legacy. To many people she will remain a writer synonymous with quality. She wrote beautiful sentences, and she thought in careful, nuanced ways. To some, though, she will always be a slight disappointment. She seemed to start out so radically with the narrator in *Promised Land*. The writing of an out lesbian character whose sexual orientation was not the drama of the narrative had critics fawning over this exciting new voice in British fiction. The follow up, *Séances*, was a good novel, but it never – and nor did any of the following novels for that matter – reached the heights of that first burst onto the scene. It must be said, though, that most writers never reach the level Darnell got to in *Promised Land*, so in a sense she was victim of her own success.

And is that a fair summary of how her fiction has been received? That it lost its radical edge as time went on?

I think so, yes. That first novel promised so much: a new literary take on identity, sexuality and narrative. It was unlike anything else published in those years. For many of us, her turn to philosophical and theological themes, the writing of more religious characters, the seeming loss of interest in tackling the conservative politics of the day, these all felt like lacks in her subsequent output. But for so many, her death will be felt as a real loss to literature. She was a singular voice and one who may well merit revisiting in the years to come.

Clara turned the voices down as the bus trundled roughly towards the slipway. The professor could not have misunderstood Christina's novels more if he had tried, which, she suspected, he might well have done. Clara found herself giving up on the argument she was gearing up for in her head. Her thoughts were stilled by the gentle roar of the engine and by the soothing shake of the bus along a quiet stretch of motorway. There were no lights on the road, and Clara had to press her forehead to the window to see outside to the dark fields. The vibrations of the bus made her nose itch and as she straightened in her seat and clicked the footrest into place in front of her, she discovered she had decided to leave Belfast. Maybe she'd known it for a few days, a week maybe, ever since Christina died. It was not a decision she had known much about, and she found herself leaning into it. And, for a moment, Clara allowed herself to feel just how sad she was.

13
Aspects of the Novel

Eleven Months Later

There were more people in the bookshop than Clara had anticipated and the sight of them made her suddenly aware of her nerves. Groups were gathered by the white pillars in the centre of the floor, some lifting books from shelves and showing them to friends; others were milling around the back of the seating in ones and twos, unsure if sitting was permitted. The staff had cleared away three large display tables earlier in the day and set out the few dozen black foldout chairs facing the front. It gave the second floor a significance, Clara thought, an air of expectation.

She stood, watching the growing number of people, most of whom she didn't know, and was uneasy about the whole thing. She moved her hand along the leather armchair, and went to fill the two glasses of water sitting on the coffee table between the chairs for something to do. The staff had set up a screen behind the armchairs which displayed the title of the book on a sage-green background in white, italicised font. The makeshift stage was walled-in between 'Big Ideas' on the right and 'Photography' on the left, and the screen the staff had built an hour ago was obscuring 'Religion and Spirituality'.

'No one ever buys anything from there anyway,' one of the women said to the manager as they clicked the steel frame into place.

Clara looked at her phone. Five minutes to go. She pulled down a message from Stacey, her mum's friend, to read in full and then swiped it off the screen. She noticed her phone light up as she moved it to her pocket, clocked the name on the new message and put the phone away.

Professor McDonagh was finishing a conversation with a tall, elderly man and gave Clara a small wave. She smiled back and looked around the bookshop again. Thirty, maybe forty people, had taken over the floor. It was a proper event. Clara spotted three of her new students leaning against a table in the Theory section. She smiled and nodded to them. They waved back and one of the women gave her a double thumbs up. Clara laughed and mouthed a 'thank you' as Professor McDonagh appeared beside her and touched her arm.

'A lovely crowd, Clara. You must be so pleased.' She spoke in a near-placeless American accent, with ghosts of the old Ulster vowels suggesting themselves in certain words. The 'ow' in crowd had a subtle 'oy' in it that gave away her childhood in Antrim, though Clara had read her bio on the university website long before she'd asked her to host the launch. Maeve had left Ireland in 1993 to take up a post in Chicago and then Iowa, where she had been for the last twenty years. She was an expert in post-war British and Irish fiction, and had been something of a mentor to Clara when she arrived in Iowa last year, taking her for coffee, then a lunch, discussing books and teaching strategies with her at length. When Clara booked the space for the launch, Maeve was the obvious choice.

'I'm a little terrified,' Clara said, and laughed.

'No need. These people have come because they want to. Remember that. They could be anywhere else.' Maeve smiled at

Clara and touched her arm again. 'Do you have any questions before we start? Are you happy with everything we talked about?'

Clara nodded. 'I think so, yes.'

'Great.' Maeve walked in the direction of a small man hunkered down beside a camera on a tripod. The man's name was Patrick. He introduced himself to Clara earlier in the afternoon and put her mind at ease a little with his kindness. Maeve leant into his ear as he adjusted the angle, and he nodded. He looked up and smiled in Clara's direction.

Maeve returned to the front, faced the room and said a loud, practised, "Good evening."

'On the way to the bookstore this afternoon, I thought to myself that on paper this might seem like a rather strange event. An Irish academic launching a book on a celebrated British writer in a bookstore in the American Mid-West. As I've been thinking ahead to today's event, these strange details have made me grateful that such a launch can happen, that we in the academic community are so connected, so invested in the creation and celebration of knowledge that these events are so well attended. That so many of you are all here is also tribute to our wonderful guest this evening, and new teaching fellow at the university, Dr Clara Wilson. She has been with us for a few months now, and she tells me she is beginning to like it here, aren't you? Let's make her feel at home and welcome the writer of this fantastic new book, Dr Clara Wilson.'

There was loud applause as Maeve concluded her introduction and Clara smiled at the crowd, aware of the muscles in her face. The applause quietened, and Maeve spoke again.

'I should say also, a hello to anyone joining us on the live-stream. I think it's around about late dinnertime back in Ireland and the UK.'

Clara looked towards the camera, to Patrick standing behind it. She wondered if her mother was watching.

'Now, tell me Clara,' Maeve continued, swivelling subtly to face her, 'why Christina Darnell?'

Clara looked from Maeve's smile to the book sitting between them. 'She was my first love, I think. Men come and go, but books are permanent, aren't they?' There were a few laughs from the crowd and then a louder laugh when a woman from the back of the seating said 'Amen!' and clicked her fingers. Clara smiled out at the crowd. 'In all seriousness, I discovered Christina's first novel when I was in first year of university. It was sitting, waiting for me in the university bookshop. At least, that's how it felt.'

Maeve looked into Clara's eyes as she continued to talk. She recounted the experience of first reading Christina's work, how it was blind luck that led her to take the novel from her bag that afternoon. Maeve seemed to really listen to her, and only broke eye contact to check her notes as Clara finished her first answer.

'And that first novel was *Promised Land*, which you all can buy after the event,' Maeve said. 'Clara, before we get into the book itself, is it fair to say that it was that novel that led to you sitting here, in Iowa, in a new city, with a new job, a new book?'

Clara looked at her glass between them and thought about picking it up. She moved in her chair. It was a question she and Maeve had discussed over coffee the previous week. Maeve had suggested it as a way of contextualising Clara for the audience, to give something of a backstory to the writing of the book. 'An audience will love to hear your own journey to the book, and to us,' she'd said. Clara agreed. It had been a sun-filled morning on the campus, and she'd just come from teaching Sarah Moss to a small group of enthusiastic students. Things had felt strangely fine by the time she was drinking coffee with Maeve, the first time Clara felt something other than anxiety in her new city, and it had made her agreeable.

'I think that's right. It's odd to have that kind of clarity about your past, I think. But it feels true. Picking up that book set me on a course that is traceable from sitting here to walking into that bookshop ten or so years ago. I've thought a lot about the impact Christina's writing has had on me. It made me want to be an academic, that's for sure. Her novels reward careful attention, and a PhD gave me three years to do that. I lived in various coffee shops in Belfast, poring over the same five books, underlining sentences, writing ideas down in spiral notebooks. It was a time of crazily intense pleasure. This book was inevitable, really. I wanted something to come from the sheer love of Christina's work.'

Maeve leant forwards, her hands pressed together. 'And this book, it's not like a typical academic monograph, is it? Talk to us about how you've written it.'

Clara felt more comfortable now that the conversation was on the book itself. She too leant forward in her seat and lifted the copy of her book. 'It struck me as I was writing the proposal for publishers that one of the gaps in Darnell studies is the writer's biography. She'd done plenty of interviews to publicise her novels as they came out, and lots of events at festivals and the like. But she always managed to get round questions about her own life. So I chanced my arm, as we say back in Ireland, and sent off an email to see if she would be up for an interview.' Clara settled back in her seat. 'Oh, and I should add,' she said then, turning back towards Maeve, 'I read an article online that said Christina was living in Belfast. You can imagine my reaction. I sent the email off the same day.'

'That's an amazing part of this story, Clara. Were you surprised when she, *the* Christina Darnell, agreed to meet you? Tell us about that. How did it all get set up?'

Clara, having told the story many times to her friends, told it again for the audience. There was a pleasant silence as she spoke.

Maeve had been right – Clara could feel a warmth in the room coming from the audience. She was grateful to be speaking personally about Christina, and the people gathered seemed to be pleased not to be listening to two academics talk theory about books they hadn't yet read.

'And it wasn't just a one-off interview,' Maeve said to the audience. She turned to Clara. 'Do you know how many times you sat opposite her?'

'Oh, I think it must have been about twelve or thirteen coffees. Always on a Sunday morning, always at nine o'clock.' Clara smiled a little. 'She liked routine, I think. But she invited me to her house for dinner, which was a really nice touch. I think it told me that she also enjoyed the conversation, that it wasn't one-sided.'

'You were friends, or so it seems from the outside at least,' Maeve said then.

Clara shifted in her seat. 'I think we were. I certainly valued all my time with her. I learned so much, this aside.' Clara laid her hand on the book and looked back at Maeve.

Professor McDonagh smiled at Clara with affection. She praised her book to the audience, telling them it was unlike most other monographs she had read. Then Maeve asked Clara to talk about the structure and the interviews she had threaded through the chapters. Clara felt her nerves calm completely as she talked about something she knew well. She finished her answer by saying that her hope for the book was that readers would get a sense of Christina's mind.

Maeve nodded her head at this. 'I'd read her work in the past, you know; in fact, as I was preparing for our chat today, I went back through my old module records and saw that I actually taught *Séances* about eleven years ago as part of a course on the contemporary Gothic. So I've been aware of Darnell's work for a long time, impressed by her writing, her erudition. However, I can honestly say that I was not quite appreciative of how much of a thinker she was until I read this book. It gave me a renewed desire to get her books off the shelf and re-read them. And if that isn't a five-star review in the academic book market, I don't know what is!'

The audience laughed at this, and Clara joined them. The whole experience, as pleasant as it was, had started to feel surreal. This was her book launch. Something she had dreamed about for years. And now she was sitting at the front of a packed bookshop, and the event felt flimsy, paper-thin.

Clara's mind flitted back to her first driving lesson. Her instructor, a family friend, had taken her on a brief five-minute journey to a quiet part of the city, talking all the while about how to use the clutch, how to handle the gear stick, which side the indicators were on. After a few moments, she pulled to the side of the road and told Clara to swap places.

'Your turn,' she had said, with a glint in her eye.

'I have no idea how to drive,' Clara had replied, fear rising in her chest.

'No, but I do,' Joan said. 'Now get out before I drag you out.'

Clara did as she was told, her legs feeling powerless as she walked around the front of the car and slid into the strange seat.

Once she had finally got into third gear, Clara felt her nerves settle slightly. She coasted around the quiet roads, enjoying the satisfyingly regular tick of the indicator as she turned left. Joan directed her calmly, saying 'Very good' as Clara changed up and down the gears. Eventually, they turned onto a busier road, and Clara was met for the first time by cars coming towards her on her right. She'd been a passenger thousands of times, so the sight of oncoming traffic was not unusual. But being a driver was different, she discovered. As an absent-minded passenger, she had assumed there was some sort of cosmic law in place to prevent the driver of a car turning the steering wheel sharply to the right and launching the car into traffic. It was an assumption she had made unconsciously, she realised, and one for which there was absolutely no justification. As she drove, Clara became increasingly aware of the fiction of the white lines in the middle of the road. There was nothing stopping her from suddenly putting her foot down and crashing into the white van coming towards her. Then she thought, without choosing to, about mounting the kerb on her left, wiping out the children and their mother who had just left the primary school from further up the road. Why do people not talk about this all the time? Clara thought as she drove. There is nothing, *nothing* stopping me. Everything is possible and nothing is real.

It was a thought that etched itself into her mind. Clara cancelled her next lesson.

'You mentioned that the book attempts to do justice to Darnell's way of thinking. There are some thornier elements to her views, aren't there? Were you nervous about including some of what she said in interviews with you?'

Clara bit her bottom lip and straightened herself in the chair. 'What views are you talking about?'

'I was thinking specifically about the interview you have transcribed where she talks about current publishing trends, how books are bought, sold and judged solely on the identity of their writers. It's a viewpoint that will no doubt be challenged by many.'

'I am sure you're right, but I'm not convinced Christina would mind being challenged. I don't think her views are quite as strong as you laid out there, but she was right about publishing. Author bios are now way more important than they've ever been. I have had a look at literary agents' pages and quite a few outwardly say they are seeking certain kinds of writers. Not mystery, or literary or crime writers, but writers who fit a certain label. Christina didn't have much time for that sort of thing. She was a lesbian, which is important to remember. She contended with prejudice. But she would say her work was good. There's no way she would have kept writing if she thought her work was only published based on one aspect of who she was. She lamented the reduction of literature to causes, as she called them. Which wasn't meant as a reduction of the actual cause, but more of a view of what literature ought to be about. But she also didn't just blame it all on the publishing world, she also lamented the reduction of people's moral imaginations, that, increasingly, we think in binaries, or in one category at a time. For her a good writer, or a good book, should be unavailable to these sorts of readings. Her mind didn't really work in either/ors.'

Maeve looked up as Clara stopped speaking. 'Did you find yourself uncomfortable with her views at all? I mean, sitting opposite her, knowing you were writing the book. Did it ever make you feel uneasy?'

'No. It might have if I thought I was sitting with someone who couldn't handle a different viewpoint, or someone who had never changed her mind on an issue. She was, right up until she died, willing to change her mind about things.'

Maeve nodded. 'And on this idea of a writer's mind, would you give us a reading from the book, Clara? I think you have a passage picked out? I'll have to help, won't I?'

Maeve had made the suggestion at their coffee meeting. Clara had initially resisted the idea. She'd never been to an academic book launch that included a reading and thought it might be pretentious, but Maeve had insisted.

Clara looked from her book to the crowd, to the camera and back to the book.

'OK, to give a little bit of context for everyone, this reading is taken from an interview I did quite late on in my meetings with Christina. I think it was just a few weeks before she passed away. I chose it as I think it gives an impression of how present she was in conversation, how she really cared about ideas. It comes about two-thirds of the way into the book, after a chapter on her novels' frequent use of religious and philosophical vocabulary. Anyway, I hope it makes sense on its own.'

Maeve had opened her copy as Clara spoke. She ran her hand down the centre of the book, flattening out the pages so she could hold it open with one hand. Then, she cleared her throat and began to read. 'So you believe in something like the soul, then? Something non-physical that makes us who we are?'

Clara's eyes cast down the page to where Maeve was reading from. She read Christina's reply. ' "Soul" is a tricky word, I think. It comes with religious baggage, and necessarily so, perhaps. I like your phrase "non-physical". That takes us into a whole realm of possible ideas. I suppose my conviction is that a human person is not accounted for entirely by an exhaustive material description, even if such a description were possible. My anthropological assumption is that an omniscient scientist would need to stray from her discipline to adequately account for what we are. There is something superfluous about a human person, a gratuitousness to our complexity that makes me suspect we might well always exceed any purely materialist explanation.'

'Where does that sense of the non-physical come from? You say it's not religious. Can you account for it?'

'It comes from writing. Undoubtedly so. I know I've only written four novels to date, so I don't have the same range of characters as a Murdoch or a Rushdie, but my experiences of inventing character have led me to these sorts of conclusions. Or, perhaps, it has led me to realise the assumptions I've always had about personhood. I think that might be it. You see, when you invent a character, you become aware of your metaphysics, unspoken though they may have been up to that point. For me, inventing Thomas Stewart for *The Hiding* or the narrator of *Promised Land*, revealed to me that I consider people fundamentally mysterious. It's not an insight unique to fiction writers. Nietzsche said, "We remain unknown to ourselves." Children and parents have to come to terms with the utter strangeness of their guardians and offspring. It's one of those intractable human problems – the fact that we never really know another person, even if we know every little fact about them. It seems pessimistic, but I think it's true.'

'How have you come to that sort of conclusion?'

'Because what I know to be true of myself must be true of other people. After decades and decades of life, writing, thinking, I am no closer to understanding myself than I am to understanding anyone else. And I really mean that. From a distance, I find myself utterly incomprehensible. I think this sort of baseline level of unknowability in every person is why the religious came up with the idea of the soul. It serves a purpose: venerating something that is, under a different light, a disturbing aspect of existence.'

'Famously, your novels are not terribly interested in plot. Instead, they've been called "novels of ideas", or "character driven". How do you write a character-driven novel when you have such major reservations about the idea of a person's character?'

As Maeve read the question, Clara felt a swell of pride in her chest, just as she had when she asked the question to Christina.

That morning, their conversation had flowed seamlessly and with little reference to the questions and notes in Clara's open notebook. Christina had sat back in her chair when Clara had responded and shaken her head, with a smile. 'Now that's a question.' Clara removed the praise from the transcript when she put the interview into the manuscript, but it came back to her as she read Christina's response.

'I wouldn't say I have reservations about character, exactly. That would be too strong. I think what I mean is that when I find myself inventing people, I never feel I have to have their entire lives under my hands before I can accurately depict them. I once heard a writer tell aspiring novelists that they had to know everything about their character: what their favourite fragrance is, what they would order in a restaurant. This is nonsense. As a writer you may well know these things, but they don't amount to a person. Character is often a thin business. What you're aiming for is the invention of a person who subtly shares in the problem common to us all: that they don't know themselves as well as they think they do.'

'That sort of claim is never explicitly in your fiction, of course. Scholars have often noted that one of your strengths as a writer is implication. They argue that your fiction finds its power in suggestion rather than in plot or revelation. Is this something you are consciously aware of as you write?'

'It's the feminist in me, they say, don't they? Well, I suppose I am aware of what I'm doing, in holding back from a big reveal or something. But I don't consider that part of my writing to be terribly groundbreaking, Clara.'

Clara paused after reading her own name out loud. It was the first time in the reading that she heard Christina's voice in her head, and it returned her to the coffee shop they had sat in for the interview, to the smell of rose perfume and sunlight streaming through the window, Christina's figure in front of her, darkened by the light behind her. Clara always hated saying her own name out loud and now, shifting in the armchair, she heard how her own pronunciation clashed with the high, clear English accent in her head. She refocused on the page.

'I think my approach to writing is, to use the academic term, as *realist* as I can manage. Real life, you see, is not really lived out in plot. Or, to echo my previous answer, real life is not accounted for entirely in terms of plot. It's the meaning of plot that gives life its character, the implications that events have, the resurgence of memories, the entire sagas that play out in a person's mind as they drink their tea. My writing is a response to that, is maybe an attempt to capture that truth: that real life teems below a still surface.'

'Your work is concerned with truth, then?'

'I think so. But that isn't a simple thing either, is it? We keep circling back to this question. The one Pilate asked. My answer to it is the body of work I'll leave behind, I think. The fiction that will outlive me. Over the many years I've been writing and thinking about those sorts of questions, I have realised that any final answer is impossible. The question of truth eludes us because we are looking for a satisfying and tidy conclusion to it. In the end, the idea of truth might well be a fiction we have landed on to help us survive. Or, it might be exactly the opposite. Fiction may well be the only truth we have. That sounds very philosophical, but it's also practical: if there really isn't an objective guidebook or definitive way to do things, then the way we string ourselves together from day to day is, under a certain light, like the writing of a novel. We all write continually as we go, and we edit and rewrite, and we reinterpret and revise. All of life is a kind of fiction. How could it be otherwise?'

Maeve looked up from her book and gestured to Clara. The audience applauded and the two women set down their books.

'Wonderful. Absolutely wonderful,' Maeve said. 'And it leads us seamlessly into my next question.' Clara took a drink from her glass and set it back on the coaster. 'Christina mentioned how often you two spoke about truth and fiction. It is one of the most interesting aspects of this book, I have to say, and you'll all see what I mean when you get your copies afterwards.' Maeve gestured to a small table with three neat stacks at the back of the room. 'Clara, can I ask you about the epigraph you've chosen for the book? It's from Wallace Stevens. Talk to us about why it's there, because it does frame the book in a very particular way.'

'Yes, it does. My conversations with Christina came back to a few central themes. They weren't exactly what I had planned to talk about with her, but they were clearly what she wanted to discuss. And I am grateful she led me there. When it came to choosing an epigraph for the book, I knew it had to be the Wallace Stevens quote. I suppose I should read it, so we are all aware of what it says.' Clara lifted the book from her lap and prised open the cover. Three pages came with it and she found herself looking at the publication details on the leftmost page. She turned another and saw the epigraph on the right and began to read. '*The final belief is to believe in a fiction, which you know to be a fiction, there being nothing else. The exquisite truth is to know that it is a fiction and that you believe in it willingly.*' I first came across the quote during the first year of my PhD. I audited a course on philosophy and poetry and really enjoyed both Stevens and Robert Frost. Wallace Stevens has a similarly philosophical dimension to his work as Christina, doesn't he? And I think that's what drew me to him. But that particular quotation only really opened up to me after Christina passed away. When that happened, I didn't want to look at her work for a while. I stopped writing the book for a few weeks and just got on with a little bit of teaching. When I went back to finish the manuscript, I was working on editing down that section we just heard. My mind summoned up the Stevens quote. It was the perfect accompaniment to the conversations I'd had with Christina, and I think it summarises her approach to life.'

'I've always loved that particular quotation too,' Maeve said. 'I have used it with my first-year students for years. You say it summarises Christina's approach to life. Can you tell us more. What do you mean?'

Clara was quiet for a moment. 'You know, after the first few meetings with Christina, I was slightly disappointed. I think I'd been gearing up for some major discovery, or for her to tell me something shocking about her life, something she'd never shared before. But she never said anything about herself. Not really. She wanted to talk about politics, poetry, music, epistemology, religion, metaphysics. I thought I was failing. I couldn't get anything personal from her. But even as I read out that section of interview, it reminded me that the way she answered my questions was gently, patiently showing me her whole approach to life. She talked then about how her characters have an unknowable centre that even she can't account for. Well, I think she was reluctant to speak about her personal life, her background, her family, because speaking about those sorts of things would begin to reduce who she was. I've come to realise in the process of reading through everything she said to me that biography would amount to a total lie. No amount of biographical detail could add up to a whole person. She knew that, I think. And she gracefully resisted my clumsy questions so she could retain some kind of ownership of herself.' Clara found herself using her hands more as she spoke. This was the one thing she could speak about with authority. Instead of putting her hands back on her lap, Clara, moved forwards, leaning towards the audience. 'She believed a person was more than a list of what happened to them. The past shapes character, but it doesn't determine it. I think that's what she might say. Anyway, you asked me how the Wallace Stevens epigraph chimes with Christina's life. It's simple, I think: she knew, more than anyone I've ever known, that authenticity comes from recognising that the only life worth living is one you've *chosen*. It is possible to live in all sorts of ways, all of them more or less futile, given the guarantee of their conclusion. She chose to be a writer, and died that way, with a manuscript just about finished. It was her *choice*, and she behaved as though it was her choice, inhabiting every inch of it, even as she knew there was no ultimate destiny being fulfilled, or some final truth in what she had chosen. Christina always said that fiction was unavoidable – she said somewhere it is "the condition of life". I think she really believed that there is genuine beauty in choosing to believe in something, knowing all the while it is a fiction. She found freedom in it, I think.'

Maeve looked at Clara as she spoke and smiled as she finished. Clara sat back in her seat.

'It's a beautiful thought, Clara. I did find myself wondering if Christina's philosophy was in some sense a justification for her own way of life, whatever that may have been. Did you ever directly question her about her own background? Her parents? How they felt about her choice of career? It seems to me that Christina came back to the idea of life being a fiction often, and I wonder, is it in some sense a response to never feeling validated in her choices?' Maeve looked to the audience. 'Sorry, I don't mean to psychoanalyse.' There was a small laugh from the crowd.

Clara picked up her glass. She found her eyes smarting a little at the idea of Christina as a young woman, alone, willing herself into writing. She took a sip and set her glass back down. 'This isn't going to be a very academic answer, Maeve. But I don't care.' There was another laugh from the audience as Maeve raised her eyebrows. Clara continued. 'What you say might well be true, but I can hear Christina's response in my head. "Just because we've uncovered the psychological context an idea comes from doesn't mean that it isn't also true." It seems entirely plausible that Christina has biographical reasons for clinging to certain ideas about life and truth. But as I got to know her, I stopped caring about what those reasons might be. The ideas themselves were worthy of attention. It's why my book is the way it is: focused on her mind, not her past. Put it this way, if I discovered all of Christina's diaries and read them cover to cover, they may well explain why she thought the way she did. In fact, I suspect they would. But we are still left with the ideas themselves. And we have to test them on their own merits, not based on her relationship with her father, or the death of her mother. Her ideas hold all we need to know about her history. All she needed us to know. She wanted more and more of everything, even as she was diminishing. There's a poem I read recently that talked about how a rose opens more fully as it dies. That's what Christina was like.'

There were some murmurs of assent from the crowd, and as Clara finished speaking she looked down.

Maeve shifted in her seat. 'You mentioned the word "authenticity" earlier. It strikes me as I hear you speak about Christina that she lived authentically. Whatever that word means, it must apply to her. Does that feel right to you?'

'It does. When I began the book and the interviews, I wondered if Christina's move to Belfast was part of a significant story waiting to be uncovered. Maybe a break-up, a falling out, a failed attempt at retiring, a last chance at love in a new place. None of these things were true, in the end, I think. Or, none of them accounted entirely for her decision to come to Ireland. She just wanted to do something different, to go and be somewhere else. There was nothing much to uncover, though I think her final novel is set in Belfast, which will be interesting. Authenticity, in some sense, relies on self-knowledge. It requires us to understand the reasons beneath why we want to do the things we do, why we actually *do* the things we do, why we avoid the things we avoid. Why we move across continents.'

'And, on that theme of relocation, Clara, we are absolutely delighted that you decided to move all the way across the Atlantic to be with us. It can't have been an easy decision, but selfishly, I am glad you made it. This is a fantastic book, Dr Wilson, and I think in the course of our conversation you have all got a glimpse of how much heart there is in this piece of work. It is not typical for me to experience a gut punch of emotion when reading a monograph, but there are many occasions across this book that I had that exact experience. It's usually only fiction that gets me like that, so credit to your scholarship and your love for Christina Darnell's work. Join me, folks, in congratulating my newest colleague on such a brilliant piece of work. Dr Clara Wilson, ladies and gentlemen.'

As Clara shook Professor McDonagh's outstretched hand and turned to face the applause, she found herself feeling very sad. Behind the camera, Patrick gave her a thumbs up and pressed a button.

'How'd it go at the bookstore?'

James was wearing grey sweats and a college hoody and came into the living room with a bowl of cereal in one hand and a spoon in the other. Over the last couple of months, Clara had discovered that the man was as near to nocturnal as someone with a university job could conceivably be. He typically left his bedroom at one or two in the afternoon, sloped into the living room with his towel over his shoulder and, after boiling an egg or toasting bread, would have his shower. After, he would cross the living room, leaving wet footprints on the pale wooden floor and make his way to campus where he might be teaching, or having a meeting with a postgraduate student.

Clara observed this pattern with wonder, having retuned to the apartment for lunch after teaching her morning classes.

'It was good, I think,' she replied. She set her bag down on the arm of the sofa and went to the kitchen counter. She found herself wanting a glass of wine. If she'd launched the book in Belfast, there would have been free wine. Cultural differences abounded everywhere, she found, but some were less bearable than others. 'Have you any alcohol?'

'I think there's whiskey on the fridge,' he said. 'Have some.'

'I didn't know about the whiskey,' Clara said, moving James's congratulations cards out of the way.

'If I can't sleep I sometimes have a bit. What is it you Irish call it? A *wee nip*?'

'That's Scottish people. Thank you, though.' Clara found a glass tumbler in the cupboard and poured herself a couple of measures. She braced herself as she lifted the glass to her lips.

Clara had been unhappy for the first month after moving. And though she had shed certain things: Daniel, the obligation to visit her mother, her lack of a full-time position, she recognised in the first week that on the whole, her unhappiness had travelled with her.

On the first Friday evening in the new accommodation, James had come into the living room to find Clara looking out of the window of their apartment. There wasn't much to look at. The window oversaw the communal car park for the building, and the sun was hidden behind the next building over.

'I'm going out for drinks tonight,' he said. 'And you're coming, too.'

He walked Clara to an Irish pub run by a Mid-Western couple who had traced their lineage back to Donegal. *Doon-e-gal.* Clara considered correcting their pronunciation, but the conversation would make her homesick, she thought, and the couple meant well.

Over their first drinks, James asked Clara questions about her research and writing. *Do you have to read much philosophy in literary criticism? Does logic play any role in how you interpret a novel? Have you ever read Stanley Cavell?*

After a few more drinks, Clara relaxed into the evening. The owners were playing rebel songs through the sound system, and the wife hummed along sweetly as she poured pints for the other customers. In the corner of the bar, an old man was unloading a fiddle from a hard case. Clara felt like the whole thing might have been a practical joke, something set up to make her laugh.

But in the end, the total absence of irony was strangely reassuring for her. This has been going on without me for years, she thought. The only difference is now I'm in the middle of it.

She turned to James and told him about how depressing it had been for her to realise her move was not a new start, that she felt like she was stuck with herself. She spoke with uncharacteristic ease, and for much longer than she could have managed back at home. 'I feel exactly the same,' she said, 'but the weather is a little bit warmer, and no one is sarcastic. Aside from that, it's like nothing has really, substantially changed.'

'It sounds like *The Omen*,' James said, setting down his Guinness.

'How?'

'Well, they remade it a while back, didn't they? I caught it on one of the cable channels late one night when I couldn't sleep. I realised a few minutes in that the script was exactly the same as the old version, as the original one. They just re-shot it with new actors and slightly better special effects. But the dialogue was identical. Isn't that weird? Anyway, that's what happened to you. You thought it was a new thing entirely, but the script is pretty much the same as before.'

'Jesus, James, we went round the houses to get to that.'

'I'm trying to help. Are you always so resistant to help?'

'Yes.'

James laughed and leant back.

'It feels like nothing ever really changes,' Clara said after a moment, staring into her half-empty glass. 'Even when you move across the world.'

'Have you read Emerson?' James asked then.

'Of course I've read Emerson, James.'

'Well, then you'll know all about his views on travel.'

Clara shook her head at James, who had looked away from her to the bottles displayed behind the bar. 'Don't huff. Go on.'

James relented and brought his phone from his pocket. He typed something in, flicked his eyes down the screen and handed the phone to her. Clara took it from him and read.

> At home I dream that at Naples, at Rome, I can be intoxicated with beauty, and lose my sadness. I pack my trunk, embrace my friends, embark on the sea, and at last wake up in Naples, and there beside me is the stern fact, the sad self, unrelenting, identical, that I fled from.

'Fuck Emerson,' Clara said, as she handed the phone back. She ordered two more pints from the woman behind the bar and paid with her phone. Clara pushed one of the glasses towards James and lifted one for herself. '*Sláinte*,' she said and clinked her glass off James's. Behind the bar, the woman's eyes sparkled.

Clara had refilled her glass before she left the living room. She set it on the bedside table, plugged her laptop in to charge and settled herself on the bed. When she had first arrived, she couldn't believe her room had only a single. Wasn't everything meant to be bigger over here? she thought. Then, she'd put the two dozen books she'd had room for in the bookcase in the corner of the room. Choosing had been difficult. Sally Rooney made the cut. All of them. She would need something comfortingly sad, she thought, especially for the first few months. *Life of Pi* made the journey, too. Clara had meant to read it for years, but couldn't ever get past the first hundred pages. Maybe America is where I will finish it, she thought to herself. A similar thought process had led to the packing of *Middlemarch* and *Wolf Hall*. Of course, she had included the five Darnell books, too. For a day or two ahead of leaving, Clara had considered leaving them behind. This was a new act of her life, after all.

Perhaps it would be better to make a clean start. But the thought of those broken, peeling, dog-eared books being across the world in her old bedroom in Derry was intolerable. And, Clara thought, when the last one came out, it would be nice to have a complete set, wherever she would be living.

All things considered, life had shrunk. In Belfast she lived in an apartment all to herself, moved in and out of her regular coffee shops, visited Felicity and Sophie in Bangor and Glengormley, spent the night in East Belfast with Daniel, had reason to go to Derry, swanned into university lecture theatres and seminar rooms, went for dinner in the centre of town, saw arthouse films in the independent cinema, splurged occasionally on West End shows touring at the Grand Opera House. Her heat map, Clara realised, would indicate the life of a relatively free woman. Now, her life was a single bed in a rectangular room. Her books had been reduced to what she could carry, and the drive to the campus cost her enough money on Ubers that she had to seriously think about when she really needed to be there.

Clara took a spare pillow and placed it on her stomach. She tilted the screen of the laptop so her image was more central and clicked the 'start' button. After a few moments, Clara's image disappeared into the corner of the screen, a smaller, passport version of herself that blinked a second after she did.

'Hello, pet, can you hear me?'

'Yes, I can hear you but I can't see you.'

'Hold on.'

Clara lifted her glass and drained it.

'Oh, there. I can see you, love. Am I on your screen?'

'You are now.'

Julie was wearing a top Clara had bought her for her last birthday. A diamond patterned shirt with a low neckline that she had described as *risqué* at first and had to be encouraged to wear by Stacey. Now, though, she wore it without comment.

Clara looked at her mother's eyes on the laptop. The light from the screen emphasised the dark circles underneath them, and the growing number of fine lines etched at either side. It was like looking into the future, Clara thought and, perhaps due to the distance, she found the thought didn't trouble her.

'How did it go? We watched a bit of it on the computer. Stacey got it up for me, but the sound wasn't brilliant. She said we can see it tomorrow when they put it up. Is that right enough?'

'Yes, that's right. The university said they'll put it on their channel. You were good to watch it, though, Mum.'

'Was there a good crowd? We couldn't see the audience.'

'It was pretty packed. Standing room only.'

Clara heard her accent coming back to her. The dropped 'g' in standing.

'Isn't that brilliant. We'd a Chinese this evening, it was good. Bit spicy, though, my mouth is still burning.'

'Stacey told me all about it. Did you have many round?'

'We did. Stacey organised a few people. It was nice. I'm tired now, though, but I wanted to say well done. It was mad watching you sitting on that chair talking away. Did you sell many books?'

'I think we did. There was a queue and all. I was embarrassed but I had to sign copies of it for people. Mortifying.'

'Not a bit of it. Those books might be worth a lot of money in a few years. You never know. Wait until you're famous. Well, you're famous already if I can watch you on the computer from Derry.'

'What's the time there?'

'Oh, it's late enough. After twelve I think.'

'It's not your birthday anymore,' Clara said then, and moved hair from her face. 'I hope you had a lovely day. Sixty! I'm sorry I missed it.'

'You have bigger fish to fry, Dr Wilson. I heard that bit alright: *Doctor Clara Wilson*. I can't believe I have a doctor as a daughter. I must have done something right.'

'You did plenty right,' Clara said, feeling the whiskey. It made her head feel heavy, pressed into the pillow.

'Did he message you?'

Clara felt her stomach drop a little and she readjusted herself on the bed. 'Yes, just before it started.'

'That's good. What did he say?'

'Something like "Good luck and congrats." I haven't opened it yet.'

'Clara . . .'

'I'll reply now. I haven't had a chance.'

'I ran into him in the supermarket last week. Must be up here now, working in the hospital. He called my name and all. He's looking well.'

'That's good.'

Clara thought back to the first weeks in Iowa. The two messages she'd ignored. Better to have some space, she'd thought. She'd replied a week later, wishing him well for his consultant's exam and he'd replied with a heart. Opening his message now would bring it all back on screen.

'He must have a new one on the go,' Julie said. 'She didn't come over, obviously. She looked a bit like you. Nice long hair like you used to have. I didn't ask any questions.'

Clara glanced above the laptop to the door. 'Might have been his sister.'

'Maybe.'

There was a silence. Her mother looked tired. She tucked her hair behind her ear and then shifted on her seat.

'I'd need to be getting to bed, love. I'm never up past eleven these days. Well done this evening. Or was it evening? It was probably afternoon for you. I'll never get used to that. Well done anyway. I was very proud.'

Clara said goodnight to her mother and closed the laptop. The sound it made died in the room quickly. Clara was aware of silence like a fuzz of white noise behind her ears and the leaning of the walls into the centre of the room. She heard the bathroom door open and lifted herself from the bed. She opened the door and saw James walking across the living room, his waist wrapped in a towel.

'I thought you were Zooming your mom,' he said.

'We just finished. It's late there.'

'How was it?' He put one hand on the band of the towel, hooking his thumb underneath.

'Grand. Fine, I mean.' Clara went to set the glass into the sink and James came alongside her. He lifted the glass.

'I need some water,' he said. 'One less dish to wash.' James rinsed the glass under the tap. Clara watched him, wondering how he stayed in such good shape. She leant herself against the back of the sofa. His shoulder blades shifted under his skin as he dried the glass and refilled it from the tap. He turned to face her and drank from the glass, lifting it as he tilted his head back to finish.

Clara's eyes went to the towel, how it stopped above his knees. James walked into his room and shut the door. It was getting dark and Clara returned to her room.

14
Time Passes (2)

Weeks later, Clara got the bus to the bookstore, bought herself the new book and returned to the apartment. She put off opening it all morning and afternoon, instead busying herself with cleaning the insides of the windows and sweeping the kitchen floor. She cooked fresh meals of pasta for lunch and risotto for dinner and washed the dishes. Then, she took her laptop and the book to her room.

After submitting the application she spent the early evening on, she closed the list of secondary schools she'd been studying. Then, Clara booked flights, shut her laptop and took the new book with her to bed.

The light from her window was strong enough to read by for the first hour, after which she turned on the small yellow lamp she'd taken from her mother's house. She read until she'd finished, her wrists sore from keeping the hardback open, her neck stiff. Clara switched onto her right side for a final time, and as she turned the last pages the outside was perfectly dark.

Reading it all in one sitting, Clara felt the book as a single effect, an entirety, and she found that time had flooded past her. When she looked up from the book, her vision was soft and blurred, her mind quiet. She had been utterly lost in the novel, and it would be a long time before she could think properly about it. But there was no deadline now, Clara recognised.

The thought crossed her mind then that she would never write about the book. Clara felt weight leave her body.

She held the closed novel and her thoughts turned to Christina. Her desk, her handwritten notes, her now empty house. The dog-eared books. Her garden. Clara sat up on the tiny bed to read the final page again, tears falling freely from her eyes, and pushed her back against the wall.

The huge oak by the house held birdsong and seemed, to the cat, to touch the sky. It had always been like this, but now, the tree was bigger, and the sky more full of blue than it had ever been. The cat was too old to be distracted by what the songs in the tree used to mean and rounded its base in search of the sun. Winter, being a difficult season for cats – even those with a bed by an open fire like this one – had commenced its sixteenth disappearance, and the cat sensed a new kind of light in the garden and set out that morning to find it. The woman had been leaving to buy eggs and milk, and had been surprised to find the cat scratching at the back door to be let out. Taking this as a good thing, the woman bent to touch the cat's head and then opened the door. The garden was new to the cat, just like it always was, and he padded over the grass to the old patch of flowers he liked to roll in. The light was indeed fresh, for it had a warmth in it that seemed to precede warmth, the way some silences beckon sound. The cat sniffed at the purple flowers and then lifted his paw to remove the blade of grass on his nose. His ears twitched a few times as a back door was opened and then closed a short distance away, and the cat returned to the oak tree. As a kitten, he'd climbed the tree. At first only to the first set of branches and then, so high, the woman put a small bell around his neck when he finally returned to the grass below. He rubbed his cheek now on the bark, the way cats do. This is how they declare ownership, it is said, though the cat did it now because he was so full of love. The cat, spotting the light's reflection in the kitchen window, bounded towards the house, and, refusing time for a moment, leapt onto the window ledge, as though to demonstrate grace one more time. He had landed exactly where he had intended, which was, of course, where the ledge met the light and had become warm. It was there that he groomed himself, licking his right paw and bathing his head and ears. And it was from there that he turned and looked into the house for any sign of the woman's return and, on seeing nothing, turned back towards his garden. The cat had not yet seen enough so when he heard a small rustling in the garden beyond his own, he jumped down from his ledge and went with intention, without thinking, to the source.

It was like that, in the end.

Acknowledgements

There are a number of people who made this book possible. Huge thanks are due to:

The very wise and patient Becky Walsh for stewarding and pruning the entire project from beginning to end. Thank you for all you've done for this novel.

My extraordinary agent, Audrey Crooks. Your intelligence, vision and enthusiasm for the book have made it infinitely better.

All at The Irish Writers Centre, who through the Novel Fair, gave this book a fighting chance.

Olivia Fitzsimons: a more generous and kind colleague could not be imagined.

Tricia Malone and Kelly O'Brien who both read early drafts of the novel and offered insightful feedback and much needed encouragement.

Pip Jaffa, who inspired the longest chapter of the novel with a healthy amount of wine.

Louise Nealon for being there from the very start of my writing, and for crisps.

Mandy Cook, Claire Humphrey and, above all, Mícheál McCann for buckets of inspiration, long conversations and fiction worth believing in.

RAISING READERS

Books Build Bright Futures

Dear Reader,

We'd love your attention for one more page to tell you about the crisis in children's reading, and what we can all do.

Studies have shown that reading for fun is the **single biggest predictor of a child's future life chances** – more than family circumstance, parents' educational background or income. It improves academic results, mental health, wealth, communication skills, ambition and happiness.[1]

The number of children reading for fun is in rapid decline. Young people have a lot of competition for their time. In 2024, 1 in 10 children and young people in the UK aged 5 to 18 did not own a single book at home.[2]

Hachette works extensively with schools, libraries and literacy charities, but here are some ways we can all raise more readers:

- Reading to children for just 10 minutes a day makes a difference
- Don't give up if children aren't regular readers – there will be books for them!
- Visit bookshops and libraries to get recommendations
- Encourage them to listen to audiobooks
- Support school libraries
- Give books as gifts

There's a lot more information about how to encourage children to read on our website: **www.RaisingReaders.co.uk**

Thank you for reading.

hachette UK

[1] OECD, '21st-Century Readers: Developing Literacy Skills in a Digital World', 2021, https://www.oecd.org/en/publications/21st-century-readers_a83d84cb-en.html

[2] National Literacy Trust, 'Book Ownership in 2024', November 2024, https://literacytrust.org.uk/research-services/research-reports/book-ownership-in-2024